FATECARVER

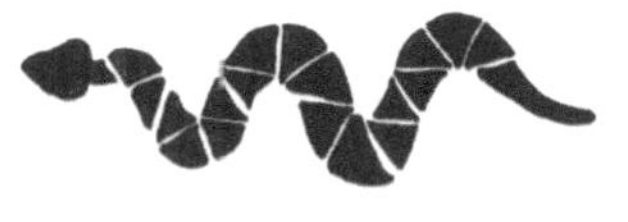

Robinne Weiss

Published by Sandfly Books

Copyright 2021 Robinne Weiss

ISBN-13: 978-0-473-57641-7

Cover design by Jenn Rackham

This book is also available in electronic formats.

Discover my other books and stories on my website:
https://robinneweiss.com

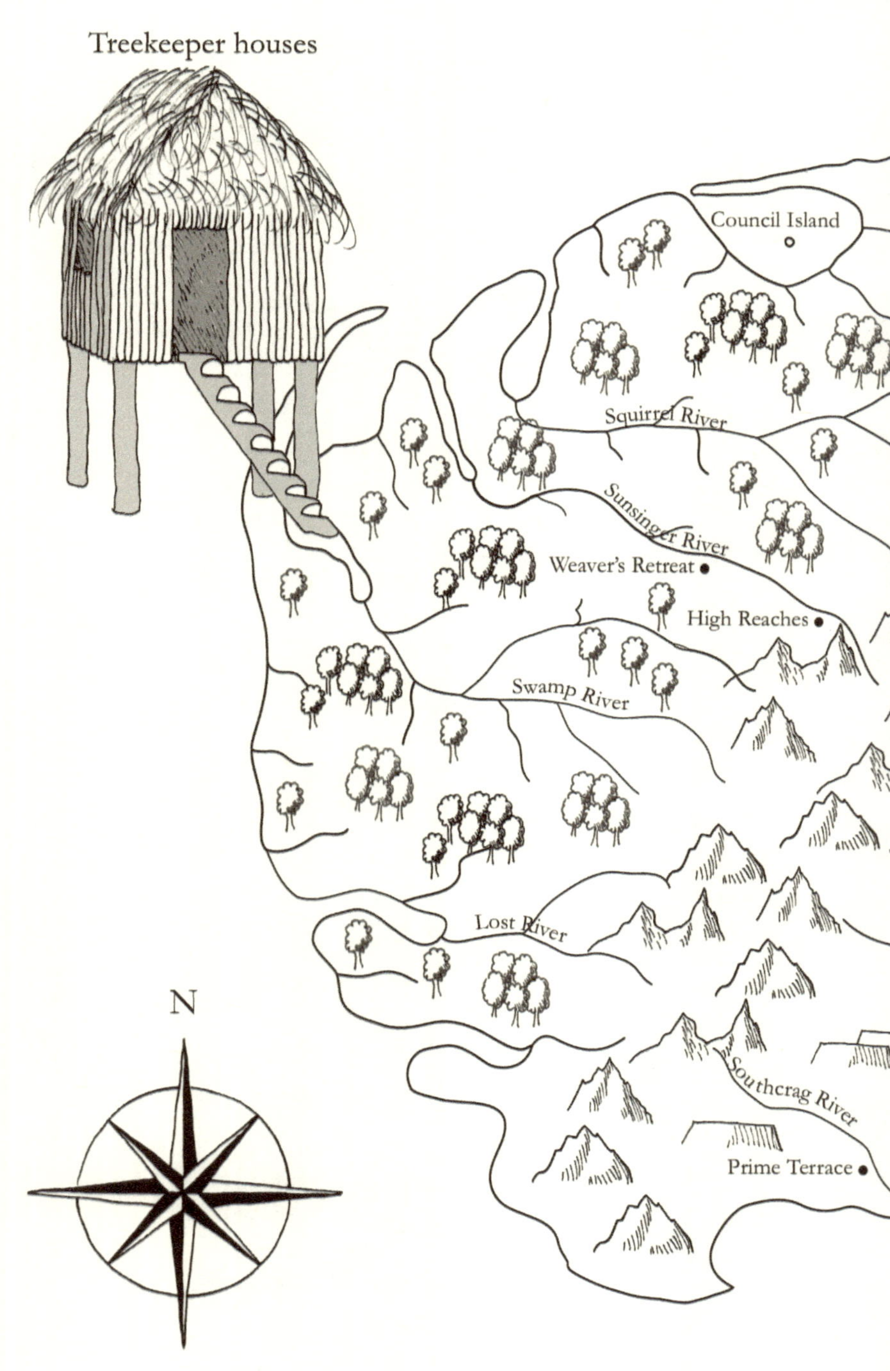
Treekeeper houses
Council Island
Squirrel River
Sunsinger River
Weaver's Retreat
High Reaches
Swamp River
Lost River
Southcrag River
Prime Terrace
N

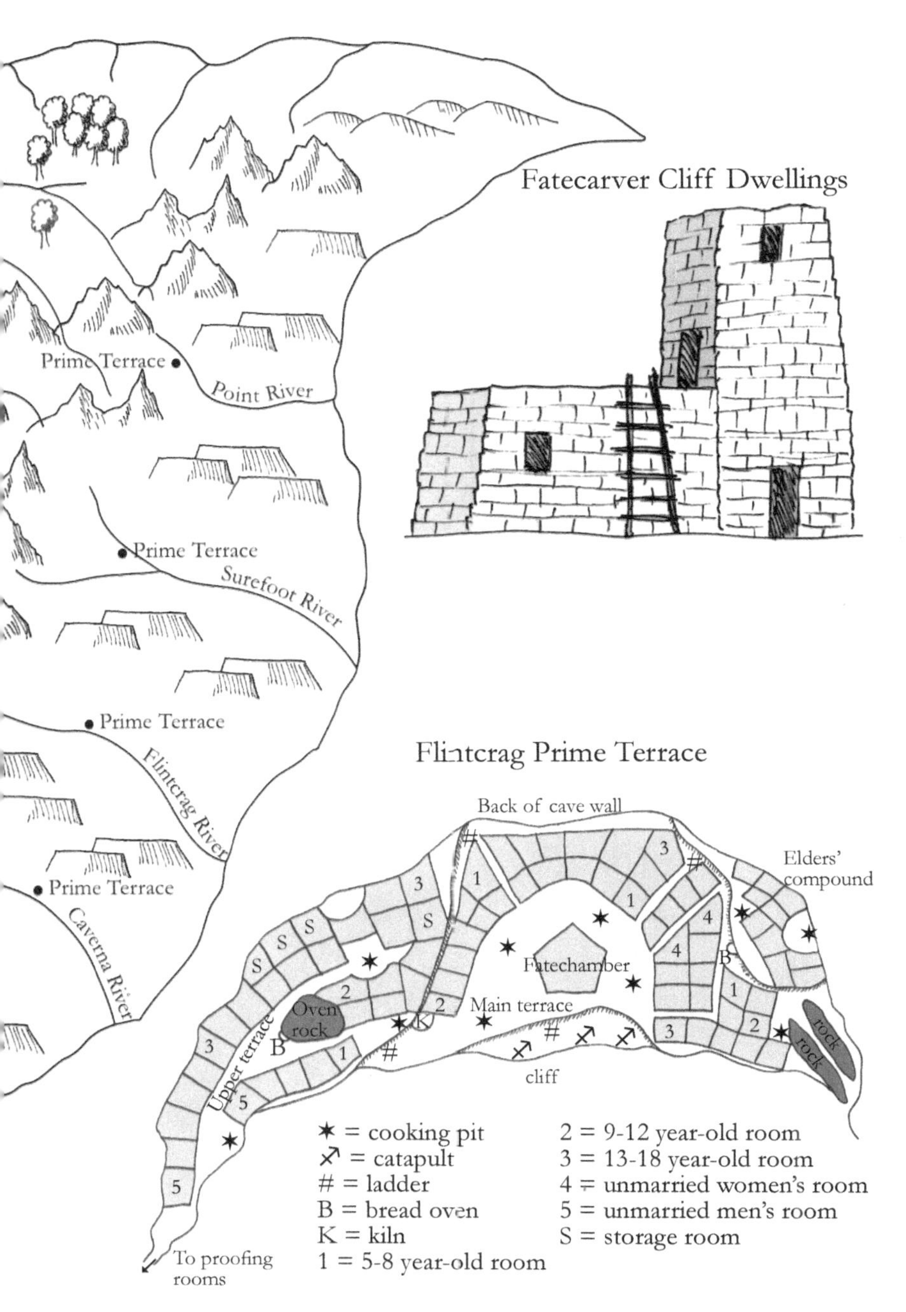

Fatecarver Cliff Dwellings
Prime Terrace
Point River
Prime Terrace
Surefoot River
Prime Terrace
Flintcrag River
Prime Terrace
Caverna River
Flintcrag Prime Terrace
Back of cave wall
Elders' compound
Fatechamber
Main terrace
Oven rock
Upper terrace
cliff
rock
rock
To proofing rooms
✷ = cooking pit
↗ = catapult
# = ladder
B = bread oven
K = kiln
1 = 5-8 year-old room
2 = 9-12 year-old room
3 = 13-18 year-old room
4 = unmarried women's room
5 = unmarried men's room
S = storage room

ONE

Drums sounded in the pre-dawn darkness. *Dum da da da dum. Dum da da da dum.* Kalish bolted upright, tossing the blanket off and snatching up her staff. "Raid!" She shook Dayo, still snoring next to her, as the others in the sleeping quarters stirred on their platforms. Within seconds, the gaggle of teens was alert and pattering quickly to their defensive stations.

Men did the raiding, but everyone, down to the toddlers, defended the terrace, and they all knew what to do. Kalish was one of the first on the street, and she pounded along the dusty grit past the upper terrace's bread oven, already lit, but now unattended. She squeezed through the narrow space between Oven Rock and the younger children's sleeping room. "Up!" she yelled on her way past. "Raid!" The forms inside began to stir, and Kalish ran on, taking the ladder down to the main terrace in great leaps. Dayo caught up with her as she leapt down to the shelf at the edge of the cliff, where the raiders would try to ascend. Others were dropping onto the shelf with them, the space filling with fighters.

Dayo yawned and rubbed his face. "How do you do it?"

"Do what?" Kalish dropped to her knees and shuffled to the edge of the cliff to peek into the darkness below.

"Go from asleep to awake faster than a lantan can strike."

Kalish slithered back from the edge and smiled at Dayo. "Maybe I'm half snake. Something for you to aspire to, little puffer."

Little puffer was what the elders called Dayo. From them, it was a scathing comment on his size and bravado—puffers were small lizards that inflated their necks to look bigger when frightened. Kalish had taken to using the name as a way to mock the elders, and Dayo didn't seem to mind when she used it.

A dart whizzed between them and clattered against the stone. They flattened themselves to the ground. "Caverna Clan," Dayo commented, glancing at the dart. "Again."

"Those new dart launchers they have are annoying." Kalish inched forward, ignoring the gravel scraping her knees and elbows. Others around them did the same, staves and rocks in hand, waiting for the enemy to begin scaling the cliff. More darts pinged off the rock. Younger children scrambled to collect them. "They're going to have to get better at aiming. All they're doing is delivering us darts to sling back at them."

The creak and whoosh of a catapult further along the shelf told her the raiders' siege engine had been spotted. Then a shout rang out; the raiders were scaling the cliff.

"Let's hope their aim stays bad." Dayo shoved himself forward until his upper body was hanging over the edge. Kalish followed, peering down into the gloom. She made out at least a dozen dark forms scaling the cliff. Fewer than the last raid. But there would be—not all the raiders had survived the last attack. Their teeth, braided into the hair of Flintcrag warriors, were evidence of that.

One of their attackers was already within range of her staff, and Kalish swung, giving it a little flick with her wrist so the hooked end would sweep away from the cliff with speed. It was a perfect swing, and she smiled in satisfaction. But at the last moment, the raider reached out and grabbed the staff. The man's weight jerked Kalish forward, gravel scraping her stomach and skittering down the cliff as she was dragged over the edge.

A weight slammed onto her legs. "Let go of your staff!" Dayo pinned her to the shelf.

Kalish let go, her staff and the climber both ricocheting off the rocks as they fell. Dayo dragged her back up, the broken cliff edge gouging new furrows in her stomach. She rolled away from the edge. "I hope my staff isn't broken." She ignored her stinging skin and scrambled to a pile of rocks ready for hurling.

Crawling back to the edge with an armful of rocks, she heard the creak of an enemy catapult. A moment later, a boulder smashed against the upper lip of the cave the terrace nestled in. The defenders scurried back to avoid the falling rocks.

"They'll have knocked some of their own off," Dayo commented.

"Aim. It's Caverna's weakness." Kalish inched forward again to drop a rock on another climber. It hit the side of the cliff and bounced, missing the raider. "Spines!"

Dayo chuckled beside her, dropping his own rock, which hit the mark and sent the man tumbling. "Aim. Maybe you should work on that." Kalish punched his arm, but laughed.

Their laughter was cut off by shouts behind them. Raiders. On the main terrace. How had they gotten there? Cursing the loss of her staff, Kalish picked up another rock and stood, turning toward the commotion.

Before she could throw, a dart sliced into her upper arm. She cried out and dropped her rock.

"Get down, you idiot!" Dayo scrambled toward her as she sank to her knees, gritting her teeth against the searing pain in her arm.

Reaching her side, Dayo held her arm firmly as he examined it. "They really need to work on their aim. Still, this is going to hurt." And it did. There wasn't time to take herself somewhere else, and the full brunt of Dayo extracting the dart made her eyes water.

"I thought you said they needed to work on their aim," she gasped.

"They do. They almost missed you—that dart just slipped in under your skin."

An explosion rocked the upper terrace, and Kalish flinched. "Great. They've brought incendiaries."

"Well, at least their aim is bad."

"Not bad enough." Kalish lifted her arm and grimaced at the ragged tear in her skin. Blood flowed freely from it and dripped off her elbow.

Another creak-whoosh from a catapult on the shelf was followed by a cheer. They'd hit the raiders' catapult. The fighting on the main terrace subsided, and before Kalish had a chance to worry about dodging darts on her way to the healers, their patter on the rocks ceased. The remaining raiders melted silently into the scrub, even before the sky was fully lit.

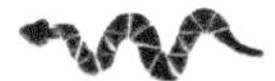

"You're late." Kalish's mother, Norili, didn't turn as Kalish entered the fatechamber.

"I was injured in the raid. I was at the healers'."

Norili turned and skewered Kalish with a glare. "There is no excuse for being late. A fatecarver's sacred duties come before all others. Did you not tell them you must be seen first?"

"Onadi was badly hurt—struck in the stomach by a dart—the healers had to tend to him immediately."

Norili scoffed. "Onadi is nothing but a farmer. You must assert yourself, Kalish. How will anyone respect you if you don't demand it?"

Kalish frowned at her feet. "Yes Fatecarver Norili."

"Don't use that tone with me, girl." Had she been that obvious? "I expect better of you, especially now, so close to your own fatecarving. Your lessons are essential. Do you want to be incapable of producing a proper fatecarving because you slacked off? How would the women of the clan feel in future if they cannot rely on the wisdom of the Fates to guide them because you couldn't be bothered to learn how to communicate with them? You will not be late again for any reason. Next time you are injured, you will insist upon being seen first, or you will come to me still bleeding."

Kalish forced her voice into a tone her mother might accept. "Yes Fatecarver Norili."

"Look at me when you speak to me."

Kalish wiped her face clean of emotion and looked into the eyes she'd never been able to meet without feeling failure. "I am sorry I was late. It won't happen again. What is today's lesson?"

As she expected, the lesson had little to do with communicating with the Fates. For the fifth day in a row, Norili set her the mind-numbing task of grinding pigment for the fatecarvings her mother performed. She suspected the task was punishment.

"But I *know* how to grind pigment," she argued. "When will you teach me how to actually do the carvings? Why can't I sit in on today's and learn?" The actual tattooing fascinated and terrified Kalish. The process was a mystery; she hadn't yet gotten her own fatecarving. She knew how to prepare the thorns, mallets and ink, and she had an idea of how the carving was done, but she'd never seen her mother at work. The process was a secret known only to the fatecarvers themselves and the adult women of the clan whose faces bore the intricate stories of their future.

"Do not question me!" her mother barked back. "I am your mother and your fatecarver. I decide what you learn and when. You are not yet a woman. Until your own face is carved, I cannot reveal the utmost secrets of the fatecarvers."

Maybe once Kalish had her storyscar, things would be different. As an adult, maybe she'd be good enough for her mother. The day couldn't come soon enough. She sighed and set to work. At least pigment grinding left her mind free. While her hands worked with mortar and pestle, her brain grappled with her latest ideas for a folding glider wing. The trouble was in fashioning a hinge robust enough to take the force of the wind on the wings. Even ironwood tended to split under the strain. Anything strong enough to take the force was heavy and required a larger wing to compensate.

With glider design to occupy her mind, the hours of grinding passed in a blur.

"Your work is still sloppy," declared her mother as she peered into one of the clay jars of ground pigment. "Did you recite the entire blessing?"

No, but she had worked out a new wing hinge design. "Yes, Fatecarver Norili."

Her mother pressed her lips together, and the weight in Kalish's stomach grew heavier. She would never live up to her mother's standards. How would she ever manage to be her clan's fatecarver?

"You will gather piromanga this afternoon," she ordered, handing a small sack to Kalish. "See that you bring it back full."

Kalish suppressed a groan. But at least it would take her outdoors and away from these Fate-pocked pigments.

Kalish grumbled as she stalked through the dry brush. This errand was senseless—a waste of her time. Mother didn't need the sacred piromanga leaves she'd sent Kalish out for—there were dozens of them stuffed into a jar in the fatechamber already. Sending her to gather the leaves was simply a way to keep her away from today's fatecarving ceremony, a way to punish Kalish for being particularly argumentative this morning. But how could she be anything but irritated when her mother gave her nothing but menial tasks day after day? She was practically a woman now—just a few five-days from her own fatecarving ceremony— and ready to start learning the skills needed to become a fatecarver herself. Yet Mother wouldn't even let her watch a fatecarving.

She ignored the pain in her injured arm, hurled herself at a cliff and began to climb. Her frustration and anger made her careless. She forgot to check each handhold, each ledge.

When the snake struck, she swore and snatched her hand away. Her other hand slipped, and her feet followed, knees and elbows bouncing off and scraping the rock as she fell.

"Spines!" At the bottom of the cliff, she clutched her knees, squeezing her eyes tight against the pain. But it wasn't her torn and bloodied limbs that upset her. She'd nearly been bitten by a lantan. And in her anger at her mother, she'd left the terrace without the herb pouch she always carried—the pouch containing the lantan venom antidote. If she'd been bitten, she never would have made it home. Her anger would get her killed.

She took a deep breath and slowly let it out. She was still angry, but forced herself to think calmly as she inspected her fresh injuries. How could she get what she wanted, in spite of her mother? Blood dripped from her knees, and her scraped elbows stung, but they were nothing to worry about. She squinted at the sky. The sun had just broken over the top of the cliff. Mother would be in the Fatewalker Realm preparing for today's carving.

If Kalish entered the Fatewalker Realm herself, might she be able to watch her mother at work? It wouldn't be the same as being there in person, but she'd at least learn something, and the idea of sneaking around against her mother's will made her smile. She scrambled underneath a bush so her body would be hidden and protected while she was away from it.

Then, ignoring the task she was supposed to be doing, she slipped out of her skin and into the Fatewalker Realm.

Leaving her stinging knees and elbows behind, Kalish trotted back to the terrace. Norili must meet the Fates in the fatechamber. There was no way Kalish could enter without being seen, but she might be able to eavesdrop from outside. She crept up the cliff to the terrace. Stopping on the ledge below the main terrace, where the fatechamber was located, she listened for any indication of her mother's whereabouts. Silence met her ears. Perhaps Mother was already in the fatechamber.

A few more moments of silence emboldened her. She crept up the ladder to the main terrace. Seeing no one, she tiptoed toward the fatechamber and pressed herself against the wall beside one of the doors. The smooth adobe bricks were warm from the sun, and she let them calm her nerves as she listened.

"Surely you can't expect me to carve *that* on the girl's face!" Kalish had never heard horror in her mother's voice before, but there was no mistaking it now.

"You must. It is her fate." Whichever Fate Mother spoke with had a low, musical voice. Soothing. How could her mother argue with such a voice?

"The elders will banish her if I do what you ask. I will not do it."

Kalish stifled a gasp. Her mother was refusing to do what the Fates decreed?

"You will." The voice took on an edge. "You must. It is her fate, and even a fatecarver cannot change it."

"But—"

"Enough. You know your duty. You are bound by it."

Footsteps sounded inside the chamber. Kalish scrambled down from the terrace and raced back to her body.

Back in the real world, with aching knees and elbows, Kalish stood. Her anger with her mother had been replaced with confusion. She'd always assumed the Fates spoke and fatecarvers listened. Did her mother always argue? What did that mean for the storyscars she carved? Did they represent the will of the Fates, or her mother's will?

And what sort of carving would get a girl kicked out of the clan? Kalish was glad she didn't know the girl her mother would carve today—someone from one of the smaller terraces—she'd hate to see a friend banished.

Slowly this time, watching where she placed her hands, Kalish resumed her climb.

Hours later, having scoured the windswept butte for piromanga, Kalish stood at the edge of the cliff and shaded her eyes against the sun as she watched a falcon soar overhead. It hovered for a moment, and then dove, folding its wings and plunging toward the tussocks below. After one of the rock skippers feeding on the nodding seed heads of the grasses, no doubt.

Moments before it would have struck the ground, the falcon pulled out of its dive. A handful of rock skippers flushed from the grass and flitted away, but one wasn't fast enough. The falcon hit it at speed. A puff of feathers marked the impact and slowly drifted to the ground as the falcon rose again, bird clutched in its talons.

Kalish sighed. If only she could fly like the kiriki falcon. Gliders were a poor imitation of the power and precision of the falcon's flight. What would it feel like to be able to fly for real, with wings of her own? She spread her arms wide and imagined the breeze ruffling wing feathers. If she could fly, she wouldn't mind so much being sent on stupid errands.

Movement on the valley floor caught her eye—the farmers returning from their daily work in the fields. *Spines!* She'd been away far longer than she thought. She glanced at the half empty bag of piromanga leaves lying by her feet. Her mother would know she'd been wasting time.

Gathering piromanga was slow and boring work. Before each leaf was plucked off its wiry bush, she had to say a long prayer to the Fates to ensure the potency of the leaf. It was forbidden to pick more than one leaf from each bush, and piromanga was sparse, so filling even a small bag could take hours.

But Kalish had been gone all afternoon, and her bag was only half full. Her stomach sank at the prospect of her mother's reaction. She'd already been yelled at enough today. Another reprimand might just push her over the edge. She'd lose control of her tongue and snap back, and then there would be a screaming match. Those always ended badly for Kalish—a month of latrine duty or hide tanning on top of the endless menial tasks her mother set her to in the fatechamber. Whatever tasks she was assigned would keep her in the terrace all day, without any chance to climb to the top of the butte and watch the falcons or hunt goats in the crags further up the valley. She wouldn't be able to sneak away with Dayo to test their latest glider design or catch bats in order to study their wing structure.

Kalish scrambled down the cliff and jogged through the scrub at its base. She reached a piromanga bush and paused. It was a scraggly little thing, with barely a dozen leaves on it. Her mother would have instructed her to leave it alone.

The men were nearing the cliff now. Their laughter filtered through the scrub as they followed the path to the terrace. If they arrived home before she did …

Without uttering a word of prayer, Kalish snatched four leaves off the plant. "Sorry," she muttered as she hurried to find another.

Two

"Kalish!" The sound of Sensa's gravelly voice brought Kalish to a skidding stop before she reached her mother's chamber. She took a deep breath and schooled her face into neutral respect. Sensa was an elder, and Kalish couldn't ignore a summons from her, no matter how much the woman annoyed her. Besides, she was now far too late to be returning with her not quite full bag of piromanga leaves. To have Sensa waylay her was a perfect excuse to keep her out of trouble.

"Sensa." Kalish nodded her respect to the woman as she ducked into her room. "What do you wish of me?"

"My granddaughter, Seeda, has finished firing the most beautiful bowls! Will you look at them?" She waved a hand across an array of brightly decorated earthenware. Deep mahogany, bright orange and yellow, and brilliant white glazes adorned the edges—an impressive display of Seeda's skill and patience in preparing pigments. Kalish struggled not to frown at them—they were far better than anything she'd ever produced.

"Here." Sensa picked up the largest and most ornate of the vessels, cradling it in her hands. "Why don't you take this to your mother."

Of course. Sensa would never pass up an opportunity to cosy up to the clan's fatecarver on her granddaughter's behalf. Only a moon cycle ago, it had been a gift of a pot of rare green clay for her mother's hair, and before that, a bag of carefully crafted beads.

"Thank you Sensa." Kalish accepted the bowl. "I'm sure mother will love it." If she didn't accidentally smash it on the way there.

But she couldn't. Sensa would surely ask her mother if she liked it—another excuse to sing the praises of her granddaughter. She would have to grit her teeth and give the gorgeous bowl to her mother, once again exposing her own failings.

Sensa smiled, and Kalish steeled herself for what was coming. "And you are looking more like a woman every day. I'm so glad you and Seeda are so close in age. You can't have too many allies, especially once you become fatecarver."

Kalish bit her tongue. Seeda was no ally, and there was no way Kalish was going to give her a prestigious job once she was fatecarver.

"Your mother's mother and I were very close. Did I ever tell you how I saved her life when the Southcrag Clan came raiding?"

"Yes, you've told me that story." About a hundred times. Kalish forced a smile. "I'm sure grandmother was grateful to you."

"She was certainly gracious, allowing me to work alongside her in the fatechamber, making sure I always had the best sugarspike fabric for my daughters. I remember how—"

Kalish tuned her out. Even as the fatecarver's daughter, she didn't dare interrupt an elder to complain she'd heard these stories before. But she would rather endure another tongue-lashing from Mother before listening to this woman try to ooze her way into her mother's favour. And all for the benefit of that cactus, Seeda.

Someday, when Kalish was fatecarver, she could breeze past Sensa and ignore her entirely. Someday it wouldn't matter that her pots were a sad shadow of Seeda's beautiful creations. She fantasised about choosing one of the other girls her age—maybe Fala or Lingle—to be her assistant. *If you wanted to be my assistant, maybe you shouldn't have been such a Fate-cursed cactus to me*, she imagined saying to a livid Seeda.

She must have smiled at the thought, because Sensa patted her arm, breaking her reverie. "Yes, it was a wonderful time, and I was happy to be of use to your grandmother."

Kalish had no idea what Sensa had just said, but she nodded. "If you'll excuse me, I'll go to Mother now. She's expecting these." She raised the bag of piromanga leaves to show her.

"Oh yes, of course. Fatecarver business must come first. Tell Norili that Seeda and I send our deepest respects and look forward to greeting her on Fateday."

Kalish assured her she would and sped off before Sensa could remember another story to tell.

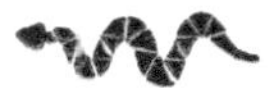

"The climbers, the darts, the incendiary ... they were only ever meant to be a distraction."

By evening, life had returned to normal on the terrace. The raiders who had been captured alive on the main terrace had been interrogated and then killed, the fire from the lone incendiary had been extinguished, and the family who had lived in the destroyed room had been relocated. Kalish was exhausted—had it only been this morning they'd been raided? The upper terrace teens were still buzzing, though, and Dayo was pleased to share his insider information.

Information he'd gotten from Kalish, who, as the fatecarver's daughter, had more inside information than he could ever dream of being privy to. But Kalish was happy to let Dayo tell the story. He was so much better at it than she was. And she enjoyed listening to his voice as she lay in the dark next to him in the bunk room with the other teens. Theirs was one of several rooms housing the teens of the terrace. She'd chosen it like she'd chosen all her bunk rooms as she grew up—because it was furthest from her mother's room.

"So, what was the raid for?" asked Tino from the other side of the room. Tino's voice had lowered dramatically since he'd moved into the room a year ago, but Kalish smiled into the dark at the squeak still evident in the word *for*.

"They were after the spinning machine."

Fala snorted. "Won't do them much good if they don't have the new loom to go with it."

"Yeah," echoed Seeda. "It'll take them a year to weave a skirt for their stick of a fatecarver on the old looms."

Kalish felt Dayo nod. "They were after the loom, too."

"What's so great about sugarspike fabric that they raided for it?" asked Meech. He was one of those boys who confirmed Kalish's mother's opinion about men in general—that they were useful only for their muscles and their ... other parts.

16

But Kalish liked Meech, so before Seeda could sneer at his question, she spoke up in a voice she hoped was gentle. "It seems silly, doesn't it? Every clan can make sugarspike fabric. But if you think about it, the fabric is as much a weapon as our catapults are. What is most of our sugarspike fabric used for?"

"Um … glider wings?"

Kalish was glad Meech answered correctly. "Exactly, and the lighter the glider, the better it flies, right? Well, with our new spinning machine and loom we can make fabric far lighter than anything we could produce with the old spindles and looms. And faster too."

Even Meech knew incendiaries dropped from gliders were the most effective way to torch rival clans' crops. And gliders were usually single-use, because they were almost impossible to control. A glider flight ended in a crash more often than not. Glider fliers were lucky to get home alive after a raid, so being able to make better gliders more quickly was a huge advantage.

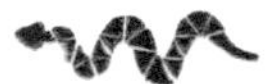

When the conversation had died out, Kalish lay on her bunk unsleeping, her injured arm throbbing, and her mind replaying her mother's scolding over and over again. On her right, Benut began to snore, something she'd done ever since she'd broken her nose playing lantans and ladders on the cliff face one day when they were seven or eight years old. The room grew close with the smell of sweat—washing happened infrequently in this land of dry, windswept buttes and seasonal rivers.

Kalish took a long slow breath, knowing sleep wouldn't come easily in this skin, in this room. She closed her eyes and stepped away from her pain, her tired body and the stink of her companions.

She padded lightly out of the bunk room and onto the street. In the fresh air outside, she stretched her arm, pain free and unblemished. The street was empty, of course. What would happen if Kalish met her mother here, in the Fatewalker Realm? Norili would be angry. Especially if she found out Kalish came here without any help from piromanga leaves, deemed the only gateway into the Fatewalker Realm. In fact, she'd decided long ago that, if she were ever caught here, she'd lie and say she'd stolen piromanga from her mother's herb pouch. Better to be thought a thief than … well, she wasn't sure what she was. But she knew she wasn't supposed to be here.

And she definitely shouldn't have taught Dayo how to come here.

Still, she smiled when she arrived at her favourite perch, on a rock outcrop far from any of the established routes along the cliff, and found Dayo already there.

His eyes crinkled. "I knew you wouldn't be able to sleep with that arm."

Kalish sat down next to him, heedless of the vertiginous drop below. She wasn't sure what happened if you died in the Fatewalker Realm, but she never once slipped or felt unsafe, no matter how difficult the climb here. She felt, though she'd never been brave enough to test it, that she could leap off the edge and spread her arms to fly like a bird if she wanted to.

They sat in companionable silence, gazing out at the view below. It was always sunny and the perfect temperature here. A falcon wheeled silently over the valley below, and then plunged after some small animal invisible to them on their ledge. Grasshoppers sawed away in the shrubby grey-green vegetation on the valley floor, and the faint bleat of a mountain goat echoed from the other side of the canyon.

"Five more days," Kalish said finally, breaking the silence.

"You're nervous." It wasn't a question. Dayo knew her.

"You would be too, if you were facing the prospect of having your own mother carve your storyscar." Then Kalish laughed. "Well, maybe not *your* mother. I wouldn't be half so worried if she were doing it." Dayo's mother had practically claimed Kalish as her own after Kalish's father died. At four years old, faced with the choice of moving to the children's sleeping room nearly two years early or staying alone with her demanding mother for whom she could do nothing right, Kalish had run. The first night in the children's room, she'd curled in the corner, sobbing, grieving for her kind, loving father, missing his warmth at her back, his arm slung over her body as they slept. She clutched the little felted wool bat her father had made for her.

The other children had made fun of her. They'd kicked her until she snarled like a cornered fox. When they saw her little bat, they accused her of stealing the scraps of sugarspike cloth the wings were made of. They didn't know she was Norili's daughter—her mother had distanced her from the rest of the terrace.

Dayo, nearly seven, but even then small for his age, had stepped between her and the other children. He'd puffed his chest out and declared her under his protection. He'd tucked her into the C of his body that night, holding her close until her sobbing subsided and she fell asleep.

The next day he'd taken her to his mother.
Wathi knew who Kalish was and why she'd fled her
own home. Instead of sending her back to her
mother's rebuke, she washed the girl's face and fixed a
tear in her little bat's wing. Without fuss, she folded
Kalish into the fabric of her own family.

Dayo laughed, breaking into Kalish's memory
of that dark time. "I don't think you'd want my mum
to carve your storyscar, given she doesn't know how to
do it. She might accidentally slice off a cheek."

Kalish sighed. "Better to accidentally lose a
cheek than have my mother carve on my face exactly
what she thinks of me."

"But she's supposed to be taking direction
from the Fates, not carving whatever she wants."

Kalish narrowed her eyes at her friend. "I believe that about as much as I believe she was sad to see
me leave home."

"But that's blasphemy!"

Kalish shrugged. "Who's here to hear it but
you?"

"But you're going to be a fatecarver, and we're
in the Fatewalker Realm; the Fates themselves could
be listening in!" Dayo's eyes were wide now. Kalish
knew he questioned authority—how could he not
when he could enter the Fatewalker Realm, where men
and boys were never supposed to be able to go, even
with the help of piromanga leaves. But he hadn't
heard what she had today.

"Let the Fates hear it, then." Kalish raised her
voice so it echoed across the valley. "Norili is an eggsucking lantan! She carves whatever the Fate she wants
on people's faces!"

20

Dayo clapped a hand over Kalish's mouth, but he was laughing. They mock-struggled for a minute before dissolving into giggles. When the giggles subsided, Kalish sighed and leaned her head on Dayo's shoulder.

"I really am scared."

Dayo wrapped an arm around her. "I know."

THREE

They woke as they often did, with Kalish nestled into the C of Dayo's body, his arm thrown over her. She didn't fit as well as she had when she was four—they were nearly the same size now—but there was still comfort in it.

Kalish woke to pain. But it wasn't her arm that caused her the most grief. It was the pain low in her abdomen that had her slipping out of bed and scurrying in semi-darkness to the privy. She squatted over the clay pot to relieve herself, thinking perhaps she had the sickness that sometimes set in after a battle wound. That sickness came with aches and pains far from the wound.

But when she carried the pot to the ledge to empty it, she saw the clots of blood.

No. Her heart sank. Not now. Not right before her fatecarving. Not when she needed all the comfort she could get.

Kalish had never menstruated before, but she knew what it was. And it was the signal she had to move from the teen sleeping room to the room for

22

unmarried women. She was no longer a child, and was no longer allowed to sleep in the same room as boys until she proofed with someone. The proofing rooms were set apart from the terrace, tucked into a little cave reached only by a narrow path from the terrace. Couples who wanted to marry moved to the proofing rooms, where they lived together for a moon cycle to decide if they were compatible.

She stood staring at the blood in the pot while a stone settled into the pit of her stomach. She always knew she'd have to move to the unmarried women's room after her fatecarving, but she needed Dayo to get through the four days before it.

"Well, we'll just have to meet in the Fatewalker Realm," he said matter-of-factly when she told him the news. Then he smiled. "Congratulations, Kalish. You're all grown up now." He laughed. "Even though you are two years younger than me."

Kalish bottled her emotions behind pressed lips and downcast eyes. He wasn't bothered by this turn of events, and that was worse than being separated from him. She wondered if Seeda would take her place next to Dayo in the bunk room. Her only consolation was that Seeda would only do it to spite her, not because she actually wanted to sleep next to Dayo. But Seeda knew as well as Kalish did that Dayo had a crush on her. And the best way to hurt Kalish was to feed Dayo's crush.

"Promise you'll meet me there?" Her voice sounded small in her ears.

"Promise." Dayo gave her a quick hug, and then pulled away. "Can you meet me, for real, on the far side of the butte this afternoon?"

Kalish glanced up at the excitement in his voice—gliders were the only things to elicit that tone. She raised her eyebrows in a question.

Dayo nodded. "I think I've done it. Those modifications we came up with seem to have worked. I want to show you."

Kalish smiled, forgetting her worry. "I'll be there."

Gliders were invented by the Point Clan the same year Kalish was born. Those first gliders were deadly— launched from the cliff tops, the flier was lucky if they didn't drop like a stone. But if the glider flew, a raider could drop incendiaries over an enemy clan's crops or smoke out a terrace dwelling before anyone knew what was happening. That is, if the glider went where they hoped it would—steering was nearly impossible, and more often than not, a glider attack ended in the death of the flier in a heap of sticks and fabric far from the intended target.

Still, the technology was coveted by all the clans, and it wasn't long before the Surefoot Clan stole one. Once the Surefoots had made a few, the Flintcrag Clan kidnapped the young Surefoot warrior, Talek, who had been tinkering with the design. Under torture, he divulged the plans, allowing the Flintcrag Clan to make their own. The Caverna Clan had recovered a crashed Flintcrag glider to start building their own and, in a daring move, Southcrag had kidnapped Caverna's fatecarver, returning her for the ransom of a glider.

So all five clans had learned to make gliders within a few years of their invention. Each clan had continued to tinker with the design, so each made slightly different gliders from the original. Flintcrag's gliders had improved dramatically in reliability—with the development of superfine sugarspike fabric and a lighter frame, Flintcrag gliders always took to the air, and with luck, a flier could bring the glider down safely, though usually deep within a hostile clan's territory.

Kalish and Dayo had been tinkering further with the design. Their aim was to make a glider that was fully steerable, so a raider could not only deliver incendiaries with precision, but also return home and land safely, without injuring the flier or damaging the glider.

Kalish braced herself against the wind at the edge of the cliff, toes automatically gripping the rock. Dayo turned a lazy circle in the air and she raised her fists. "Woo hoo!" She watched for a moment longer as Dayo shifted his weight under the stretched fabric bat wings of his glider and came out of his spiral to glide toward the dry riverbed below. Then she turned and scrambled down the cliff face.

"That was amazing!" she called when she finally pounded across the gravel to Dayo's side, where he was dismantling the wings' frame.

His bronzed face split into a grin. "You think she'll like it?"

The question punched Kalish in the stomach, but she held onto her smile. "Yeah. Seeda will love it." She would, too. Seeda would see immediately that here was a weapon to give the Flintcrag Clan a huge advantage over the other Fatecarver clans. She was greedy enough to even imagine this glider giving them the ability to invade the Treekeeper peoples on the other side of the mountains, or crossing the endless waters. But Kalish doubted it would make Seeda want to marry Dayo. She would string him along and probably claim the glider design as her own, purely to torment Kalish, but she'd never agree to marry him.

At least, she hoped not. Even if Kalish didn't want to keep Dayo for herself, her best friend deserved better than that prickly cactus.

"It looked like shifting your weight was difficult," she said, to change the subject.

Dayo nodded. "I nearly fell off the seat when I started into that spiral. I'm thinking we need to add a rope to tether the rider, just in case."

This was what she loved about Dayo … well, one of the many things she loved about him. He obsessed about flight, just like she did. Kalish considered the problem for a moment. "What if we actually suspended the rider from the wings? Then they could shift their weight by pushing or pulling on the frame, without any risk of falling." She bent down and smoothed the dirt at their feet. "If you made some sort of harness …" She drew in the dust with a finger, sketching a figure suspended below a glider by an arrangement of ropes.

Dayo's eyes narrowed as he considered it. Then his mouth crept into a smile. "That might just work. You, Kalish, are amazing." He gave her a quick peck on the cheek.

Kalish crossed her arms. "So does this mean I get a go?"

Dayo grinned. "Your mother would kill you if she knew. 'The future fatecarver of Flintcrag Clan does not risk her life testing gliders! That's men's work!'" He did a passable imitation of Norili's bark, having been on the receiving end of it often enough.

"Well, I'm not going to tell her, so if she finds out, I'll know who to beat up." Kalish grabbed the

neatly folded wings and headed back toward the cliff,
Dayo laughing at her heels.

That night, in the unfamiliar darkness of the unmarried women's sleeping quarters, Kalish blocked out the
chatter and the giggling and took herself to her cliff-
side retreat.

Dayo wasn't there. Kalish sighed and wrapped
her arms around her legs, resting her chin on her
knees. She gazed out over the scrub, eyes unseeing
while her ears focused, listening for any sound of
Dayo approaching. But the only noise was the buzz of
a grasshopper below.

Time could be deceptive in the Fatewalker
Realm, because the sun didn't move in the sky, but
Kalish waited for what felt like forever, and Dayo still
hadn't appeared. Had he forgotten her? Was he with
Seeda? She tried to ignore the questions drumming at
her mind. Dayo was easily sidetracked. No doubt he
was scribbling diagrams in the dust, planning the
glider suspension system she'd suggested earlier. The
thought brought a smile to her face. She stood and
stretched. Maybe she should go find him. She scrambled back along the cliff and padded silently past the
proofing rooms and along the narrow path to the terrace. Her new sleeping quarters were on the far side
of the terrace, and it was an eerie feeling to walk
through the entire village and find it silent and still in
the middle of the day. She scrambled down a ladder
from the upper terrace to the main terrace and
stepped into the plaza around the pentagonal fatechamber. The fatechamber was the religious hub of
the community. It was five-sided, with each side repre-
senting one of the Fates: Life, Death, Love, War, and

the Unknown. In each wall was a low, tunnel-like entrance that led to the domed chamber inside where religious services were held, proofing couples were married, and storyscars were carved.

Kalish froze mid-step. A voice chanted the
names of the fates—her mother's voice. Kalish
ducked behind the corner of one of the younger children's sleeping rooms. The voice grew louder, and
Kalish peeked out to see her mother rounding the fatechamber. Her eyes were closed, her fingers trailing
the wall to guide her steps. Her heavy beaded capelet
clinked with each step.

"Life, Death, Love, War, Unknown. Guide my
steps and let the path be shown. Life, Death, Love …"
She rounded another corner.

Strong hands grabbed Kalish from behind,
and she would have cried out in surprise, were it not
for the palm against her mouth.

"Quiet, or your mother will hear you."

Kalish stilled instantly, and the hands relaxed.
She turned eager eyes toward the voice she knew.
"Grandmother Ma!" she whispered.

Grandmother Ma's eyes crinkled. She was just
as Kalish remembered, her wiry body vibrating with
energy, her spiky hair stiff with grey clay, making it
look frozen upright. Kalish threw her arms around her
grandmother, tears threatening to spill from her eyes.
She thought she'd never see her father's mother again,
after she died. But of course she'd show up in the
Fatewalker Realm—sneaking around, no doubt, just
like Kalish was. It had been Grandmother Ma who
taught Kalish how to enter the Fatewalker Realm, long
before her mother showed her the *proper* way to do it.

"Sometimes, your body will be in places, situations, where your mind doesn't want to go," she had
28

explained. "You must learn how to take your mind somewhere your body can't follow."

"But only the fatecarver can enter the Fatewalker Realm," Kalish had replied.

Grandmother Ma's eyes had flashed. "That's what your mother says, but she doesn't know everything."

Kalish had long been thankful for Grandmother Ma's teaching. Without the Fatewalker Realm to escape to, she might have wallowed in self-pity for years after her father's death. Now she was doubly thankful. She opened her mouth to speak, but Grandmother Ma held up her hand and pulled her away from the central plaza until they were far enough to talk without risk of being heard.

"It is good to see you, child." She cupped Kalish's face in her gnarled hands. Kalish took in the sight of her grandmother's face—her intricate storyscar, blurred and faded with age, telling how she would leave her birth clan and join the Flintcrags. For the thousandth time, Kalish's gaze travelled over the ropy scar where Grandmother Ma had sliced her own skin away to remove the part of her storyscar that decreed she would wed a man whose name Kalish didn't know—a man who had raped Grandmother Ma when she was a girl.

"Grandmother," Kalish's voice broke, and the words she wanted to speak stuck in her throat. Instead, she threw her arms around the old woman again. As her mind grasped the concept that her dead grandmother could be here, it flew to her father. She pulled away, eyes wide with the thought he might be here, too.

Grandmother Ma, always perceptive, raised a hand. "I never taught him how to come here." Her smile vanished. "If only I had. If only I had known."

Kalish slumped, her flash of hope dashed. But before she could give in to grief, Grandmother Ma grasped her by the shoulders. "Listen to me, child. I've been poking around here for a long time now. I've seen and heard a few things you need to know."

Kalish frowned. "What things?"

"Well, some of them you already know. Like the fact your mother is a greedy, self-important cactus. But I've also learned that the Fates do not have our best interests in mind." Kalish sucked in a breath at the suggestion her people's gods were against them. Grandmother Ma continued. "I'm sure the devout would claim otherwise, but I have seen the Fates conspire to prevent us from advancing our technology, to prevent us from looking beyond the confines of our current territories. I've seen them pit clan against clan, planting seeds of conflict in the storyscars of all clans. They're whispering poison into the ears of every fate-carver, turning clan against clan, even family against family."

"But why? Why would the Fates seek to destroy us when we worship them every five-day?"

Grandmother Ma shook her head. "That I do not know. Perhaps we do not follow their strictures properly. Perhaps they are capricious gods, toying with their subjects. Perhaps it is a test of our own faith—will we destroy ourselves to follow our gods?" She pressed her lips together in distaste.

"But—"

Grandmother Ma shook her head, cutting off the question. "You are nearing your fatecarving, are you not?" Kalish nodded. "Then you must flee."

"What? Before I get my storyscar?" Kalish was nervous about the carving, but it was the pivotal moment in every woman's life. A woman without a storyscar was … not a woman.

"Yes. Before your fatecarving. I don't trust anyone under the influence of the Fates, least of all your power-grabbing mother. I caught her deep in conversation with Life recently, and she has become altogether too smug in her dealings with the Fates."

"But what will I do if I flee? Where will I go?"

Grandmother Ma waved a hand, like it was no issue. "To another clan. You're a smart girl; you'll figure something out, just as I did. I don't even care if you want to get a cursed storyscar, but not carved by your mother. No good will come of it—she will carve your face only to fuel her ambition."

"But—"

"No buts. I'm serious, Kalish. The future the Fates and your mother are forging is one of death and destruction, one in which brothers and sisters turn on one another, in which people fight over scraps. We have to stop playing into their schemes or we'll destroy ourselves."

"How does me running away help that?" Could Grandmother Ma have gone crazy? Many elders did get a bit strange, but in life Grandmother Ma had been sharp-witted to the end. Had death changed her?

Grandmother Ma sighed and cupped Kalish's face in one hand. "I see myself in you. I see the young woman who questioned her own fate. The young woman who loved her people in spite of their faults, who faced challenges with a keen intellect and dogged determination." She dropped her hand and rubbed her own face. "I missed an opportunity to change things when I escaped my own fate. I was afraid. I didn't give credit to my own thoughts, and I had no one to talk to about them. But now I know. The Fatecarver clans must break with the Fates. They must come together as one to preserve their lives and culture."

Kalish laughed. "But I'm going to be a fatecarver! How can I tell people to break with the Fates? Besides, do you think I can just whistle a tune and make everyone forget the Fates and stop fighting? And if I've fled from my own clan and don't even have a storyscar, no one will listen to me."

"Change has to start somewhere. You are strong. You will find a way to make them listen."

"But—"

"Who's there? Kalish, is that you?" Her mother's voice echoed through the terrace, and Kalish sucked in a breath.

Grandmother Ma took Kalish by the shoulders, turning her and pushing her toward the small gap behind the sleeping room next to them. "Go. She can't know you're here. I'll distract her."

"Hello?" Her mother's voice grew closer. Kalish turned and squeezed through the gap.

Four

Dayo found Kalish in the main plaza the next morning, where she sat putting the final touches on the beaded capelet she would don for the first time after her fatecarving—a display of her skill and her womanhood. He approached from behind, but she didn't need to see him to sense him. She gritted her teeth and refused to show him how much his desertion the night before had hurt her. She focused on her work and refused to acknowledge him. In private, they ignored social customs, but here in the plaza, Dayo couldn't speak to her until she spoke first—as a female, and especially as Norili's daughter, she was his better and she must initiate any interactions. She let him sweat for the time it took her to affix four beads. When she did speak, it was one curt word. "Dayo."

Dayo knelt in front of her and whispered, "Kalish, I'm sorry. I was about to come to you when Seeda lay down next to me. *Seeda*!" The excitement in his voice tore at Kalish's heart, and she swallowed hard and forced her voice to calm disinterest before responding.

"And Seeda was more important than me?"

Dayo rolled his eyes. "Well I couldn't exactly slip away while she was there, could I?"

"You could have pretended to be asleep."

"But she wanted to talk. To *me!*"

And if her aim had been to hurt Kalish, she'd done it. Seeda was only two five-days younger than Kalish. Daughter of the clan leader, she had always bullied her way around the terrace. She had a special hatred of Kalish, the only girl of higher rank than her. If Kalish had to hear all about Dayo's pillow talk with Seeda, she might crack someone's head open during fighting practice later. "I thought you might have been working on the glider design."

"Oh! I was. For a long time. I was going to try to make the changes this afternoon. I've got to help in the fields this morning." He might have said he had to roll naked in a bed of cactus, for all his enthusiasm. Dayo was desperate to be classed as a fighter when he reached his coming-of-age trial. To be stuck as a farmer would kill him. Unfortunately, his stature made becoming a fighter unlikely. Kalish didn't know whether to hope her friend managed to become a warrior and fulfil his dreams, or to hope he failed. Seeda would never deign to talk to a farmer.

"Well, good luck with the glider." Kalish draped her capelet over her arm and stood, forcing Dayo to rise and step backward.

"Will you come and help me?"

Finally, Kalish looked him in the eye. "I have other things to do this afternoon." She strode away before he could see her blink away tears. It wasn't until she reached the ladder to the upper terrace that she realised she'd taken off in the wrong direction. She couldn't get used to living on the other side of the terrace from her old room. Well, she wouldn't let him see her turn around. She climbed the ladder, and when she finally rounded Oven Rock and was out of sight, she scurried back to the main terrace by cutting through a few rooms and following the narrow path along the back of the cave wall.

When she returned to her room, a few of the other women were passing by carrying small pigment pots. She feigned interest in their work and made sure she was engaged to help them with a pot firing in the afternoon.

In the evening, she forced herself to chat with Lanzen and Infali, two of the women in her room, and refused to enter the Fatewalker Realm. Let Dayo search for her tonight.

The conversation with Grandmother Ma echoed in Kalish's mind for two days. She wanted to tell Dayo, to talk it out with him and try to make sense of it. There was no one else she could trust with the knowledge that she could, and did, enter the Fatewalker Realm, no one else she could trust with the things Grandmother Ma had said. But by herself, she couldn't decide if she should take her grandmother's advice; she didn't know if she could do it. Survive alone as a fugitive? The thought tied her stomach in knots. Survival might be possible—she knew how to find water and was decent with an atlatl—but how did someone live without a clan? Kalish had never slept without others breathing at her back. She'd never cooked or eaten a meal alone. She'd never travelled except in a group of her clan members. She'd always had elders and others to lead the way, show her how to behave, what to do.

She was a Flintcrag first, and Kalish second. Who would she be if she left the clan?

Only Dayo could help her.

But it wasn't until the day of her fatecarving that Kalish was able to talk to him. And by then it was too late.

Kalish shut her eyes and willed herself not to wince as her mother's mallet beat a rapid tap-tap-tap-tap on the back of the sugarspike thorn ranging across her face. Each jab of the ink-dipped thorn was a tiny wound, but it took thousands of stabs to create a storyscar. Her mother worked intently, and each prick welled with blood, drawing lines of crimson beads on her cheeks. As she lay on her back in the fatechamber, two women pinned her arms, while another steadied her head in the vice-like grip of one who remembered her own coming-of-age ceremony.

The thorn-wielder was Kalish's own mother, but that didn't mean Kalish was spared any pain. On the contrary, she was in for a longer ordeal than most. The fatecarver's own daughter could have nothing less than the most intricate storyscar in the clan. By the time her mother finished, Kalish's entire face, hairline to neck would be traced in the bloody tale of her future.

Kalish held back her tears—the salt would only sting in her wounds—and took herself elsewhere. Her mother would be flitting in and out of the Fatewalker Realm, so Kalish would have to slip away quickly if she was to go unnoticed. As the thorn stabbed again into Kalish's cheek, she left her body behind.

She made her way to her favourite perch, relieved to escape the sting of the carving. Even here, though, her face ached with an echo of what was happening to her body. She sat on the outcrop, warm from the sun, and wrapped her arms around her legs.

She wasn't there long before Dayo appeared. Eyeing her warily, he sat down beside her. "I thought I'd find you here."

Kalish said nothing. She didn't trust her voice, so happy was she to see Dayo hadn't forgotten her.

"If you want me to go I can—"

"No. Stay." She met his eyes. She was tired of acting cool and aloof. Her friend was here for her, when she needed him. "Thank you for coming."

Dayo's body relaxed and he wrapped an arm around Kalish's shoulders. "Is it bad?"

A tear leaked from Kalish's left eye. She wasn't sure which was worse, the fatecarving or the pain of her estrangement with Dayo the past few days. But it wasn't either making her cry now—it was the comfort of Dayo's presence.

Dayo took a deep breath. "Right, then. I can stay here as long as it takes. Should we do something fun? We could hunt mountain goats, or climb to the top of the butte and—"

Kalish didn't want Dayo to let go of her. "Tell me a story."

Among the young members of the terrace, Dayo's stories were legendary. He squinted into the distance for several breaths, and Kalish waited. "At the close of time, all the land began slipping into the sea, to be eaten by great scaled monsters. A girl named Kalish watched her people slowly tumble over the rocks to slip under the devouring water. But Kalish was not afraid. Her grip on the cliffs was as sure as any golo beetle's, and more importantly, she knew how to save the people."

Kalish smiled and settled in to listen. By the time she slipped back into her body, Dayo had turned her into an epic hero, and she had to check her smile, lest she ruin the final touches her mother was applying to her storyscar.

Her face was a mask of pain, and she couldn't help wincing as her mother's assistant gently pressed a cloth to her bleeding skin. When the blood and excess ink had been wiped away, her mother peered down at her with narrowed eyes, scanning her work. She frowned, and Kalish was about to ask what was wrong, when her mother barked at her. "You mustn't talk." She stood, turning her back to Kalish and addressing her assistants. "Wash it four times a day. And use the salve every time."

"Every time? But for the others you just had us use it twice a day." The woman, Neesa, flinched as Kalish's mother glared.

"Every time. And she may not talk for five days." Without a backward glance, she ducked out of the fatechamber through the Unknown's entrance.

Kalish's chest tightened. The Unknown? Why would her mother leave by the Unknown's entrance? It had to be intentional—the door through which one entered and exited the fatechamber was deeply symbolic, and her mother would have chosen her exit with care, knowing the entire population of the terrace would be watching or, if unable to find an excuse to be hanging around the fatechamber, then waiting for the news of her exit.

What fate adorned her face? Her mother's assistants worked silently, cleaning up and then bringing food and water into the chamber. Sitting, Kalish tried to catch their eyes in the hope of reading something in their own faces, but they studiously avoided her gaze. When they exited, they also used the Unknown's entrance.

The silence they left behind was suffocating. How was she to wait ten days, not knowing her fate? Her friend Santha, who had had her fatecarving a year ago, said she was glad for the wait, because she didn't want to be seen for the first time as a woman with a puffy, bleeding face. Kalish didn't give a spine what she looked like—she wanted to know her fate.

Nerves drove her to her feet, but the world swam and her vision darkened. She sank back to the floor. Maybe she shouldn't stand yet. She found the clay jar of water left for her and lifted it to her lips. The liquid was cool and sweet. It must have come straight from the spring—it hadn't yet taken on the earthy tones of the jar.

Kalish gingerly touched her burning cheeks. They felt hot and puffy under her fingertips, as though scorched by the sun. Blood and lymph oozed from the wounds. She brought her knees up and wrapped her arms around them, but when she tried to rest her chin, she felt the sting of the storyscar—it wrapped her chin and even crawled down her neck, by the feel of it. Suddenly weary, Kalish lay down on her back and closed her eyes.

The day after her fatecarving, Neesa veiled her in a black shroud that covered her to her fingertips. Without a word, the woman guided her to one of the exits and through the terrace to a tiny cell where she would remain for another nine days. Through the shroud, Kalish heard the daily life of the terrace fall silent as she passed, and she felt the weight of hundreds of eyes pressing against the fabric. She held her head high and tried hard to walk confidently without stumbling.

Ten days of enforced solitude would have been unbearable without the Fatewalker Realm to escape to. Leaving behind the pain and, later, the itching of her storyscar, Kalish spent hours scaling cliffs, hunting birds and lizards, and simply enjoying the sun on her skin on her favourite perch. But even this would have been hard to take if Dayo hadn't joined her occasionally.

She tried not to wonder what he did on the nights he didn't join her in the Fatewalker Realm. She didn't ask about Seeda, and Dayo was kind enough not to offer any information.

The first time he came upon her, sitting on the perch, his eyes widened and his steps faltered.

Kalish snorted a laugh. "Well, that answers my question about whether I'd have the storyscar here." Her stomach knotted as Dayo eased himself beside her, his eyes roving over her face. What did he see? Kalish revised her attitude toward being seen with a red and puffy face—she wished Dayo hadn't seen her this soon after her carving, and hoped that here in the Fatewalker Realm the inflammation was absent.

"You're a woman now."

"I was seven days ago, even before this." Kalish waved a hand at her face.

Dayo blushed. "Yeah, but now it shows." His eyes flicked back to her storyscar.

Kalish swallowed. "What does it look like? Can you read it?"

"You know they don't teach boys to read storyscars."

"They don't teach them to enter the Fate-walker Realm either, but that hasn't stopped you."

Dayo nodded an acknowledgement, but said nothing.

"Well?" Kalish's pulse quickened as Dayo hesitated.

"There's no fatecarver mark. You're … you're not going to be a fatecarver."

"What?" It felt like someone had jumped on her chest. No fatecarver mark? Everyone, including her, had assumed she would be the next fatecarver—the role often ran in families. Her mother had been training her.

"But …" She wanted to say, *I'm the fatecarver's daughter, I have to be fatecarver.* But her grandmother's words came back to her. *I don't trust anyone under the influence of the Fates, least of all your power-grabbing mother.* This wasn't a twist of the Fates, this was her mother's doing. Her mother didn't want her to be a fatecarver. Didn't want her to hold the most powerful position in the clan. She swallowed the sour taste in her mouth. "What else do you see?"

Dayo shook his head, knitting his brows. "I don't know. There's a swirl here, and a pair of what could be wings here." His finger traced her skin, and his eyes glittered as he stroked the wings. It sent a shiver through Kalish.

"What else? What's down my neck?" Kalish turned her head so he could see better. Most storyscars didn't extend to the neck.

He shrugged. "Some sort of plant? I really can't tell." He swallowed. His eyes kept flicking to her forehead, and every time they rested there, they looked more troubled.

"What is it? What do you keep looking at?"

"You have lantan eyes."

"What? On my forehead?" Kalish ran her fingers over her brow, as though she might be able to feel them.

"Why would you have lantan eyes?"

What had her mother been up to? Why had she marked her daughter with the eyes of a deadly snake—an animal that embodied deceit and treachery in the way it camouflaged itself among the rocks to strike at unwary climbers, in the way its venom stung only briefly, but then, when all seemed well, turned muscles to quivering sludge?

Dayo's eyes flashed with fear, as if he were looking at a real lantan. Then he pressed his lips together and wrapped an arm around Kalish's shoulders. "The Fates must have had a reason."

Kalish grunted. She still hadn't told Dayo about her meeting with Grandmother Ma. He didn't know what she'd said about the Fates. Kalish wasn't sure she wanted to tell him right now—his belief in the goodwill of the Fates was clearly the only thing preventing him from believing she was a poisonous snake. She bit her tongue.

When she wasn't escaping to the Fatewalker Realm, Kalish paced the semi-darkness of her cell, listening below the small high window in a vain attempt to hear what was going on outside and chafing at her captivity. The only bright spot was that she didn't have to attend the regular Fateday ceremony, held every five days—the stuffy, crowded fatechamber on Fateday had never been her favourite place, and since her talk with Grandmother Ma, she had seen nothing but empty ritual in the service.

Four times a day, Neesa came in silence to wash her face and apply a salve that soothed the pain and itching. Her mother never checked on her.

FIVE

Kalish greeted the tenth day with eyes red from lack of sleep. She'd waited for ages in the Fatewalker Realm for Dayo the previous night, and he never came. When she finally returned to her body, sleep had eluded her as her mind flitted between visions of Dayo with Seeda and the outcome of her fate reading the following day.

Her agitation increased with the light of day, and she paced her cell, blowing on her sweaty hands to dry them. Her stomach was knotted, and she hoped she wouldn't be expected to eat anything before her reading. She tugged at her clay-spiked hair, pulling it down over her brow, hoping it would hide the snake eyes. After ten days of neglecting her appearance, there wasn't much clay left anyway, and it flopped easily.

Neesa entered carrying Kalish's beaded capelet. She would wear it for the first time today. The garment's reassuring weight calmed her as she fastened it around her shoulders. She took a slow breath, stilled her thoughts, and looked up into Neesa's eyes. The

44

woman, whose face had been a rock for ten days, gave her a nod, and her eyes softened. She tossed the veil over Kalish's head and led her out.

The reading was done in the elders' private courtyard. Kalish had frequented the elders' quarters when Grandmother Ma had been alive and living there, but it had been years since she'd last entered the cool silence of their courtyard. The elders had frightened her a little as a child—their wrinkled skin, confident walk, and dusty smell made them seem like a different species, as though they were truly gods, like the Fates. But now, Kalish refused to be frightened. These women held power over her within the clan. They would, indeed, read her fate today. But Grandmother Ma had shown her their power was not absolute—her fate would be read, but not sealed today. Whatever game her mother was playing, whatever the elders decided, Kalish was not bound unless she wanted to be. The thought of defying the clan, defying her fate, was more frightening than leaping off a cliff hanging onto an untested glider, but she clung to it because, like a glider, it offered the possibility of freedom.

Sounds of the terrace were muted in the elders' courtyard, and the elders themselves didn't speak as Neesa lifted the veil from Kalish's head and left her in the centre of a circle of frost-haired women, their own storyscars faded with time. Neesa stepped away and the elders closed in, peering at her face in silence. Kalish focused her gaze on a crack in the rear wall of the cave that formed the back of the courtyard.

One of the women reached out and brushed Kalish's hair off her forehead. Kalish flicked her focus to the woman, watching for her reaction as her lantan eyes were revealed. But steady breathing was the only response the elders gave; their faces were as still as rock, and about as soft. The women's shrewd eyes scrutinised every detail of Kalish's face, and the examination grew more excruciating by the moment. Would they say nothing? Give no hints? She knew they would need to discuss it and come to a consensus, but surely they would tell her *something* before she left.

But they did not. Just as Kalish thought she would explode with impatience, Tanala, the most elderly of the women, nodded. All the elders stepped back and, summoned by some signal Kalish didn't see, Neesa reappeared. She draped the veil over Kalish's head again and led her back to her cell.

Impatience turned to concern and then panic as Kalish waited to be summoned for the elders' reading. She couldn't eat the goat stew Neesa brought her at midday, nor the roast tubers she delivered as the sun began to set.

"You should eat. Have you at least been drinking?" They were the first words Neesa had said to her in ten days.

Kalish wrapped her arms around her roiling stomach. "I can't." Her voice felt dusty with disuse.

Neesa frowned and pointed at the jug of water on the floor. "Drink. That's an order." She crossed her arms and watched until Kalish had taken several swallows.

"When will they send for me?" She knew the elders had already taken an inordinate amount of time discussing her fate.

Neesa pressed her lips together. "I don't know." She opened her mouth as if to say something else, then closed it again. After a moment's hesitation, she pointed to the food she'd brought. "Eat. You'll need your strength." Then she was gone.

She waited in the dark cell for what felt like an age before Neesa returned to toss the veil over Kalish's head and lead her back to the elders again. The elders' courtyard was bathed in the amber light of dozens of torches. Others were present, in addition to the elders, arrayed in a circle. Her mother was there—as fatecarver and her mother, she was twice expected. Kalish searched her mother's face but her thoughts were veiled. Then Kalish's eyes widened as she recognised Wathi, her face registering pride as she surveyed Kalish. Wathi was no blood relation of Kalish, and as such had no right to be at her storyscar ceremony. But the entire terrace knew how she'd taken in the frightened and grieving fatecarver's daughter after her father's death. Kalish glanced between Wathi and her mother, but neither gave any indication of how they felt about the other's presence.

Kalish stepped into the centre of the circle of women, forcing her head up as her stomach threatened to reject the little food she'd managed to choke down. Tanala stepped forward. "The elders have examined the storyscar of Kalish, daughter of Fatecarver Norili, daughter of Warrior Tanja, fosterling of Wathi." Kalish caught a flash of her mother's eyes, her nose pinched and her face hard. "The Fates have spoken through their conduit, Fatecarver Norili. They have guided the hand that drove the thorn. They have inked their will and wisdom on the face of this young clanswoman. We, the elders, faithfully recount the will of the Fates."

Kalish took a breath and held it, desperate to still her shaking hands.

"Kalish of Flintcrag Clan. Your fate is revealed for all." Tanala's face clouded for a moment at the close of the prescribed words. "However, your patron Fate is the Unknown, and not all of your fate can be understood."

What did that mean? Is that why it had taken the elders so long to discuss her fate? Tanala continued. "Kalish, you are fated to fly as the kiriki falcons. The wind will be your guide and conveyance. Your understanding will encompass the unknown. Innovation will guide your life, and save it." That all sounded positive. Tanala's eyes flicked for an instant to Norili. "However, your life will not be lived within the Flintcrag Clan. You will betray the clan, its interests, its survival. You will bring disaster among us and turn clanswomen against clanswomen. Your fate holds the deceit of the lantan—unseen but deadly."

Tanala might as well have kicked Kalish in the gut. She opened her mouth to object, but Tanala's sharp look stopped her. "Your loyalty to your clan will be tested, and you will fail." Tanala bowed her head. "This is a fair and accurate reading of your storyscar, as determined by the council of elders."

Before Kalish could overcome her shock, Manari, one of the more sprightly of the elders, stepped forward. "The elders have decreed you should be expelled from the clan. We will not suffer a live lantan in our midst, but out of respect for Fatecarver Norili, we will not kill you immediately. Before first light, you will be gone from the terrace, and if you are seen within Flintcrag territory after three days, you will be counted an enemy and treated accordingly."

The weight in Kalish's stomach threatened to buckle her knees. The elders' gazes were impassive. Wathi looked stricken, her mouth hanging open as she stared at Manari. Kalish's mother gave her one hard glare—a glare that conveyed the sum of all the ways Kalish had failed—then strode out of the courtyard.

The elders retreated to their rooms, their task accomplished. Wathi recovered herself and hurried to Kalish's side. She wrapped an arm around her shoulders. "Come. You must go before word gets out. You won't leave empty-handed."

Without Wathi's support, Kalish wasn't sure she would have been able to walk out of the courtyard. Her body had turned to stone, and her brain was as sluggish as the trickle from a drying spring. She vaguely registered the hurried walk to Wathi's room, and the way Wathi angled her body as they passed the few people out after dark so as to conceal her. She was dimly aware of Wathi bustling around her room by the light of a lamp, gathering supplies into a bundle and whispering instructions to her husband, who slipped out into the darkness.

It wasn't until Wathi pressed a bowl of cold stew into her hands that Kalish's mind snapped into focus again. "You must eat."

Kalish blinked at the stew, prepared hours earlier by Wathi's husband and her neighbours over communal fires in communal pots for any residents of the terrace who needed food. It would be her last meal in her clan. Her last meal prepared by someone else. "I don't even know how to cook."

"You are an excellent hunter, and you know how to find water and light a fire—you'll live. You'll find a clan to take you in. You're clever." Wathi poured water from a jug into a water skin.

Kalish's chest tightened. "Dayo."

"There's not time." Wathi glanced at Kalish, and in spite of her clipped words, her eyes brimmed with compassion. "Eat. As soon as Jenti returns, you will leave."

Kalish ate.

A short time later, she gazed up at the terrace from the bottom of the cliff. Her home, silent and dark, and no longer welcoming. She doubled over and vomited. The food was gone, but the weight in her stomach remained. She blinked tears from her eyes and scanned the stars. Wathi had been right. There was no time. She'd be lucky to clear the end of the canyon before dawn. Shoving her emotions deep inside, she shifted the bundle on her back and set off up the valley.

Six

Kalish stumbled with grief and fatigue. She'd made it as far as the upper reaches of the gorge the prime terrace nestled in. As dawn coloured the sky, she threw herself into a tiny crevice behind a sugarspike plant and fell into an exhausted sleep.

Waking to the sound of voices, she realised her mistake. She should have moved further off the path before bedding down. Her cramped quarters were separated by only a few spiky leaves from what was clearly a well-travelled route. Kalish knew the gorge was dotted with small terraces—most housing no more than one or two families—but she'd never paid them much attention. Why would a future fate-carver concern herself with the poor cousins of the clan? Those who didn't rank enough to inhabit Prime Terrace were beneath her notice.

Unable to remain in her rocky crevice all day, Kalish tumbled out when she thought the path was empty. Cramping legs made her clumsy, and she tripped, landing hard on her knee and peeling much of the skin off. The injury wouldn't have fazed her under normal circumstances—blood flowed as often as water in Kalish's life—but the reality of her banishment crushed her, and the pain in her knee and her heart overflowed in anger. As Kalish cursed and picked herself up, a young woman came skittering down the path from above. "Here, let me help you." She caught Kalish around the waist and pulled one of her arms over her shoulder with practised ease. As she helped Kalish up the steep slope, she kept up a soothing monologue. "That section of the path is deceptively treacherous. Even those of us who live here sometimes take a tumble there. Just a five-day ago I slipped and spilled an entire jug of water. Lucky I didn't break the jug. I had to go all the way back to the stream and refill it. It's not your fault you slipped. Of course, the path works wonders on our enemies, but it's hardly welcoming."

They reached a tiny terrace nestled in a shallow cave. Just three rooms reaching from floor to ceiling filled the space, with barely enough room outside for a small bread oven and a cooking fire. The woman overturned a tall pot and gently lowered Kalish onto it. She lifted Kalish's bundle off her back and set it beside her. Then she knelt, grasping Kalish's knee to examine it. "I'll need to stitch that." She ducked into one of the rooms and returned with a cloth, a pot of water, and a small bundle of rolled leather. She dipped the cloth in the water and gently patted Kalish's knee.

It was the kindness that undid her. Had the woman fought her off or even told her to go away, pride would have kept Kalish bound together. But the woman's gentle care reminded her too much of her father, Dayo, and Wathi. It reminded her too much of what she'd lost. She sucked in a great shuddering breath and covered her face with her hands as tears coursed down her cheeks. The woman worked in silence, cleaning and stitching Kalish's knee.

"Verlent, who's there with you?" The querulous voice came from one of the rooms.

"A visitor, Grandma. She's injured and I'm tending to her wounds. Some of them," she added under her breath. She finished her stitching and rolled her needle and thread back into the leather bundle. The pain of the stitching had helped bring Kalish back to her senses, which were raw and exposed, as though she'd scraped her insides instead of her knee. She lifted her face and swiped the back of her hand over it to dry her tears. Verlent stood up and disappeared into one of the rooms, returning with her grandmother, supporting her just as she had supported Kalish. The elder's right leg was twisted, and her foot struck the ground at such an awkward angle it made Kalish wince. But her face was clear and her eyes bright as she examined Kalish. Her granddaughter set her on another overturned pot, and the old woman smiled up at her. "You're a cool summer rain, my dear. Sorry I'm such a burden."

The young woman's eyes crinkled in response. "Oh, stop it Grandma. You're no burden."

The affection between the two almost brought Kalish to tears again, but she pressed a finger against her freshly stitched knee and the pain grounded her.

The elder narrowed her eyes at Kalish, and Kalish shrank away. She knew that look. The woman was reading her storyscar.

"Your storyscar is no more than eleven days old. It does not mark you as Flintcrag Clan, but you couldn't have come all the way from Surefoot or Caverna since your reading, so I'm guessing you've been banished." Her lips puckered in distaste, and Kalish

swallowed her nerves, not certain how to respond to
the accusation without risking a fight.

The elder's eyes continued to rove over
Kalish's face. "Yes … I see why they banished you."

Kalish snorted. "I bet you don't." She pushed
her limp hair off her forehead, showing her lantan
eyes. The old woman let out a surprised "Oh!" and
Kalish shook her hair down again.

"You look familiar, girl. Whose daughter are
you? It's been years since I've been at Prime Terrace,
but you came from there, didn't you?"

Kalish nodded. "I'm Norili's daughter."

Both women's eyebrows rose, and the younger
spoke in hushed tones. "And your mother carved that
storyscar." She shook her head. "You poor thing."

She should flee. Surefoot Clan was still days away, and
the longer she stayed in Flintcrag territory, the more
likely she was to have to fight her own clanspeople.
But the affection between Verlent and her grandmother reminded Kalish of Dayo. She couldn't bear
the thought of not saying goodbye to him. Maybe she
could even convince him to come with her, if only she
could see him again.

She lurked around Flintcrag territory for days,
hoping to catch him on the way to the fields or up on
the mesa tops where he tested his gliders. But he never
appeared.

At night, she entered the Fatewalker Realm
and haunted their special meeting spot, but he didn't
appear there, either. It was as if he was avoiding her.

Or being kept from her.

Then six days after her banishment he materialised in her campsite. "I thought you might be hang-

ing around." His body was stiff and his voice expressionless. When Kalish jumped to her feet and moved to embrace him, he stepped away from her. "You need to leave. I know what your storyscar means."

Kalish swallowed the lump rising in her throat. This wasn't her Dayo. "You believe what they say about it."

"You will betray us." He said it like it was a personal insult.

"Dayo, you know me. You know I'm loyal to the clan. I've spent my entire life preparing to be its fatecarver."

"It's written across your face, Kalish." He grimaced. "Go."

"Come with me." Kalish took a step toward him.

"Go, or I'll have to kill you." His voice shook. "You're an enemy of the clan now."

"But I'm not. You *know* that." She reached out to touch his arm, but he shoved her away, making her stumble backward.

"Go!"

She blinked to keep from crying as something squeezed her chest. How could Dayo believe the elders? How could he do this to her? *The same way he pursued Seeda while ignoring you,* said a voice inside her head. Maybe he had never been the friend she thought he was. The thought churned in her stomach.

Well, if he was going to be hard and cold, she would be too. She squared her shoulders. "I need to gather my things." Though in truth, she kept her bundle ready to snatch and run. She picked it up and slung the strap over her shoulder. "Seeda will never marry you, no matter how good a glider you make. She only pretends to like you because she hates me." It was the most hurtful thing she could think to say, and she didn't wait for his reaction. She turned and strode into the night.

She made good time once the moon was up, lighting her way. Anger gave her stamina and she ran through the night toward Surefoot Clan. Having finally turned her feet and heart away from home, her mind turned to the future. She was an enemy in Surefoot Clan, but if she could prove her value to them, they might take her in. What could she offer them? She'd spent sixteen years preparing to become her clan's fatecarver. Could she offer that? No. She didn't have a fatecarver's mark, and the truth was, all she had learned was how to grind pigments and chant prayers. What else did she have to offer?

Morning found her still within Flintcrag territory, exhausted, hungry, and still without a plan for how to approach Surefoot Clan. After a brief rest, she focused on satisfying her immediate needs—food and water. The scrub she stalked through hid plenty of game, and she hoped for a rabbit. She pulled out her atlatl and held it at the ready.

A family of goats browsing its way through the scrub was even better than rabbit, and Kalish crouched, watching intently as one youngster strayed from the others. That was her goat—food for several days. Her mouth watered as she crept toward it.

The soft roll of bare feet on dry earth behind her made Kalish freeze. She inched under a thorny bush and flattened herself against the ground, ignoring the pain of the spines pressing against her legs and back. Breathing shallowly, she listened. More than one set of feet were creeping through the scrub. She caught a glimpse of a man with an atlatl at the ready, his gaze locked ahead. Locked on *her* goat. *Spines!* She wasn't confident the straggly bush would conceal her from the hunting party. Her only hope was that their focus was firmly fixed on the very goat she had hoped to bring down.

The steps came closer, and she pressed herself into the ground, willing her form to disappear in the dappled light under the bush. From the corner of her eye, she watched a pair of crouched legs creep by, so close she could have reached out and grabbed an ankle. Dayo would have urged her to do it, simply for the fun of watching the man's reaction. But Dayo wasn't here, and by now, word of Kalish's fate would have reached all but the most remote terraces in the Flintcrag Clan. Kalish had overstayed her welcome in Flintcrag territory. Everyone here was an enemy now.

The hunters padded past her hiding spot. One whistled like a rock skipper, and the sound was followed by the whoosh of at least four atlatls. A clatter of hooves on rock, and then the pounding of feet signalled Kalish's release from the thorn bush. She sucked in a breath and rolled out from under the prickly branches. Several spines remained embedded in her legs, and she plucked them out with a wince. Crouching, she raised her head just enough to see the hunting party. They'd bagged the goat. A shame. Kalish had been looking forward to something other than jerky for her dinner.

But now wasn't the time to worry about food. It wouldn't take the hunters long to tie up the goat's legs and sling it over a shoulder for the walk home. By the time they passed again, she needed to be far enough away to avoid being seen. She adjusted her dwindling bundle of supplies and scuttled toward a series of rocky spires where she intended to take shelter for the day.

Grumpy and tired, she spent the day alternately dozing and nursing resentment for Dayo, her mother, and all her clan. She thought of Dayo and all the hours they'd spent together—on the cliff tops by day, and in the Fatewalker Realm by night, planning, dreaming, laughing—the memories twisted in her chest, strangling her heart and her breath. Why had Dayo befriended her in the first place, all those years ago? Maybe he hadn't meant for her to become attached to him. Maybe he regretted his kindness.

He certainly didn't return her feelings. Seeda! If anyone was a lantan, it was her. Kalish had an urge to spy on Dayo, just to be there when Seeda dashed his hopes.

Her bitter thoughts filled her stomach with bile, which was fine—she felt limp and listless in the heat of the day. She had a small quantity of dried meat still, but the thought of eating anything made her ill. She closed her eyes and wrenched her thoughts from Dayo to consider how she would approach the Surefoot Clan.

Hours later, she jerked awake to the sound of her name.

Seven

"Kalish!"

Her eyes flew open. *Spines!* She'd slept well into the night. She should have been moving, not sleeping. And now someone was nearby, calling her name. She held her breath and listened.

A breeze hissed in the dry grasses.

A fox barked far in the distance.

Something scrabbled near her head, and her heart raced. It moved again and she rolled her eyes at her own fear. Mouse. Probably going for what was left of her food. Cautiously, she reached out and shifted the bundle. The mouse scurried away.

Well, she must have been dreaming the voice. All was calm and silent. Still, there was no reason not to be cautious. She quietly slung her bundle over her shoulder and stood. The moon wasn't yet up, but the stars were out. She scanned the dark mounds of tussock and light sand, looking for any darkness out of place.

There was nothing. She should be on her way. She crept out of her hiding place with silent hunting steps, though she felt like the hunted rather than the hunter. She kept to the jumble of rocks where she'd hidden, trusting in their bulk and shadows to disguise her.

But it seemed her caution was unnecessary. The night remained quiet, and after a few minutes of furtive creeping, she straightened her shoulders and broke into a comfortable travelling lope in the hope of making it to Surefoot territory before dawn.

"Kalish!"

Her vision flickered and she stumbled. "Dayo?" she whispered.

"Kalish!"

She fell to her knees. He was calling her from the Fatewalker Realm. Dragging her into it with him.

"Kalish!"

She scrambled under a thorny bush—her body was at the mercy of the world when she was in the Fatewalker Realm, and she didn't want to collapse out in the open. Under the bush she curled into a ball and dove after Dayo's voice.

She saw him right away in the bright sun of the Fatewalker Realm, frantically running this way and that, calling her name, peering around rocks and under tussocks. Her first instinct was to call out and run to him—he looked terrified—but her anger surfaced, and she crossed her arms and silently stood her ground.

"Kalish! I need you! Kalish!" He was nearly sobbing, and it took all of her self-control to remain still. It was a relief when he finally spied her. He ran to her, and she thought he might embrace her, but he pulled up short, eyeing her warily. "I need you. I've been bitten by a lantan."

Kalish narrowed her eyes at him. "And you don't have alna leaves?" Everyone carried a pouch of the leaves with them—if you swallowed them quickly after a bite, you'd probably survive.

Dayo nodded. "I did, but they'd gotten damp—they were mouldy. I ate them, but they're not doing anything." A sweat had broken out on his forehead, and he panted, as though he were in pain.

Kalish's heart twisted and her resolve crumbled. "Where are you?"

Two hours of hard running in the dark brought her to the foot of the mesa Dayo had been scaling when he was bitten. She hardly slowed, but threw herself at the rock, grabbing handholds wherever she could, not planning her route, but powering upward blindly. Her muscles burned with the effort, and she forced herself not to think about the fact Dayo could already be dead, but to focus on getting to him as quickly as possible.

Three quarters of the way up, she pulled herself onto a ledge, only to hear the telltale staccato tapping of a lantan's warning beside her. *Spines!* Of course there was a lantan here. She leapt off the ledge and continued her climb—at a more measured pace now, looking out for snakes as she went. Not that she'd see them in the dark, but her slower pace allowed the snakes to get out of her way.

Her muscles shook and her lungs heaved by the time she clawed her way to the top. But she didn't stop. Dayo's form was visible in the moonlight, inert, sprawled no more than a dozen body lengths from the cliff.

"Dayo, I'm here," she panted, staggering towards him. "Dayo?" She fell to her knees beside him and rolled him onto his back. His head lolled and his limbs flopped. His eyes stared at nothing. "Dayo!" She couldn't keep the anguish out of her voice as she lay her head against his chest, listening for a heartbeat, feeling for a breath—anything to tell her he lived. After an eternal few moments, he drew in a shallow, rasping breath.

Kalish tore off her bundle and unwrapped it, scrabbling around to find her alna leaves. In his state, with lantan poison paralysing most of his muscles, he wouldn't be able to chew them, and he might not even be able to swallow. Kalish popped a bundle of dried leaves into her mouth and chewed until she tasted their sharp bitter bite and the leaves had turned to a vile paste. Then she spat them out into her hand, eased Dayo's mouth open, and slid the squishy ball under his tongue. She closed his jaw and waited, her hands cradling his face. After a moment she turned her head and spat—alna wasn't something you ate unless you were dying, and her saliva glands were trying to purge the flavour from her mouth.

"Come on Dayo," she muttered. "Live."

He took another shallow breath, and she could see the effort it cost him in the shudder it sent through his body.

"That's it. Breathe." She blinked back tears. "Come on, breathe!"

Another breath.

She wiped a damp clump of hair off his forehead, smoothing it back into his braids. "You have to live, Dayo. You have to come back." She felt four years old again, holding her father's head though he was already gone. A tear rolled down her face and splashed onto Dayo's cheek.

Another breath.

Kalish swiped her tear away with her thumb. "You have to live." She bent down and kissed his cheek.

His face spasmed and he swallowed. Then he opened his mouth, as if to spit.

Kalish clamped her hands over his jaw. "Oh no you don't. Swallow." She could feel his trembling resistance, but she kept her hands over him like a vice. "Swallow."

He swallowed, and then took another breath, smoother this time. His eyes blinked twice, and then closed. His chest rose and fell twice more in quick succession. Kalish relaxed her grip and sobbed a laugh, and then the tears came in great rivulets down her cheeks.

After that came hours of waiting. Kalish did her best to make Dayo comfortable, but she couldn't alleviate the pain of muscle cramps the lantan poison caused. As Dayo moaned and twitched, drifting in and out of consciousness, she sat, his head cradled in her lap. She spoke soothing words to him and stroked his face, just as he had done to her when she was little and frightened.

When the sun rose, she saw his swollen purple foot—the site of the bite. She wished she had a salve for it. With the sun came a fierce hot wind. There was no shelter on the mesa top, but Dayo had been carrying a glider. She stripped the fabric from the frame and draped it loosely over both of them to create some shade and block the grit that skittered along the ground.

By midday, Dayo's condition had improved dramatically. With his increasing lucidity came an awkward silence. Kalish let his head rest on the ground and shifted to a crouch beside him.

He eyed her warily. "Water," he croaked.

She lifted his head and helped him drink from his water skin. A muscle spasm juddered through him and water spilled down his face. Kalish reached out to wipe it away, but pulled her hand back as Dayo jerked his face away from her touch. She lowered his head again and shuffled away from him.

He shut his eyes again against another muscle spasm. When his body relaxed, he said, "Thank you. You should go."

Kalish pressed her lips together. She wanted to tell him she wasn't about to leave her best friend helpless and exposed like this. But it was clear they were no longer best friends. They were no longer even fellow clan members. She was the enemy. A lantan waiting to strike. Ironic, really, given the situation. She blinked back tears and silently slipped out from under the makeshift shelter.

Dayo might have mentioned he was with others.

Kalish had barely reached the bottom of the cliff when four young men trotted up to her. Meech, Tino, Janth, and Sala—she knew them all from Prime Terrace. "Dayo's on the mesa." She pointed up. "Lantan bite. I gave him alna. He'll live, but he—"

"It's her! The lantan!" Meech's eyes widened.

Janth lunged before Kalish could react, grabbing her arm in a vice grip. "What have you done with Dayo?"

Kalish struggled against him, to no effect. "Get your hands off me!" No man would assault a woman like this. "I told you. I saved his life."

"Don't lie, snake." Janth shook her.

"I'm not lying. Let me go!"

Janth was half again larger than Kalish, and strong too—she couldn't dislodge his hand, which only gripped tighter the more she struggled. His hard stare never left her as he ordered Tino and Sala up the cliff to check her story. "You're not welcome in Flintcrag territory."

Kalish rolled her eyes. "I'm aware of that. I wouldn't be in Flintcrag territory, except that Dayo called for help."

Janth glowered. "We've been looking for him most of the night. How did you hear him and we didn't? You were supposed to be gone over a five-day ago."

Spines. He had her there. She couldn't possibly explain that he'd called her through the Fatewalker Realm. "My hearing must be better than yours. Let me go." She jerked her arm again, and then winced as his fingers dug into her muscles. She shifted her gaze to Meech, watching with wide eyes. "Meech, you know me. We roomed together not that long ago. Tell him to let me go."

Meech swallowed nervously, his glance darting to Janth's face. "Um …"

"Don't let her fool you. She's a lantan. The elders read it in her face. She'll betray us."

"Betray you? Who's betrayed whom here? Who's been kicked out of her clan for no reason?"

"The reason's written all over your face." He gestured to Meech with his free hand. "Give me your knife. We'll kill her now."

Meech stepped back. "Um …"

The Fate he would kill her. They thought her a lantan? Well, she'd act like one then. Kalish lowered her head and bit Janth's wrist. She ground her teeth until she tasted blood. Janth howled and let go.

"What the Fate?" Janth clutched his wrist. Kalish didn't wait to see what he'd do next. She ran.

Eight

Janth and Meech pursued Kalish all afternoon into the night. She didn't lose them until she was well into Surefoot territory. But if she thought she might find the Surefoot Clan more welcoming, she was soon relieved of the notion. Curled in a clump of tussock trying to catch a few minutes of sleep as dawn neared, Kalish was too exhausted to wake before the Surefoot hunting party stumbled across her.

Six men ringed her, a variety of weapons at the ready, when a kick roused her. She blinked, confused and weary. Expecting Janth and Meech, she frowned at the unfamiliar faces. She rubbed her eyes and tried to sit up.

"Don't move or you're dead," an older man barked as the others tensed for the kill. Kalish froze. Against three axes, two atlatls and a knife, she hadn't a chance. "Who are you?"

She had no clan mark on her face. She could claim to be from anywhere. She could claim to be anyone. But the truth was probably her best ally. If they thought she had information they could use against Flintcrag, they'd let her live.

"I am Kalish, daughter of Norili. I was driven from Flintcrag Clan after my fatecarving revealed I would betray them."

Six sets of eyebrows rose. "You have the eyes of a lantan," said the older man. "How do we know you speak the truth?"

Kalish brushed her hair back over her forehead. "There's a pair of Flintcrag men who've chased me here. They can't be far away."

One of the younger men leaned in, raising his axe higher. "She's brought a war party with her. She's a decoy to distract us while the men attack."

The older man raised a finger. "That's no reason to kill her … yet. Tana, Maled, Riven—see if you can find this pair." Three of the men melted away. "You." He waved his bow at Kalish. "Get up."

Kalish rose slowly, keeping her hands visible and open. She gave no resistance when one of the men approached and tied her hands behind her back, and then slipped the knife out of the sheath strapped to her leg. She'd expected as much. In an ideal scenario, she would have approached a terrace on her own, with a plan and a gift, but this could work too. One of the men picked up her bundle and rifled through it. "An atlatl, water skin, some dried food, herbs. Nothing of interest." He dismissed all her worldly possessions.

"Bring it," ordered the older man. He turned his attention to Kalish. "You will come with us. If you try to escape, we'll kill you before you take ten steps." Kalish nodded. They would have to take her to their prime terrace to be judged by the elders. If they didn't simply kill her. She had never been to Surefoot's prime

terrace, but she knew from Flintcrag raiding cam-
paigns that it was three days from the border.

They set a swift pace toward the mountains
and deeper into Surefoot territory. At first, one of the
younger men kept a hand firmly clamped on her arm,
but after a few hours, when it was clear she wasn't
planning on bolting and the terrain grew rocky and
challenging to navigate as a pair, he let go. "I'm a step
behind you," he warned.

The men were silent as they travelled. When
the three who had gone searching for Janth and
Meech returned, they muttered a few words to the
older man. He nodded and glanced at Kalish, but his
face gave no clue as to what the searchers had found.
Or whether Janth and Meech still lived. Kalish was
surprised to find she didn't care. Janth had been willing to kill her, and Meech hadn't had the backbone to
speak out against him.

The path they followed took them along a dry
riverbed dotted with boulders. Kalish struggled to
keep her balance with her hands tied. The men didn't
slacken their pace for her, but when she slipped on a
loose rock, the one behind her grabbed her arm and
kept her from falling. She raised her eyebrows at him,
and he shrugged. She was a prisoner from a rival clan,
but she was still a woman and was glad to see that
commanded some respect.

The day grew hot, and Kalish's exhaustion began to catch up with her. As they climbed out of the
river valley into a maze of hoodoos that made her jaw
drop, only the stunning scenery kept her on her feet.
When they finally stopped for a rest, she threw herself
into the shade of a scraggly tree and shut her eyes.

She opened them with a start when someone
loosened her bonds. It was the older man. "You'll
68

need your hands soon." The man who had been carrying her bundle handed her water skin to her.

"Thank you." She drank eagerly, glad she'd refilled her skin before Dayo's call for help.

The older man scrutinised her. "Kalish, daughter of Norili. Norili the fatecarver?"

Kalish blinked at him. "You know my
mother?"

He shook his head. "My wife is from
Flintcrag." A smile flitted across his face. "We met at
the Assembly years ago." The Assembly was a gathering of all clans on neutral ground, where intermingling
and intermarriage were encouraged in order to ease
tensions among clans. Kalish had never gone—it was
an adult-only affair—but her terrace hosted several
members who had arrived with a spouse from the Assembly. Some adopted their new clan wholeheartedly,
as fiercely loyal to it as native-born members. Others
never quite forgot their roots. Kalish wondered which
this man's wife was, and whether it would make a difference to how she was treated when she arrived.

"Tana, you may as well tell her what you
found." The older man nodded to the tallest of the
three who had searched for Janth and Meech.

Tana's grin was predatory, and Kalish fought
the urge to run. "You'll be happy to know we found
your two clansmen and no one else. And at a guess,
you'll also be happy to know they won't be chasing
you or anyone else ever again." He narrowed his eyes.
"That was quite a bite on the taller one's wrist. Looked
like it had gone bad already."

Kalish didn't hide her own smile. "Lantans are
dangerous." It was probably a stupid thing to say—she
was their captive, and any indication she might fight
back could go badly—but there was a note of respect

in Tana's voice that emboldened her. The men believed her story, that she'd been chased out of her clan. They knew she came with them willingly.

Of course, they also knew she had no choice in the matter. Willing or not, she was going to have to face the Surefoot elders and prove her worth to the clan. Her stomach flipped. How was she going to do that? She hadn't worked out a plan yet. She frowned. "How long before we reach the prime terrace?"

"We're not headed to Prime. Not yet, at least. We were only out for the day, and aren't prepared for a journey that long. We're headed to Western Terrace. The women will decide what to do with you."

"How far to Western?" She scanned the towering hoodoos rising like a petrified forest around them. "Do you live among these?"

The awe must have shown in her voice, because the man smiled. "Lofi was enthralled by them too, when she first arrived. I take it you don't have anything like them in Flintcrag."

Kalish shook her head. "Not that I've seen."

The way grew ever steeper on loose scree. They wound between spires until Kalish lost track of the way they'd come. Once or twice she was certain they were passing the same formations twice, and she wondered if they were deliberately confusing her so she couldn't escape or tell anyone how to find Western Terrace. If they were, it worked. Fear began to nibble at her like a mouse. There was no going back now.

As she expected, the final approach to the terrace was vertical—a narrow chimney shooting upward. The terrace itself was invisible until she pulled herself up onto the ledge where it nestled.

Tana took her by the arm, his grip firm and commanding, but not painful. When all six men had gained the ledge, the older man spoke. "We'll put her in the granary. Tana, stand guard for now. The rest of you, get something to eat. I'll let the women know what we've found."

The men dispersed, and Tana escorted Kalish toward the back of the terrace. It was a tiny village compared with Flintcrag's prime terrace. Two rows of no more than a dozen rooms were separated by a narrow alleyway. The back row was stepped up on a higher ledge, and some of the rooms had short ladders from alley to door. Though small, the place was crowded. Tana stopped several times to explain Kalish's presence and where he was taking her, and as they traversed the alley, a gaggle of young children chasing each other nearly bowled them over. Tana pushed her up one of the ladders into a tiny cell of a room mostly filled with stacked clay pots. He loomed in the doorway, his arms crossed, axe in hand, watching her. For the first time since her capture, she felt imprisoned.

She was hungry, thirsty and tired, too. The room offered little space, and Kalish wouldn't have stretched out to sleep anyway, with Tana a step away watching. She tucked herself between two pots and curled into a ball, resting her head on her knees. She tried to stay watchful, keeping her eyes on Tana without meeting his gaze, but exhaustion won out. She'd hardly slept for two days, and had spent most of her waking hours on the run. Before long, her eyelids drooped.

She woke reluctantly, savouring a dream involving goat stew eaten on the top of a mesa while laughing at

Dayo's jokes. It was only when she realised the smell of stew was real that her eyes opened.

A woman crouched before her, bowl and jug in her hands. Tana was gone and another man stood in his place. The light was dim—it must have been evening. "Eat. The women will want to see you soon." She set the bowl in front of Kalish and poured water from the jug into a cup.

"Thank you." Kalish's voice was a dry croak. She straightened her kinked back and neck, and took a long gulp of water before picking up the bowl of stew.

The woman watched Kalish closely, her lips pursed and her eyes narrowed.

"Boled says you're Norili's girl." So, the older man's name was Boled. And this must be his wife.

Kalish nodded, her mouth full of warm stew. The woman's eyes traced Kalish's storyscar, and Kalish felt the room grow smaller with her scrutiny. Unlike the men who had brought her here, this woman would be able to read her scar. After a moment, the woman grunted and stood. "I never liked your mother."

Kalish snorted a laugh. "Try being her daughter."

The woman's lips curled up. "I'm Lofi. I'll be back to get you soon."

Kalish finished her meal and drained the jug of water. She was pacing her tiny cell, stretching the aches from her arms and back when Lofi returned for her, along with the six men who had captured her. They formed a phalanx around her as they led her to the terrace's tiny fatechamber, entering through the chamber's Unknown entrance.

Inside sat a dozen women, ranging from Kalish's mother's age to elders. Lofi took her place among them, and the six men arrayed themselves around Kalish as she stood before the women.

The oldest of the women spoke. "Boled, tell us how you came by this supposed Flintcrag."

Boled explained how the party had been hunting when they'd stumbled across Kalish, curled in a tussock. He recounted what Kalish had told him, then turned the story over to Tana to describe the two Flintcrag men they'd killed. It was the first time Kalish had heard the entire story, and she winced in spite of herself when Tana described how Maled and Riven had held the men while Tana sliced them with his knife to make them talk.

When the men had finished their tale, the elder dismissed them. All the women's eyes were on Kalish now, and as they scrutinised her, the silence stretched, prickling her neck and raising sweat under her arms.

Finally, the elder broke the silence. "Do you have anything to add to the men's story?"

Kalish swallowed. "It is as they say. I was banished from Flintcrag. I was on my way to Surefoot territory in the hope of gaining acceptance here."

"And what is your gift? Nothing of value was found among your belongings." The only way of changing clans, aside from marriage, was to bring a gift—often some rare, difficult-to-find item that showed daring and prowess. Kalish hadn't had time to consider what her gift would be, let alone actually procure it. She shuffled nervously, her mind whirling.

"It is a gift of knowledge I bring." And what would she tell them? What did she know? She'd barely become a woman—how could she know things the elders did not?

The elder frowned, and the women muttered among themselves. A younger woman spoke up. "The men say you have lantan eyes. Show us."

Grimacing, Kalish brushed her hair off her brow. Another murmur arose from the women, and her palms grew sweaty. The women huddled and whispered to one another and Kalish let her hair drop. Their voices sounded like the hiss of a snake. Kalish wrapped her arms around herself, trying to quell the shaking that had started.

After several fits of hissing and muttering, the women's huddle broke up and they turned to Kalish. Their faces showed little, but Lofi nodded ever so slightly to her, easing the knot in her stomach. The elder spoke again. "We do not have the authority to grant you a place with us. You have the eyes of a lantan, and your face speaks clearly of treachery. There are some among us who would kill you outright. And yet, as the daughter of an enemy clan's fatecarver, you could indeed have valuable information. We will send you to our elders at Prime Terrace for their judgement."

Kalish slowly let out her breath and lowered her arms. "Thank you."

"You will go under the guard of the six men who captured you. I remind you that, though we have chosen not to kill you today, the men are authorised to kill any enemy within our territory. You are an enemy until the central council determines that you are not." She fixed Kalish with a warning glare, and Kalish had the feeling this woman was one of those who wanted to kill her outright. She swallowed her fear and nodded.

Nine

The night in the tiny granary was long and uncomfort-able. The air grew chilly, and the silent stare of her guard made it impossible to sleep.

Sometimes, your body will be in places, situations, where your mind doesn't want to go. You must learn how to take your mind somewhere your body can't follow. Grandmother Ma's words came back to her. Kalish took a slow breath, closed her eyes, and left her body behind.

The sun shone as she stepped to the edge of the terrace's ledge. As she expected, she encountered no one in the Fatewalker Realm here. It was eerie to see such a crowded terrace deserted. She stopped to consider what she would do. Travel in this realm was swift, as long as you knew where you were going. Kalish hurried down the chimney and stepped into the hoodoo maze.

In the real world, she would have had no chance of finding her way through before she per-ished of thirst and exposure. In the Fatewalker Realm, all she had to do was envision her destination, and her feet took her there in land-eating strides. Before long, she was climbing the cliff where she'd left Dayo.

He wasn't there.

Not that she'd expected him to be. Even if he were in the Fatewalker Realm, he wouldn't have stayed up here. He would have gone hunting, or …

Or looked for her on their ledge. Before, anyway. Not now.

She blinked back tears and squinted toward her former home. She wouldn't go there to search for him. She couldn't show that weakness.

And the moment she decided she couldn't go there, she knew she would.

It wasn't hard to sneak up on him. He obviously didn't expect her. She pressed herself against the rock and peeked at him. He sat on their ledge, gazing out at the valley with his arms wrapped around his legs. A lump formed in her throat, and it was all she could do to keep herself from going to him. He seemed lonely. Or maybe it was her own loneliness she felt. After all, he had Seeda and the rest of the clan. Why would he feel lonely?

Her foot dislodged a pebble, which skittered off the cliff. Dayo turned toward the sound and Kalish snapped her head back and pressed herself against the rock, cursing herself for having come. Careful to remain out of sight, she crept away from the ledge, and then hurried back to her cell.

She woke desolate, with a hole in her chest that had nothing to do with hunger or thirst, though those needs plagued her too. Her guard had changed—another one of the men whose names she didn't know.

Lofi appeared some time later, as black night crept toward the grey of dawn. Kalish sensed sympathy—this woman's story also involved leaving Flintcrag Clan. She wondered what her storyscar revealed. Lofi carried Kalish's bundle along with a breakfast of warm flatbread stuffed with the congealed remains of last night's stew. "I've refilled your water skin and put some food and a few extra things in your bundle." She pressed a finger to her lips. "Don't open it in front of the men."

Kalish squeezed the bundle out of curiosity and thought she felt the hard length of a knife. "Thank you."

"You will find the elders at Prime Terrace more … challenging than the women here. I know Boled will speak in your favour, but he is just a man. I hope your information is valuable." She looked Kalish in the eye with an intensity that shot fear through her veins.

"I hope so too." Kalish bit into the bread, savouring the smell and warmth. "Thank you for your help."

Lofi smiled and stood. "May the Fates guide your footsteps."

A moment later, Boled appeared. "It's time." Kalish bolted down the remainder of her breakfast, emptied the water jug Lofi had brought her, and swept up her bundle.

The other men fell in around Kalish as they left the terrace. She noted they all carried staves as well as axes and knives now. And they were dressed to show off their status—in capelets that highlighted their skill and bravery, and with enemy teeth braided into their hair. Not a hunting party any more, but an armed escort.

They shimmied down the chimney and wound their way through the hoodoo maze in silence, Boled leading the way, and Kalish sandwiched in the middle of the column. The sun was just cresting the horizon when they exited the maze. Boled stopped to gaze at the view.

"How long will it take to get to Prime Terrace?" Kalish asked.

"Three days, unless the springs are dry. Then we'll have to detour for water, and it will take at least four." It was a common occurrence in the Fatecarver lands—water was scarce, and springs could be fickle. Several of the water sources Flintcrag's prime terrace relied on had dried up last summer and never returned.

The armed men flanking her made her nervous, but she took a breath and reminded herself she was a woman, even if she was also a prisoner. The thought gave her confidence—if she were in her own clan, she would have authority over these men. "Well, if I'm to travel with you for at least three days, I think I should know your names."

Boled's lips twitched. He might look fierce in his rare black goat pelt capelet, but Kalish sensed the same sympathy in him that his wife showed. "I suppose you should."

"You are Boled; Lofi told me that." Kalish nodded to him and then turned to Tana. "And I've worked out you're Tana." Tana's capelet was nothing special—ordinary goat fur—but his braids rattled with teeth, and Kalish wondered how many were her clansmen's. He inclined his head, as though they were being formally introduced. "And you?" She turned to a stout man with round features and wide-set eyes.

He smiled. "I'm Nenu. That's my big brother Zev." It was clear Nenu was a child-man—a child inhabiting an adult's body. Child-men were thought to

78

be specially gifted with happiness by the Fates. He wore a child's rough woven wool capelet.

Kalish couldn't help smiling back. "Nice to meet you Nenu." She turned to Zev's more severe visage, noting his auburn fox pelt capelet. Clever then, to kill a fox. "Zev." She acknowledged him with a nod. "That leaves Maled and Riven, if I remember correctly—but which is which?" Her confident demeanour slipped a little as she waited for their response. They, along with Tana, had predatory looks that reminded her of the great tawny cats that lurked in the brush of the unfarmed valleys, picking off unwary travellers and solitary hunters.

"I'm Riven," replied the one sporting a cat hide capelet. Not only did he act like a cat, he apparently hunted them, too. Kalish didn't like his gaze, but she did her best to hide the trembling in her stomach and nodded at him.

"And I'm Maled." The sixth man wore a capelet of lantan skins that shimmered in the sunlight. What sort of crazy did you have to be to hunt lantans? She'd heard rumours that some clans dipped their darts in lantan venom, and she shuddered. She'd have to be careful around Maled.

Kalish nodded, trying to quell her discomfort and exercise as much control over her situation as possible. "Well then, let's go."

She caught Tana's raised eyebrow and Boled's twitch of a smile before they turned and continued on.

Surefoot territory was very much like Flintcrag. River valleys, mostly dry at this time of year, were planted in corn, wheat, and a variety of root crops. Sugarspike plantations studded the valley slopes, and extensive clay aqueducts siphoned water from streams and springs to all the crops.

Men and boys were already in the fields, taking advantage of cool morning temperatures, and Boled greeted many as the group passed. Further from the terrace, fields grew sparse, and tussock and spiny shrubs took over the valleys. The path they travelled narrowed from a broad, well-packed road to nothing more than a faint game trail.

Her six guards spoke little at first, but once they settled into a rhythm, Tana, Maled and Riven began trading jibes and gossip.

"Tana, you didn't return to the room last night. Did you get lost on your way past the women's quarters?" Maled's voice mocked the taller man, but if Tana was embarrassed, he didn't show it.

"At least I know where the women's quarters are."

"I'm saving myself for some elder's granddaughter at Prime Terrace. Then you'll all have to defer to me and my woman."

Tana snorted. "Elders' granddaughters. They'll keep you out of the raids and demand a baby every year. You'll get stuck waiting on them hand and foot because that's what they're used to."

"At least I know I can give them a baby every year, unlike you."

Nenu giggled, but Boled cut off the conversation with a short, "Enough. You wouldn't talk like that around Surefoot women. Have some respect."

Tana sneered. "This girl's fatecarving hasn't even healed yet. Besides, she's an enemy, not a woman. We could kill her without needing to explain it to anyone, and you're worried about offending her?"

Kalish tensed, sandwiched between Tana and Boled on the path. Boled was Tana's senior by at least two decades, and Tana had not only talked back to him, but he'd just called an adult woman a girl and ignored the fact Boled's wife was from Flintcrag.

Boled suddenly pivoted around Kalish toward Tana with graceful ease, but there was no mistaking his aggression. He grabbed a fistful of Tana's tooth-crusted braids, yanking the taller man's head to eye level. Tana failed to hide the surprise on his face. "Address any woman with disrespect and you'll feed the scavengers." Boled's voice was low, but menacing. "That goes for all of you. I'm not bringing a bunch of badly behaved boys to Prime Terrace to offend the elders." Then he laughed and shoved Tana away from him. "You'll thank me for it. The elders will give you to their daughters and granddaughters for punishment if you offend them. They'll make public examples of you. I'll just slit your throat."

Tana, Maled and Riven shared nervous glances while Boled glared for a moment longer. Nenu smiled. "I'm a good boy."

The tension in Boled's shoulders eased and he smiled back.

"You are, Nenu." Zev patted him on the shoulder, and they continued their journey in silence.

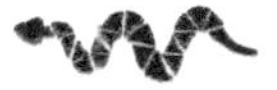

They passed two tiny terraces, little more than one extended family in each, before sunset. The curled leaves of the corn in the fields below the terraces hinted at dry springs, and so it was no surprise when they reached the spring where Boled intended to camp and nothing but moist clay greeted them.

He sent Maled and Riven to hunt dinner, and pointed Zev and Tana to the riverbed where they might dig to find water.

Kalish was at a loss. She felt she should help, but having been cooked for her whole life, she knew her camp skills were probably more pathetic than Nenu's—she could light a fire and roast meat on a stick, but that was it. He would at least know how to properly boil roots for stew. As a captive, what did they expect of her?

Boled sat Nenu down with a knife and a few twigs to shave them for tinder. "Remember to cut away from your fingers, every time." There was fatherly affection in his voice, and Kalish wondered who in the terrace had taken responsibility for Nenu's care. A child-man needed more adult support than others. Often they stayed with much younger children than themselves.

When Nenu was happily employed with his tinder making, Boled turned to Kalish. "I apologise for the young men. They are big goats on a small ledge. None has ever even been to our prime terrace, and they think only as far as their hunting grounds extend. They have no idea of what you have been through. They don't understand what it is to lose your clan."

Suddenly Kalish's eyes stung and she blinked hard. The fast pace the men set had kept her thoughts at bay all day. But with this kindly man in front of her, telling her he understood—and of course he did, because of Lofi—images of her mother, Dayo, Janth, Wathi, and even her dead grandmother and father flickered through her mind, each one a prick to her heart.

He must have seen her distress. He cleared his throat. "Nenu likes stories. And he often needs reminders about the knife. Can you keep him company while I see to a fire?"

Kalish nodded, unable to speak through the lump in her throat. She took a steadying breath and sat down next to Nenu.

By the time the other men returned with water and a pair of rabbits, Nenu's feet were lost in a pile of wood shavings, and Kalish was muddling her way through a sixth story. She didn't have Dayo's skill in making up her own tales, but she was able to recount his. Nenu was captivated, and Boled and Zev joined them while the rabbits cooked, leaning toward her and smiling. Briefly, she forgot she was their prisoner, forgot she had fled her home, forgot she belonged nowhere.

But only briefly. A woman should have been the first to eat and should have been given the best parts of the kill, but Tana, tending the rabbit, ensured she was the last, and she had to make do with gnawing sparse flesh off the front legs and picking gristle off the pelvis. Then, when it was time to sleep, the men set up a watch—two at all times—one focused outward to ward off cats, one to keep an eye on her. They didn't even allow her to relieve herself in private, but sent Maled with her to sneer at her discomfort.

Her blanket formed her bundle, and she nearly forgot Lofi's warning not to open it in front of the men. As she unrolled it, a knife in a leather sheath tumbled out. Sucking in her breath, she flipped the blanket over it and acted as if she were straightening it before wrapping it around herself. Her hands shook. Had anyone seen the knife? After a moment, she glanced around. The men were all busy with their own

night-time preparations. Her first guard, Zev, was distracted helping Nenu with his blanket. She breathed
again and slipped into her blanket.

She curled onto her side, around the contents
of her bundle. With creeping fingers she furtively felt
everything Lofi had provided her with. Dried meat
and fruit, several pouches of what she assumed were
herbs, and two thick fabric pads that confused her for
a moment. With relief, she recognised them as men-
strual cloths. Then there was the knife. It was contained in a leg sheath. Ordinarily both men and
women wore knives on the lower legs, below the hem
of the short leather skirts everyone wore. Sheaths
were often lavishly decorated and were as much a part
of the wardrobe as they were a place to hold a tool or
weapon.

But Kalish couldn't wear this knife openly. She
would either have to leave it in the bundle, where it did
her little good and where it could easily be found, or
she'd have to hide it under her clothes. Moving at a
snail's pace, she pushed up her skirt and tied the
sheath to her thigh. It wouldn't be as convenient to access as it would be on her lower leg, but she could get
to it if she had to.

Ten

The second day of their journey was similar to the first, except that Nenu begged for stories as they walked. Kalish obliged, until the foul looks Maled cast her shut her down.

Around the fire in the evening, though, she told more stories and was pleased to note Tana and Riven listening as intently as the others. Only Maled curled his lip at her or snorted in derision when the others laughed.

"Are all Flintcrags storytellers?" Zev asked.

Kalish laughed. "No." She swallowed hard. Only her best friend. "We like stories, but not everyone tells them."

"Well, you're a natural," Boled said.

"Not really. I'm just repeating stories a friend told me." A friend no longer. She rose quickly, before the men could see the pain on her face. "I'll sleep now."

Wrapped in her blanket later, she gritted her teeth, willing her grief to harden into anger. She would not mourn for her clan—they didn't want her. It was foolish to love those who hated you. In fact, she didn't love them; she hated them. She would make a new life here with the Surefoot Clan, just to spite the Flintcrags. Maybe they'd let her train as a fatecarver, even without the proper storyscar. Maybe she would betray her clan after all—carving fates to crush Flintcrag.

But that was silly. She didn't have a fatecarver mark. Why would Surefoot train her as one?

What else could she do? What else could she offer?

Gliders. She and Dayo had spent every free moment improving and testing gliders. Kalish could teach the Surefoot Clan how to weave the extra fine sugarspike cloth for the wings and how to create the steerable frame she and Dayo had designed together. It would be a good gift.

And if that wasn't enough? Well, she was clever. She'd show them the snares she'd fashioned to catch the live bats she and Dayo studied when design-ing their gliders. And the pulley system she'd worked out for hauling heavy water jugs up to the terrace. And they could see the skill of her craftsmanship in her beaded capelet, with its unusual shaped beads and bat motif.

She drifted to sleep with Grandmother Ma's words echoing in her head. *You're a smart girl; you'll figure something out, just as I did.* She looked forward to some-day telling Grandmother Ma about how she joined the Surefoot Clan.

She awoke with a start in the middle of the night, her whole body on alert. Something was wrong. She glanced toward the men. All six of them were sound asleep. A frisson of danger washed over her skin, raising every hair on her body. Slowly, she reached down and pulled out her knife. She raised herself to a crouch, eyes wide and ears alert for any sound.

A slight shift of gravel was the only thing she heard before the cat's sleek body arched through the air to land on Nenu's sleeping form.

Kalish sprang to her feet with a cry that startled the cat mid-attack. It had barely landed when it sprang again at Kalish. The move was so fast, she didn't have a chance to react, and before she knew it she was sprawled in the dust, the cat's front paws on her chest, and its jaws around her shoulder. She froze in a moment of pure shock, and then she remembered her knife, still in hand. She growled and struck at the cat, feeling the knife hit a rib and slip sideways without going deep. The cat pulled away with a snarl, and then lunged for her head. She jerked to the side just in time, and the cat's jaws closed on her shoulder again. With a scream, Kalish stabbed a second time, and the knife slid deep into the cat's chest. It howled and leapt off her. Her hand slipped from the knife and she scrambled away as the cat turned to run.

It didn't make it more than three steps before it stumbled, wavered for a moment, and then collapsed.

It was only then that Kalish felt the pain. While the men around her exploded into action, she tried to assess her wounds in the dark.

"Tana. Fire!" Boled barked.

Her fingers flew to her shoulder where the cat had bitten twice. But the gaping wound she expected wasn't there. Instead, she felt sharp grit embedded in her flesh. Even in the dark, she recognised the shape of crushed beads. The beads of her capelet had acted as armour. No doubt she was bruised and scratched, but her shoulder was intact.

Her legs had fared worse. The cat's hind claws had scored deep gashes from mid-thigh to shin. They bled profusely, and in the light of Tana's fire, she saw her blanket growing dark with blood.

Boled came to her then. "Spines! Riven, my bag." Riven dumped it at his feet, echoing Boled's curse when he saw Kalish's legs. "Let's get her over to the fire where I can see better. Lie down," he instructed Kalish. They pulled up the corners of her blanket and bundled her to the fire. She squeezed her eyes shut and gritted her teeth to keep from whimpering.

"You're covered in blood, girl," Boled muttered as he rummaged through his bag and extracted a pouch of herbs.

Kalish ignored the use of the word girl—right now she felt small and vulnerable like a girl. The adrenaline that had coursed through her and given her the strength to fight the cat drained away and left her shaking. "Not all the blood is mine. Some is the cat's."

Nenu whimpered as Zev crouched over him, and Kalish turned her head toward the sound. "How is Nenu?"

"Untouched. He says the cat leapt on him first, but jumped off right away," Zev replied.

"Yes. I yelled at it and it came after me instead." Kalish's voice sounded breathy to her ears, and a funny ringing made her shake her head. She sucked in a breath as Boled rinsed off her wounds.

Maled bent over the cat's body. He pulled the knife from the animal's side and examined it. "How did you get a knife?" His words were measured and menacing. Boled raised his head and Kalish saw recognition flash in his eyes. Kalish hoped she hadn't made life difficult for Lofi.

The sky was lightening in the east before Boled was done tending to Kalish's wounds. "The muscle was ripped. Your legs'll hurt for a long time," Boled warned. "But the wounds are clean, and I had enough spider webs to close up most. They should heal." Fatecarvers, forever fighting one another, were adept at treating wounds. Herbs to prevent infection, herbs to drive away established infections, herbs to speed healing, spider web and sugarspike thread for closing wounds, even surgery for badly broken bones and skull injuries. In the grand scheme of things, Kalish's wounds were nothing. But freshly reeling from the attack, she was consumed by them.

"I feel like I've been chewed up and spat out," she groaned as she finally sat up. She gingerly removed her capelet, and Boled swore. Her shoulder was a mass of blossoming bruises. Blood welled slowly from a few small puncture wounds. She peered at it and winced. "I think there are some beads embedded in there." While Boled picked out bead fragments, she inspected her capelet. The pattern she'd painstakingly crafted in polished stone and clay beads was muddied by crushed beads and torn threads. She brushed the bits away and frowned at the damage.

"It saved your life." Boled smeared a paste of herbs over her shoulder.

"Yes." She lowered her voice to the barest of whispers, so only Boled would hear. "So did your wife."

She pulled her capelet back around her shoulders, feeling its weight anew, as a protective mantle.

Boled stood and Maled addressed him. "What do we do about this?"

The older man held out his hand for the knife. "I'll take it."

"No, I mean what do we do about *her*? She had a knife. Stole it, no doubt."

Boled took the knife and calmly examined it. "How could she have stolen it? Hasn't she been guarded since we first found her? Are you saying one of you was lax and let her out of your sight?"

"Well how else could she have—"

"Because someone was definitely lax last night. Maled and Riven, you were meant to have the last watch. Why was Kalish the only one who saw the cat before it attacked?" His eyebrows rose as he skewered Maled with a glare.

"I … I'd just shut my eyes for a moment."

Zev grunted. "You were sound asleep when I woke to her screams. If we'd been relying on you, Nenu would be dead. She saved his life."

"She did." Nenu's voice shook. "That cat would have eaten me if she hadn't distracted it."

"She had a stolen knife!"

"And a good thing she did." Zev crossed his arms, daring Maled to contradict him.

"Riven, what do you have to say for yourself?" Boled turned his gaze to the young man who had hung back from the conversation.

Riven rubbed his eyes. "She must have made us fall asleep somehow. She's a fatecarver's daughter; she must practise the same magic. She put us to sleep and then called the cat."

Tana stepped forward. "I've heard of some strange things the fatecarvers do. When my sister came of age, she said Glilith put her in a trance and talked to bats—that piromanga smoke is powerful magic."

Kalish wanted to snort her derision, but to admit her familiarity with the Fatewalker Realm would be worse than what they believed of her now.

It was Boled who waved away the young men's conjectures with a hand. "You know the women can't tell you the truth about their fatecarvings. Have any of you boys actually met Glilith or had a fatecarving? No. Save your breath for things you actually understand." He hefted the knife. "I will keep this. Maled and Riven, you will both take double watches, and not together tonight, to make up for the one you slept through. Tana, skin the cat. Give the pelt to Kalish—it was her kill. We'll cook what we can eat this morning and take the rest with us."

"But what about her?" Maled stabbed a finger at Kalish.

"She will be judged by the elder council."

"She's an enemy!"

Boled met Maled's anger with a frigid gaze. "That is not for us to decide. We have been tasked with bringing her safely to the elder council, and that is what we will do."

Eleven

Maled's stare for the rest of their journey was nearly as uncomfortable as Kalish's wounds. And that was saying a lot; every step felt like the cat was clawing her legs anew. Her stride was stiff and her pace slow. Boled quickly adjusted for her, but it was clear Maled resented her pace.

Nenu, on the other hand, fawned over her, filling her water skin when they stopped by a muddy spring, offering to carry her bundle, and even offering to carry her.

Kalish giggled at the last. "No thank you. But it's kind of you to offer."

Zev steered Nenu onward, suppressing his own smile. "She doesn't need you to carry her. But I'm sure she'll let you cook dinner."

"Oh! And I can cut up her meat for her!"

"Don't be ridiculous." Zev rolled his eyes and flashed Kalish an apologetic look. Kalish smiled. She liked the way Zev cared for his brother, helped him fit in as best he could. She was glad none of the other young men were Nenu's brother.

Without seeming to hover or intervene, Zev managed to place Kalish between himself and Nenu as they walked. When they stopped for the night, he offered to help her scrape the cat hide, and she suspected it was his way of keeping Tana and Maled away. Boled kept the other men busy with cooking and collecting firewood and water. But when Tana and Maled drew straws to see who would watch Kalish and who would watch the perimeter the next night, Maled won. He chose Kalish.

She rolled up in her blanket and turned her back on him, but she could still feel the prickle of his watchful eye on the back of her neck. She'd rather face a hungry cat every night than Maled. She struggled to stay awake for the whole of his double shift on watch, but her body, pouring everything it had into healing, had other ideas.

Sometime in the deep of night, she woke to a knee in her back and a hand over her mouth. She arched her back to try to get away, but froze at the bite of a knife on the back of her neck.

"I can kill you and make your body vanish. Tana won't care, and he'll back me up that you used fatecarver magic to escape." Maled's breath hissed in her ear. "I don't know how you stole that knife, but everyone at Prime Terrace is going to know about it, you little lantan. And when the elders reject you, I'll be the one to slit your throat. You have nice teeth. And I think I'll take those lantan eyes too, and add them to my capelet." He shoved her face into the dirt and stood.

Kalish spat dirt. "Why do you hate me so much? What have I done to you?"

"You exist. Your clan killed my entire family." He stalked away.

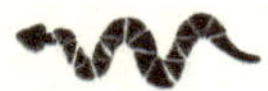

With Kalish's slow pace and a detour to find flowing springs, it took five days to reach Prime Terrace. Nights were tense; she was glad to have the cat hide to tan, because it was something to occupy her hands and mind. Later though, rolled in her blanket in the dark, she struggled to relax. After Maled's nocturnal threat, she wondered how many of the other men had lost family to her clan, and she worried about her reception by the Surefoot Clan. She remembered a Caverna man who had married Dayo's eldest sister a few years back. She and the other girls had delighted in taunting and tormenting him, calling him Rat, because of the single braid the Caverna men wore, like a rat's tail hanging down their backs. They spat at his face, knowing he couldn't do anything to retaliate, and made sure he knew he didn't belong in their terrace.

They had no reason to hate him other than the history of fighting between their clans. Eventually Rat and Dayo's sister had moved to a small outlying terrace. Kalish had instantly forgotten him. Now she wondered what had become of him.

The approach to Surefoot's prime terrace was not a cliff, as she expected, but a steep scree slope that defied a frontal assault. Any attackers would have to wind their way slowly up the exposed face, making them easy targets for darts, rocks and spears. Jutting stumps and hacked tussocks indicated regular maintenance to keep the slope free of vegetation—protection against fire as well as attacks.

Before they started up the slope, Boled took Kalish's bundle and bound her hands. She understood why, but a shiver of unease coursed through her all the same. This was it. She looked up the rocky slope at the terrace that was either her future or her death, and swallowed her fear.

Maled shoved her forward. "Move it."

As they neared the top of the slope, Kalish's eyes widened in astonishment. The terrace was enormous. The main level was at least as large as her home terrace, but the community sprawled upward onto every ledge and crevice the land afforded.

"It's huge!" she breathed.

Boled, leading the way, nodded. "Goes all the way across the top of the butte."

"Really? On top?" She'd never seen a terrace on top of a butte—they were exposed to rain and snow during the winter and felt the full brunt of the hot spring and summer winds. Who would want to live up there?

The entrance to the terrace was a narrow space between rock walls studded with sharp pottery shards. Now there was a good idea to take back to Flintcrag. Except she wouldn't be going back to Flintcrag. A pair of guards armed with axes stepped out to bar their entrance. "Friend or foe?"

"Friend." Boled nodded politely to the guards.

"And foe," Maled called out from behind. "We bring a prisoner."

Kalish saw Boled's shoulders stiffen, but his tone was diplomatic. "We bring Kalish, daughter of Norili of the Flintcrag Clan, who has been expelled from her clan and wishes to join Surefoot. The women of Western Terrace have decreed she should be brought here to be judged by the elder council. We who first encountered her have been tasked with ensuring her safe arrival here."

"You have been to Prime before?" asked the second guard.

"I have," Boled said. "I know the way to the elder compound."

The guard nodded and stepped out of their way.

The terrace teemed with activity. Men passed with jugs of water or grain balanced on their heads and shoulders. Groups of women wearing intricately beaded capelets sat weaving in plazas. Children scampered up ladders and down cliffs, laughing and shouting in their play. Kalish recognised a game of lantans and ladders being played by a group of youngsters on an outcrop rising through the centre of the terrace. The smell of bread and wood smoke sent a pang of homesickness through her.

They wound through narrow alleys and broad streets. They passed three Fatechambers, and Kalish wondered if the terrace had more than one fatecarver. She couldn't imagine such a thing, but she also struggled to wrap her mind around the size of the community she was being led through. They might need more than one fatecarver in order to keep up with the work. As they passed a long row of granaries, she thought about the sweeping agricultural fields they'd travelled through to get here. The land needed to support this sprawling metropolis must be enormous.

If she was awed by the size of the population, she was overwhelmed by the innovation she saw. Pulleys like the one she had fashioned, but used in threes or more so that a single man could easily lift enormous vessels of grain. Water races running through much of the terrace, and some form of pump people used to draw the water up to higher aqueducts from lower races. Huge round stones fashioned into some sort of grinding tool for grain. Her head spun with the array of astonishing tools so casually used around her.

96

By the time they reached the elder compound, she worried her 'special gifts' for the Surefoot Clan would be limp roots, rather than the sumptuous feast she'd expected to offer.

Twelve

She was placed in a cell purpose-built for containing prisoners—one of several identical cells in a dark side alley, and another Surefoot innovation she'd never seen before. Unbroken walls sloped inward to a small opening in the roof. She was ordered down a ladder into the cell, and then the ladder was taken away. It was like being stuck in a huge clay jug, and about as pleasant. The air was stale and reeked of urine and faeces, though the floor had obviously been swept clear of debris since the last occupant vacated it—it was bare as the granaries in early summer, before harvest.

Her legs and shoulder ached, and she was thirsty. How long would they keep her here? When would the elders see her? Would they judge her in absentia, or would she have an opportunity to make her case?

Time stretched on. Kalish shifted from pacing to leaning against the wall to slumping on the floor. The meagre light grew dim. A scrabbling at the rim of her cell caught her attention. A form silhouetted against the opening lowered a small jug to her. She met the jug on its way down. It was full of water. She glanced up at the figure. "How long will I be in here? When can I see the elder council?"

The voice, male and disinterested, echoed back to her, "How should I know? Are you going to take that jug off the rope so I can send down some food, or are you planning on starving?"

Kalish quickly loosened the cord and slipped it off the neck of the jug. A minute later the figure lowered a curious covered bowl. She untied it from the rope, and both rope and figure disappeared.

It took several tries for her to work out the mechanism by which the cover was locked to the bowl. It involved turning the cover to release interlocking protrusions on the bowl and cover. For a moment, she marvelled at the clever idea and the potter's skill. Then her stomach growled, and she eagerly devoured the cold cooked roots the bowl contained. The food and water were welcome, but didn't quite satisfy her thirst and hunger.

As the light faded to black, Kalish resigned herself to spending the night in her prison. She closed her eyes. Whatever happened tomorrow, she'd face it better if she slept.

At some point in the night, a sharp thud woke her. She lay staring into the darkness, holding her breath. The opening of her cell was a dim outline of lighter black above her, and for a moment, she thought she saw a form there. But when she blinked it was gone.

She rose silently and crept to the centre of her cell, certain the sound had come from there.

Her feet met an object and she bent down to feel it. It was a knife in a leg sheath. She looked up again, but the opening remained empty.

Had Boled returned the knife Lofi had given her? What if she were caught with it here? And if Boled had tossed it down to her, what did that mean? Did he expect her to need it? Her heart sped up and the cell seemed to close in on her. She quickly strapped it on under her skirt.

By the time a ladder was lowered to her mid-morning, she was so on edge she nearly drew the knife at the sound.

"You've been called before the elder council," came the call from above.

She scurried up the ladder, glad to escape the stench of her desperate early-morning deposit in the corner of the cell.

Outside her cell, she was met by one of the guards, who bound her hands again. He led her to the end of the alleyway, where Boled, Tana, Maled and Riven took charge of her. She searched Boled's face for any recognition he'd dropped the knife to her, but if he had, he didn't give any sign of it. "Where are Zev and Nenu?" She'd been relying on them as allies alongside Boled.

"Nenu was overwhelmed by the terrace—too many strangers. Zev is taking him home. Come. We mustn't be late." He took her by the arm and led her into the street.

The entrance to the elder compound was another guarded slit in a fortified wall. They were admitted without questioning—obviously expected—and the men were stripped of all weapons. They didn't check Kalish—they'd checked her before she entered her cell. A young woman met them on the other side
100

of the wall and directed them to a circular chamber with ornately decorated walls. The doorway marked the low point of the room, and the floor stepped up from the centre in several large tiers that were crowded with elders. Kalish sucked in a breath. So many! But of course, in a terrace this large, there would be many elders. Her knees weakened and she stumbled as Maled pushed her to the centre of the room. The men arrayed themselves behind her and stood silently.

The rumble of conversation in the room quieted as all eyes turned to Kalish. She couldn't have felt more exposed had she been stripped bare and tied to a rock in the sun. The shrewd eyes of the elders raked her from head to foot, and she felt the knife against her thigh like a hot coal. She should have left it in the cell. Hidden it in the water jug and denied all knowledge of it.

The silence pooled in the bottom of the chamber until Kalish felt suffocated by it. But she wasn't foolish enough to speak until an elder asked her to.

Finally, a wizened woman with a storyscar so faded it had all but vanished amidst the lines of her face leaned on a stick and rose. "You will tell how you captured this Flintcrag woman."

Boled stepped forward and nodded. "We were out hunting and found her asleep in a tussock." Laughter rippled through the room. "She claimed to be the daughter of Flintcrag's fatecarver, fleeing her own clan after being expelled. We corroborated her story by finding and questioning a pair of Flintcrag men chasing her."

A voice called out, "And the Flintcrag men?"

"Dead." Tana grinned and shook his toothy braids so they rattled. More laughter. Kalish swallowed and tried to keep her face impassive.

Boled continued. "The Flintcrag prisoner claims she bears a gift, and wishes to join our clan. The women of Western Terrace ask you to judge her gift and her worthiness to join us."

"You forgot to tell them about the knife," Maled interjected. "The one she stole."

Eyebrows rose around the room, and the knife flamed against Kalish's thigh.

"Tell us about this knife, young man."

Maled drew himself up. "When we captured her, we stripped her of weapons, but on our journey here, we discovered she carried a Surefoot knife hidden where we couldn't see it."

"And if you couldn't see it, how did you find it?" A note of warning coloured the speaker's voice. Kalish might be a Flintcrag, but she was still a woman, and she suspected that if Maled had violated her in any way, his punishment would make anything they did to her look pleasant.

Boled stepped forward. "Our camp was attacked by a cat one night while the two who were supposed to be on guard slept." He shot a sharp look at Maled and Riven. "Kalish detected the cat's approach and distracted it as it leapt for one of our party. The cat then attacked her, and she fought it off and killed it. We found the knife embedded in the animal's side."

"She killed a cat? With a knife?" There was approval in the voice.

"And she saved the life of a member of our terrace," Boled added.

"But she stole a knife." Maled was insistent.

"I think that says as much about whoever was guarding her as it does about her character." The comment rang out and was followed by laughter. Kalish failed to suppress a smile as her stress eased. Instead of turning the elder council against her, Maled was only highlighting her strength.

The wizened woman rapped her staff on the floor and the room fell silent. "If the men have no more to add, they are dismissed and can consider their duty fulfilled to the women of Western Terrace."

As the men left, Kalish hoped she would have a chance to thank Boled later. Now her attention was commanded by a second woman who rose as the first sat. She stepped down off the terrace and onto Kalish's level. She walked slowly around her, examining her with a measuring look on her face.

"You say you are your fatecarver's daughter. And yet you have no fatecarver mark upon your own face."

Kalish shrugged. Fatecarvers didn't always follow family lines, although most of the time they did. "It is not my place to question the Fates." It was the safe response, whatever she thought about the Fates.

"You will have been pampered, as the fatecarver's daughter. You will receive no special consideration here if we allow you to stay."

Kalish raised her head higher. "I expect none. I come ready to join your clan on my own merits, not those of my mother, who banished me." She had to swallow hard to retain control of herself.

The woman before her sucked in a sharp breath and swept the hair off her forehead.

Spines! Kalish knew eventually she would have to show her lantan eyes, but she'd hoped to put it off for longer.

"Lantan eyes," the woman announced. An agitated buzz arose in the room as the elders reacted. Her eyes roved over Kalish's face. "There is flight as well as treachery in your face."

Kalish jumped at the opening. "Yes. And flight is part of my gift to the Surefoot Clan. I can show you how to create a fully steerable glider—one you can launch, guide to a destination, and then guide back home again."

"We have a team already working on a steering mechanism for gliders. Why do we need yours?" a woman called out from the topmost tier, her voice haughty and bored.

"Mine is simple and elegant. Easy for anyone to make and use." Her palms were sweating. "And I also know how to weave the superfine sugarspike fabric that makes Flintcrag gliders lighter and more portable. I can show you how to prepare the fibres and make the special looms needed to weave the cloth quickly."

"Again, how do we know if your ideas are any better than ours? Have you brought examples of your glider and your fabric?"

"I was driven from my home. There wasn't time to collect anything."

The old woman with the staff rapped it on the floor. "I will appoint a committee to hear the details of the Flintcrag's gift, rather than waste the entire council's time on this matter. The committee will advise us tomorrow whether they believe the gift worthy."

She rapped her staff again, and a pair of men entered and led Kalish to a small chamber nearby. They stood at attention, each one gripping one of her arms until five of the elders arrived.

104

"Untie her hands," one of them directed. "And then guard the door."

Another woman laid a large clay tablet on the floor and produced a piece of the soft white stone found along the coast. She handed the stone to Kalish. "Draw your glider."

Kalish crouched, and the five women watched as she carefully drew and explained the working of the steering system she and Dayo had invented.

"And you have built and tested this glider?" asked one of the women.

Kalish squirmed. "We've tested a prototype without the hanging harness, and it is easily steerable. We haven't actually tested the harness, but we know the concept works. The harness is really more a safety measure than anything."

"Hmm. I see your wings are shaped differently than ours. Tell me about the support structure you use."

Kalish was pleased by the question. She and Dayo had wanted a truly portable glider—one that could be carried and deployed by a single person, rather than the team of three it currently took to transport and launch a glider. She explained how the unusual shape used tensile forces to help hold the wing in position, allowing a lighter support structure. This led on to a discussion of the lightweight sugar-spike fabric, and Kalish wiped the tablet several times to draw additional diagrams of looms, fibres and other aspects of the process.

The women's questioning was astute and detailed. The tone of their voices shifted from dismissive to intrigued to—Kalish imagined—impressed. When she'd explained everything to the committee's satisfaction, they left her alone again with the guards.

They didn't bind her hands again, and Kalish took it as a good sign. Still, her nerves sang when she was summoned back into the full council.

She couldn't read the elders' faces—they were blank as fresh clay. The woman with the staff rose and banged for quiet, though there was barely a whisper in the room.

"The committee has examined your gift and recognises the value of the weaving knowledge and the cleverness of the glider design, which we understand is largely yours." She nodded to Kalish, and she breathed more easily, the knot in her stomach easing a little.

"However, we question whether we can trust one who would divulge these secrets so freely." The woman's gaze sharpened, slicing into Kalish like a knife. "One with lantan eyes and a fate tied to treachery. The only way to prevent a lantan bite is to kill the snake. The council of elders does not believe the knowledge you bring is sufficient to counter the fate you wear on your face." The woman smiled. "But thank you for your gift. We'll be sure to use it well."

Kalish's heart began to pound. She opened her mouth to protest, and then shut it again. Talking back to the elder council wasn't going to save her. She cast around for a sympathetic face in the room, but the women were statues.

"Ordinarily, we would not allow you to leave this room alive, but we have had an unusual request." Kalish's brief moment of hope was dashed with the woman's next words. "It seems you've made quite an impression on one of your captors."

Kalish turned at the sound of footsteps. Maled approached with a grin.

"Maled has requested to be the one to kill you. We have granted that request, provided it is done by nightfall and within the terrace. We expect to see evidence of the kill as soon as it is done."

Maled grabbed her arm and nodded respectfully to the elder. "As you wish. Thank you for granting my request. It will mean much to my family's spirits."

THIRTEEN

Panic set in as Maled yanked her toward the exit. "But … but my gifts! I gave them in good faith!"

Maled slapped her across the face, shocking her to silence. "Shut up." He shoved her through the door to where Riven waited with a cord to tie her wrists again.

"You can't do this to me! I'm a woman!"

Riven laughed. "No. You're a Flintcrag, which makes you dirt."

"And we're going to have a little fun. It's still a long time to nightfall, and I have ten family members to avenge." Maled shoved her forward, and Riven caught her other arm. The pair dragged her away from the elders' compound.

"You can't do this!" Kalish struggled, but it was no use—the men were bigger than she was, and she couldn't reach her knife.

"Watch us," growled Maled.

They made quite the spectacle in the crowded streets. Maled and Riven made no secret about who they escorted and what they intended to do with her.

Soon they'd gathered a following. Dozens of Sure-foots—men, women and children—paced along with them, taunting Kalish and laughing along with Maled and Riven.

Kalish didn't know where they were going, but she knew she didn't want to get there. She dragged her feet, tried to trip the men, went limp to make herself as heavy as possible. Nothing stopped their forward motion. At some point, a man with a spear joined the pack, following behind and poking Kalish in the back every time she slowed.

They wound through several broad streets and into an alley. The men shoved her up a ladder, laughing when she slipped and cracked her jaw soundly on one of the rungs. They led her into a small plaza quickly filled by the curious onlookers.

"Cousin!" A young man approached and clapped Maled on the shoulder. "I see you got your wish. We've prepared everything." He waved them forward to a spot in the centre of the plaza where a post had been set in the ground. The man produced a thick rope and the men bound her to the post by tying her wrists behind her.

"Shouldn't we tie her more firmly, so she can't move?" Maled asked.

His cousin grinned. "I thought it would be more sporting to give her a chance to dodge the darts. Let's see how fast she can spin around that post."

Maled chuckled. "Good thinking. Since we're in for a bit of sport, shall we make a game of it? Who can inflict the most pain without killing? We should assign points to each body part and keep score."

They walked away laughing and discussing how many points to assign to kneecaps, thighs and feet. Kalish's stomach churned and her knees trembled as the men organised onlookers for the sport. People ran to collect atlatls and darts. Kalish struggled against her bonds, but only succeeded in rubbing her wrists raw.

As the first contestants were lining up to fire at Kalish, a flash behind Maled made her blink and flinch. Someone screamed, and then chaos erupted around her. Thick black smoke billowed up from one side of the plaza.

Riven raced to Maled, screaming, "Fire! Incendiary! The terrace is under attack!" He pushed his friend ahead of him and into the crush of people racing away from the plaza. The smoke grew thick, and Kalish coughed, her heart racing. Bad enough to be shot at, worse to be burned alive. She pulled at her arms again and felt the entire post shift slightly. With a desperate cry, she hurled her back against the post, putting all her weight into it. The post rocked, and she pulled forward, wrists complaining as the cord bit into them. She threw her weight against the post again and again as the plaza emptied and the smoke seared her lungs. Finally, the post gave way and she tumbled painfully on top of it. She wasted no time slipping the post out from between her arms and scrambling to her feet.

Just as she started to run, someone called her name.

"Kalish! This way." Boled materialised out of the smoke and beckoned her away from the direction the others had run.

"My hands!"

Boled whipped out his knife and made quick work of her bonds. Then he grabbed her hand and they ran through the smoke. He led her through a doorway into a warren of heavily populated rooms.

110

"Slowly. Be calm," he whispered, keeping hold of her hand. Most people ignored them, but when they didn't, he claimed to be looking for his cousin Tirith, who lived in the complex. Kalish couldn't believe they weren't caught out, but the further they went, the better she understood how vast the complex was—no one could have known who lived in every one of the rooms.

They climbed several ladders and went through dozens of rooms before they came out into bright sunshine at the top of the butte. Boled pulled her into a small sleeping room, empty at this time of day. "You won't make it out of the terrace by the main entrance. The guards will know to look out for you, even if Maled doesn't come looking for you there." His voice was low and urgent. "You'll have to go down the back of the butte. There are some routes you can climb, if you're skilled. They're exposed from below, but they might be your only chance. Do you still have the knife? Bless my wife for her foresight."

Kalish smiled. "I do. Thank you. Thank Lofi for me."

"Don't thank me yet. Now go, before the commotion dies down and they realise it was just a smoke bomb."

"Smoke bomb?" Kalish had never heard of such a thing.

Boled smiled. "A bit of Surefoot technology. Now go!"

Kalish strode from the room, hurrying but trying not to show the panic she felt. Hoping to blend in with the busy life of the terrace.

She followed the flow of people, sticking to the busy streets as she increased her distance from the plaza where smoke still billowed up to drift over the terrace. *Walk with confidence,* she told herself. *Act like you belong.* But if she belonged, she'd be busy at this time of day—weaving or beading or making pots, not hurrying along the street, eyes darting left and right scanning for danger. With an effort, she slowed her steps, nodded politely at other women she passed. In her own terrace, she would have already been caught—everyone knew everyone there—but here she had a chance of passing unnoticed. She needed an excuse to hurry, and even more important, she needed a disguise, so Riven and Maled wouldn't recognise her.

Passing a pair of middle-aged women chatting in a doorway, she heard a snatch of their conversation. "… must go and collect my new cape today." It gave her an idea.

She stepped out of the flow of people and pretended to take a pebble out of her sandal, listening hard as she dawdled.

"Garlanti's finally finished it?"

"Yes. I thought it would never be done. But I suppose it takes extra time to make it waterproof."

Waterproof? Surefoot Clan clearly had a whole range of innovations her clan didn't.

A young woman called across the street. "Morning Yelita!" The woman planning to collect her cape waved. That was all Kalish needed. She slipped her sandal back on and hurried away.

Once out of sight of Yelita and her companion, Kalish asked the way to Garlanti's room. It wasn't far. When she arrived a woman was sitting outside weaving on a loom Kalish would have liked to stop and study in detail—it was nothing like the looms the Flintcrag Clan used.

Instead, she stepped up and nodded. "Garlanti?"

112

"Yes?" The woman looked up from her weaving.

"Yelita has sent me for her cape."

Garlanti jumped up from her stool. "Ah, yes. Let me get it." She stepped into the room, calling out from inside. "Did she send the beads with you?"

Spines! There would be payment, of course. "She said something about coming around later to bring them and thank you for it." Kalish clenched her hands into fists, tensing to run if she needed to.

Garlanti returned, cape in hand. "She never pays on time." She rolled her eyes. "But I know she's good for it." She laid the cape gently in Kalish's arms. "Tell her she'll want to rub it with goat fat a couple of times a year to maintain the fabric." Kalish nodded, accepting the cape with wide eyes. It was lighter than she expected, and felt slick and oily under her fingers. Guilt stabbed her, but then she heard a commotion down the street and recognised Riven's tall form coming toward her.

She took the cape and hurried away. *Not too fast. You're just taking a cape to Yelita. Blend in, blend in.* It was easier to control her feet than it was to curb her racing heart. Riven and Maled would pick her out if she ran, but they'd catch up to her if she moved at the pace of the crowds.

She turned left into a smaller street, out of sight of Garlanti, and flicked the cape over her shoulders. Then, turning right into an empty alley, she broke into a run. The only way out at the other end was a ladder; Kalish took it at a sprint. She burst out above the buildings onto a wide expanse of rooftop where huge racks of meat were spread out to dry in the sun and wind. Several men walked among the racks flipping strips of meat to speed their drying. One raised his head and frowned.

Men's work. She'd walked into the middle of it. So much for blending in.

She straightened her back, striding purposefully down a row of racks and stopping now and again to examine the meat.

One of the men met her halfway down the row and bobbed his head at her. On the street, he would have had to wait for her to speak, but this was his domain. "You must be one of Uranga's inspectors. You'll see we've implemented her suggestions for the racks." He waved his hand at the nearest rack. "This batch only came in yesterday, and you see it's quite dry already."

Kalish nodded. "Yes. Well done. Uranga will be pleased." She angled between the racks, crossing the roof to the far edge where she could glance down on the street below, picking up a piece of meat now and again, as though she was checking it. The man followed, rubbing his hands nervously.

The street below was busy. She didn't know where it led, but from up here she could see the edge of the butte she was aiming for. It wasn't too far.

She turned to the man. "It all looks satisfactory here. I'll let Uranga know." She clapped her hands together. "Now, I'll be off. Is there a way down to this street?" She indicated the one below.

The man nodded, clearly relieved to be rid of her. "Of course, you'll be on your way to inspect the grain next. I hear they brought up twenty pots of it yesterday. This way." He waved her toward the corner of the roof.

Kalish had no idea what a pot of grain was. She envisioned the pots her terrace stored grain in—

114

waist high, with narrow bases to deter mice—and
twenty didn't seem like many. She nodded her thanks
to the man as he showed her a ladder leading down to
the street.

Halfway down the ladder, a shout rang out.
"There!" Kalish jerked her head up to see Maled
pointing at her, an angry scowl on his face. So much
for her stolen cape as a disguise. He had ample time to
examine her as she descended from the roof.

She leapt the rest of the way down the ladder
and hit the ground running. No point in trying to
blend in anymore. People fell away from her as she
shoved through the throng. She dodged men with jugs
of water sloshing on their shoulders, a baker with a
basket piled high with bread, and a gaggle of children
following a tiny rock skipper fluttering on a leash.

"Stop that woman! She's a Flintcrag!" Riven's
voice boomed out behind her, and she picked up her
pace. Left, right, left—she tried to keep heading toward where she knew the edge of the butte was. The
commotion behind her grew.

Finally she burst out from between two buildings and onto an expanse of well-trampled earth at the
edge of the butte. If Maled and Riven hadn't been
nipping at her heels, she would have skittered to a halt,
her eyes wide, gawking at the scene before her. Long
neat rows of enormous fat pots paraded through the
space. The pots had narrow bases and the sides flared
to wide shoulders at about Kalish's head height before
narrowing again to rolled rims. Each pot was wrapped
in a snug rope net. Sweating men used the nets as han-
dles as they deftly tipped and rolled the pots along
broad aisles and into a row of enormous rooms. Near
the edge of the butte, they hauled on ropes running

through a series of pulleys affixed to a massive wooden frame.

She ducked behind one of the huge pots, lungs heaving. Maled and Riven pounded out from the street, heads swinging back and forth looking for her. Maled pointed, and they took off away from Kalish.

The workers ignored her until she approached the edge of the cliff. As she peered over the edge, one of them shouted, "Hey! You! What are you doing there?"

Kalish ignored him. At home a man would never question a woman's right to be wherever she wanted to be. The men here were bold, and it was going to cause her trouble.

The man who had shouted headed toward her. She began walking along the edge, away from him, desperately looking for a way down. It was no wonder the terrace focused its defences on the other side— this cliff would challenge the best of climbers, even if they weren't worried about being seen and captured.

The man gained on her, and she moved faster, breaking into a jog. "Hey!" the man shouted again. "Get away from there!"

"I'm trying," Kalish muttered. "How the Fate am I supposed to climb down?"

Another shout behind her made her look up. *Spines!*

Maled.

Kalish broke into a sprint, veering away from the cliff edge to weave among the giant pots. She rounded one brightly painted pot and nearly bumped into a man marking something on it. "Excuse me," she said breathlessly, "I'm looking for the route down from this side of the terrace."

The man frowned. "There is none. Not unless you're a grain pot."

Kalish clenched her fists. "I was told there's a way down."

"Well, the kids try now and again. Some make it, but unless you're half goat, your best bet is to go out the front." His eyes narrowed as he scanned her face. "You're not from here. Are you even Surefoot?"

Kalish didn't wait around to explain. She took off running. How was she supposed to make it all the way across the terrace and back down the other heavily-guarded side? She burst out from a cluster of pots to see Riven only a dozen paces away. He had his back to her, but before she could react, he spun. His eyes widened and he lunged as Kalish turned and ran.

She flew down the row of pots, Riven inching closer with every step. Where to now? He was faster than she was. Thinking of the rabbits that skittered away from the much speedier foxes, she dodged left between two pots, and then raced along a narrow corridor between rows of pots. A moment later, Riven ducked into the same lane. She dodged left again and immediately pelted back the way she'd come. With luck, he'd be so focused on where she'd vanished, he wouldn't notice her passing him in the other direction. As she whisked past each pot, she glanced to her left. *There!* She caught sight of Riven's leg in the other aisle. *Keep running!* She pumped her legs faster.

But she'd forgotten about Maled. When he stepped out from between two pots mere paces from her, she couldn't stop, but careered right into him.

He was as surprised as she was, and they bounced off one another like rocks ricocheting down a cliff. Adrenaline pumping, Kalish was back on her feet in an instant, but not faster than Maled, who snatched her arm in a vice grip.

She yanked her arm away and ran. Maled's nails left ragged scratches in her skin, but Kalish ignored the sting. She reached down and pulled out her knife as Maled cursed at her heels. Then she dodged left. *Be like a rabbit. Dodge and turn. Bite if they catch you.*

Left, right, left—Kalish's breath grew ragged as she tired. Riven had picked up the chase again, as had a group of workers nearby, and Kalish understood no one in this terrace would help her. She was the enemy. She would have to get herself out.

FOURTEEN

As Kalish reached the edge of the cliff, she took in the hive of activity as the pots were lowered and raised.

No way down unless you're a grain pot. The man's words flashed through her mind and gave her an idea. She darted into a jumble of pots near the lift apparatus, weaving in and out among them, keeping an eye on her pursuers. The instant she was out of sight, she sheathed her knife and leapt at the nearest pot. Catching the lip, she pulled herself over the edge and dove headfirst inside.

She landed with a thud, rolled to a crouch, and then stilled her body. Her breath came in heaves, but she forced herself silent as the men searched for her.

Feet pounded just outside the thick clay walls. "She went this way!"

"Catch her before she comes out the other side!"

"Over there!" Maled and Riven's voices were joined by others.

"Where'd she go?"

Feet slowed down, then passed by her in several directions. Kalish eased herself against the wall of the pot, shimmying up the sloped side as far as she could. The pot's shoulder would hide her if someone peeked down from this side, at least. It was the best she could do if they decided to look into the pots.

Slowly her breathing evened out, but her heart still raced as she listened to the increasingly frustrated voices outside. As far as they could tell, she'd vanished like a lantan among rocks.

But Maled was every bit as cunning as she was. "Check the pots—inside."

Kalish grimaced and tried to inch her way higher up the sloped wall of the pot. She wondered if she should pull her knife out, but didn't think it mattered. If they found her, she was trapped. She questioned her sense—maybe she should have kept running, headed back into the terrace to lose herself among the rooms.

Too late now. A slap at the top of the pot jerked her eyes up. Hands gripped the rim opposite her position. Feet scrabbled at the pot—whoever was trying to climb wasn't very good. Under cover of the man's noise and shaking, she hurled herself to the other side, tucking herself as high as she could up the wall and holding her breath.

The movement outside stopped, and Kalish felt the man's presence through the clay. A moment later he grunted directly overhead. His breathing was loud as he scanned the inside of the pot. Then he dropped off the side.

She heard him move on to the next pot and slowly let out her breath. Still, she didn't move. Now that the men weren't running and shouting, they'd hear her. She waited until she heard them check all the pots

120

around her. She waited until she heard Maled cursing. She waited until she couldn't hear Maled or Riven at all. She waited until her legs trembled with the effort of standing on the near-vertical wall.

Silently she let herself down into the bottom of the pot. She took a deep breath, and the shaking in her knees subsided. She rolled her shoulders and patted her thigh, reassuring herself her knife was still there.

Footsteps outside made her tense, and a moment later, she nearly cried out in surprise as the pot tipped, sending her sprawling.

"Hey! Watch it! You can't push that hard, boy," a man's voice called. "Now, gently this time. It's not a race, and if you break the pot, you'll be on latrine duty for more five-days than you can count."

The workers were moving her pot, exactly as Kalish had hoped they would. What she hadn't thought through was exactly how she'd manage to avoid being seen … and survive … as her pot was tipped and rolled.

She raised herself to a crouch, thanking the Fates the 'boy' was just learning. The man barked instructions to him that clued Kalish into what would happen next.

The pot stabilised so it was almost upright, and then the men began to roll it along the ground. In a crouch for balance, Kalish tried to keep up with the rolling pot. She made her movements fluid like the slinking run of an attacking cat—no jarring motions or noise to give away her presence.

The rolling started off slow, but increased in pace, presumably as the boy grew more confident.

"Hold it there!" The pot came to an abrupt stop, tipping upright, and Kalish struggled to maintain

her balance. She felt bad for the boy as he was repri-
manded yet again for shoving the pot, knowing it was
her own weight throwing the pot off balance. "Two
more," the man said, and their footsteps faded.

Moments later new footsteps approached.
These men were silent, and Kalish didn't know what
they were doing as the pot shuddered under their
touch.

"Up!" One man barked a signal, and the pot
shifted, scraping across the ground for a moment before stabilising in a gentle swing. She was hanging!

A creaking sound to her right accompanied the
rhythmic chanting of several men, and the pot shuddered and swayed as it dropped downward. Before
long she could see the top of the cliff through the
mouth of the pot.

The descent was rapid, and before she had a
chance to decide what to do when she reached the
bottom, she was there. She crouched on the floor of
the pot as more men worked around it, presumably re-
moving the ropes it had been lowered with. What
would happen then? She guessed the pot would be
filled with grain, but did they move it somewhere else
to fill it? How long before they started pouring grain
in? And would they check the pot first to make sure it
was empty?

The answer to all her questions came with the
first shower of grain a moment later, pelting Kalish
and catching in her hair. She bent and shook her head
to dislodge the grains, only to receive a second shower
down her back. She staggered to the side of the pot,
underneath the shoulder, and watched the grain tumble down. Hands appeared, holding a small jug at the
lip of the pot and tipping it in. Then another and another, from all sides of the pot, like miniature water-

falls. How many people were out there? How was she going to escape unseen?

The grain piled higher and higher, the stream nearly constant. Before long, Kalish was knee-deep in it. At this rate, she'd suffocate in grain before she could make a break for it. Part of her marvelled at the vast fields the Surefoot Clan must cultivate in order to produce this much grain. They must have innovations in the fields as well as in the terrace. If only she'd been able to stay in the Surefoot Clan—the glimpses of technology she'd gotten in her flight away from the terrace excited her curiosity—had she not been running, she would have stopped to ask questions and study things like that smoke bomb and the lifting apparatus. She'd been a fool to think she had valuable innovations to give them—they were far beyond her own clan.

Or rather, the clan she used to call her own. Where was she supposed to go next? If she got out of this pot alive, where would she run to?

Don't worry about that now. First you have to get out of this situation. No point in worrying about what's next until you're sure you'll have a chance.

The grain rose higher and higher. Kalish tried to stay on top, but struggled to keep her footing. Before long, she had to crouch to keep her head below the rim. She had no plan except to hope there would be a lull in activity and everyone would leave so she could escape unnoticed.

The grain kept flowing. Any moment someone was going to notice her, crouched on top of the pile. She was going to have to move. But maybe she didn't have to run. She took a deep breath to calm her nerves and slid her knife out, tucking it out of sight in her folded arms. She straightened the cape on her shoulders and stood abruptly.

A man about to pour grain into the pot gasped and jerked away. Others awaiting their turns to empty their grain jugs stepped back and froze, staring wide-eyed at her. Kalish glared down upon them with what she hoped was an imperious air. There were at least a dozen men gathered around two of the enormous pots. Hundreds of smaller vessels lay scattered around, some empty, some full, and a stream of other men carried them to and from the fields. Those arriving slowed to a halt as they took in the scene. There were possibly a hundred men near enough to give chase if she ran, and nowhere to hide in the expanse of fields that spread out from the base of the butte. Kalish prayed no one noticed her jittery knees.

"Pathetic." She stepped up to the lip of the pot and jumped to the ground. "It took too long for you to fill that pot." She glared at the man in front of her and he fell away. She paced away from the pot and out of arm's reach of her enemies. "You're slow and weak. A bunch of boys could do your job better. It's no wonder you're here in the fields and not out raiding." Those who had withstood her gaze dropped their eyes to the ground. She paced along the row of waiting men arriving from the fields, moving further and further from the cliff. "Yes, I see why the elders sent me out here to inspect your work." One man's eyes flicked to her face and he frowned. She was going to have to make this quick, or they'd notice she wasn't a Surefoot, was barely an adult, and *hadn't* been sent by the elders. "I am going to inspect the fields. I hope when I return, you have picked up the pace so I need not take an unfavourable report back to the elders."

124

She waited a beat, and then barked, "Well, don't just stand there. Move!"

The men jumped into action and Kalish turned and strode away, her back prickling with the stares she knew some of the men were giving her, and listening keenly for sounds of pursuit. The muttering she left behind turned to arguing, and she hadn't gone far before running footsteps sounded behind her.

She knew that the minute she ran, the game was up. She gripped her knife more tightly and picked up her pace. The footsteps gained quickly, and it took all her self-control not to break into a sprint. She was a woman, and she was supposed to be a representative from the elder council. She would not run. Not until she had no other options.

The men pounded toward her. She didn't know how many, but it was certainly more than she could fight. She gritted her teeth, waiting and listening to their approach.

When they were mere paces away, she whirled, snarling at them, "Didn't I tell you to get to work?" Some skidded to a halt, but a few kept coming, and she slashed her knife at them. Most dodged the wild movement, but she caught one man's arm as he reached for her. He staggered away dripping blood.

The men surrounded her. Ten of them. "You're not a Surefoot," one growled.

Another spoke up. "You're that Flintcrag I heard about, aren't you? The one that hunting party brought in the other day."

"I am no Flintcrag!" Saying it aloud, with a sneer in her voice was like plunging a knife into her own gut, but pretending to be angry gave her strength. "I was sent by the Fates to your terrace bearing a warning. One you would all do well to heed."

The men shared nervous glances, and a few stepped back. "Wh … what's the warning?" asked a young man in the back.

I have no idea. I'm making this up as I go. Kalish gave a haughty laugh. "The men of this terrace think to meddle in matters of women?" She turned a scowl on the man who had spoken. "I have spoken to the elder council. Your job is to do as they command. And they command that you *get back to work!*" Kalish spat. Then she turned and continued on her way. The men fell back, allowing her to pass.

Spines! Spines! Spines! The fields seemed to stretch forever, and they crawled with Surefoot men. Her whole body shook from that last encounter. How long before someone else knew who she was? How long before her ruse was up?

Fifteen

Kalish pulled her stolen cape tighter around her shoulders, gripped her knife firmly, and moved as fast as she could without breaking into a run. It was too hot for the cape, but she wore it like armour. She would need it if she made it away from the terrace, if she was to survive long enough to make it through Surefoot territory to … where?

Beyond Surefoot lay Point Clan. She knew little about the Points, except for the rumours they had strange ideas about men. Kalish didn't know what those ideas were, but the way the women of Flintcrag Clan whispered behind their hands about them, they were scandalous.

Well, she was scandalous, too. Maybe the Point Clan would accept her.

Her haughty demeanour was working—most of the men she passed, lugging full pots of grain, lowered their gaze at her approach. She began to breathe easier. Her grip on the knife relaxed a little, but her pace didn't slacken.

She passed through fields busy with harvesters. Not only did the fields cover the valley floor, but they carpeted the dry slopes too. Kalish wondered how they watered the higher fields.

A path sliced between two fields, angling uphill. In the distance, a dark smudge of scrub drew her on. Scrub was a place to hide and usually meant water, and she was parched after her headlong flight. Maybe she could rest there, work out a plan.

The path grew steep, and she breathed a sigh of relief as she passed the last of the harvesters. The way ahead was free. She glanced behind her—only two men were headed toward her, and they were a good distance away. She sheathed her knife and broke into a run.

She was panting by the time she passed through the grain fields. She didn't slow down, but plunged off the path into the prickly scrub. Branches snagged at her cape and scratched her legs, but she pushed through the bushes until she was clear of the path before stopping to catch her breath.

Listening intently, she heard no sound of pursuit. Even so, she wanted her knife easily accessible, and there was no point in hiding it now. She took the hidden sheath from her thigh and strapped it to her lower leg. She pushed further into the scrub, heading for the deep V at the centre of the vegetation where she was sure she would find a spring. She wanted to avoid using the path and creep up unseen—there were certain to be people at a spring so close to the terrace and the agricultural fields, and she wasn't keen to meet anyone.

Thirst would be her main enemy, even this deep in Surefoot territory, surrounded by an enemy clan. Without a water skin, she would be forced to find a new water source every day. That meant sticking to well-travelled routes near human habitation, hiding from her enemies along their most well-travelled paths.

Her steps faltered. She had nothing but a knife and a stolen cape to get her from deep within the Surefoot Clan to the Point Clan, where she would face all over again the same danger from which she had just escaped. She clutched her stomach against a wave of despair. She'd never make it. No one wanted her. Not with this fate carved into her face. Not with lantan eyes flashing treachery. She sank to her knees, the impossibility of her situation dragging her down. She would spend who knew how many days suffering from thirst, running from enemies, only to be caught and subjected to the horrors every Fatecarver clan longed to see its enemies suffer. She shuddered as a vision of her teeth braided into Maled's hair flashed into her head.

She knelt in the bushes and forced herself to focus on more pleasant things, but each time she brought up a soothing image it morphed into a nightmare. Dayo, shoulder to shoulder with her, planning their next glider, turned to his scowling face telling her to leave. Her father's gentle smile shifted to his slack face and unseeing dead eyes. Grandmother Ma's wise sayings switched to her stark warning. Everything good had turned against her. Everyone she thought loved her was gone, one way or another.

She swallowed the lump in her throat. Was her only option to die?

Something rustled behind her, and she jumped, knife raised in defence. She wasn't ready to die yet. Another rustle and she was on her feet, weaving silently between the bushes away from the sound.

A low murmur of voices filtered through the branches. Surely someone making that much noise wasn't following her—could they be on the path to the spring? She stopped and listened intently.

A grasshopper buzzed nearby, and another answered from further away. All else was silent.

She waited. Hunter and hunted both knew patience was what filled bellies and kept you alive.

A moth flitted over her shoulder and landed on a branch, instantly folding its wings and vanishing into the bark. Kalish tensed. Whatever had disturbed the moth was behind her. Slowly she turned. The tangled branches behind her revealed nothing but dappled light. Again she waited, keeping her breathing slow and silent. One breath, two breaths, three breaths. The silence continued. Gradually, Kalish's muscles relaxed. The noises she heard must have come from someone passing on a nearby path. They were gone now. She sheathed her knife and continued toward the spring, rolling her feet silently on the dry ground, and moving with the fluid grace of a cat. Hunter, not hunted.

"Pst! Kalish!"

The hiss made her jump, and in a flash her knife was back in her hand. She turned, darting her eyes about, searching for the source of the voice.

"It *is* her! See, I told you so."

She almost smiled. And then she made them out—Nenu and Zev. Nenu grinned and waved at her, and she resisted the urge to wave back. Instead she tensed. She remembered the two men she'd seen from a distance before she sprinted into the scrub. She wasn't about to trust anyone who had pursued her all the way up here and had been creeping along behind her.

130

Zev must have seen her wariness. He nodded gravely, and then turned to smile at Nenu, who was tugging on his arm and whispering none too quietly, "Where are her things? I found her, I should be the one to give them to her."

He pulled a familiar bundle off his back and handed it to Nenu, then watched as his brother picked his way through the bushes toward Kalish. She stood her ground, her eyes on Zev, so that when he switched his gaze to her, she saw the compassion on his face.

"Kalish!" Nenu's smile was irresistible, and this time Kalish smiled back. He held out her bundle, but when she reached for it, he pulled it back, a mischievous twinkle in his eye. "Tell me a story first?"

Zev stepped forward. "There's no time, little brother. Kalish needs to go." He turned his eyes on her, though still speaking to Nenu. "There are others searching for her. People who must not find her."

A shiver shot through Kalish's chest. "Maled and Riven?"

Zev nodded. "And others. At the moment I think we're the only ones who know you're here, but it won't be long." The corners of his mouth quirked upward. "You *did* make a bit of a scene back there."

"Well I wasn't exactly going to be able to slip away unseen."

Zev held up a hand. "You did well to get this far. But you won't get much further without your things. And you need to go now." He raised his eyebrows at Nenu, and he handed Kalish her bundle.

"But I wanted a story." Nenu sounded as forlorn as Kalish felt.

She clutched the bundle to her chest. "Thank you."

"No. Thank *you*. For saving Nenu's life." He frowned. "Where will you go?"

Kalish swallowed. "I guess I'll try Point Clan."

Zev nodded. "It's at least twelve days to the border. Best not to be seen at any of the springs, but you know that." He smiled. "Maybe don't fall asleep in a tussock either."

Distant voices made Kalish jump. She slung her bundle over her shoulder and gave Zev a nod. He held out his hand, palm up—a gesture of friendship—and she placed her hand over his. "May the Fates be with you."

"And also with you."

Before they broke apart, Kalish was nearly knocked over by Nenu, wrapping her in a hug. "Be safe Kalish!" There were tears in his eyes.

"I will Nenu. You take care of your brother, okay?" She pried his arms from around her neck and smiled at him. With one last nod to Zev, she turned and crept away into the scrub.

It should have been simple to make her way to the Point Clan's territory—keep the mountains to her left and travel at night to avoid being seen.

Should have been. Maybe if she'd spent less time talking to Zev and Nenu or if she hadn't stopped to fill her water skin so close to the terrace, it would have been.

Or maybe the Fates were simply against her. Either way, before the sun set, Kalish was being pursued. She saw them—a handful of men—at the bottom of a slope she had just climbed. They were pointing to the ground and arguing. One glanced up, and Kalish froze. She wasn't hidden, but they might not see her if she stayed still. *Be a lantan.* When no one was looking, she fell to a crouch and scurried around a rock before leaping up and sprinting away.

Tracking was difficult on the dry ground, and Kalish did her best to make her own trail as hard to follow as possible. She stepped on rocks whenever she could and moved carefully past plants to avoid breaking branches. But speed was her best ally, and mostly she ran.

Forgoing sleep, she pushed on through the night, and then snatched only a short rest once the sun was up. Under the hot sun, she soon ran out of water and had to search for a spring. Following a trail was the surest way to reach one, but dangerous. Still, dehydration was deadly. As the sun sank below the horizon that evening, she approached what she hoped was a source of water. She kept her head up and her eyes open as she passed a few children lugging jugs home, water sloshing onto the dusty path. None of them paid her any attention, and she breathed easier as she came to the spring and found it deserted. She admired the smoothly carved rock bowl placed to receive the slow trickle of water issuing from the rocks above. She bent and dipped her water skin into the bowl.

The hair on the back of her neck rose, and Kalish jerked to her feet, clutching the water skin to her chest. In the same instant, a dart whizzed through the space where she had crouched.

Without waiting to see who had launched the dart, Kalish bolted down the path, jamming the stopper in her water skin as she ran.

A wild war cry rose behind her, its ululations echoed by other voices nearby.

Spines! Kalish sprinted down the path, eyes peeled for somewhere to turn off and disappear into the scrub. But the further she went from the spring, the more sparse the vegetation. Soon she flew through a plain of tussocks dotted with rock spires. A glance behind her revealed three men giving chase. She darted behind a spire and continued on, letting the bulk of the rock hide her as she ran toward the next spire.

Dashing from rock to rock, she distanced herself from the men. It seemed they weren't trying very hard to catch her—every time she glanced back, they were further away. As dusk turned to night, she slowed her pace and caught her breath.

The same scene was repeated five times over the following four days. Every time Kalish arrived at a spring, there were warriors waiting to drive her away. Each time, they drove her closer and closer to the mountains. She was making no progress toward Point Clan territory, and the terrain was becoming more and more forbidding. She was desperately thirsty, chewing sugarspike leaves to relieve the dryness in her mouth, though they gave little moisture.

She needed water, and her enemies knew it. They didn't bother to pursue her cross-country, because eventually she'd be caught at a spring or she'd die of thirst. On the morning of the fifth day since her escape from Surefoot's prime terrace, Kalish climbed a rocky slope, her head pounding and her vision swimming from dehydration. At the top, she was surprised to see the slope continued on. From her vantage point, she could see it was part of a ridge that rose up and into the mountains.

Sixteen

The mountains. Few Fatecarvers ventured there, and even fewer returned. Rock and snow, little prey and none of the familiar plants, hungry cats—it wasn't an inviting place.

It was exactly the sort of place her enemies expected her to avoid.

It was exactly the sort of place she *should* avoid.

Kalish turned back toward the dry mesas of home. Every source of water there was blocked to her. Every person her enemy. The path to Point Clan was one of death—probably at the hands of her enemies. That familiar landscape of mesas, canyons, and grain fields was no longer home.

A falcon keened high above, and the sound drove Kalish to her knees with a sob. She curled into a ball and let her tears flow. All hope of a new home within another clan drained out with the tears, leaving her hollow inside. She lay on the ground as the falcon stooped to circle lower, unmoving as the sun rose and warmed the rocks around her. A golo beetle crept into the sun to bask, but still, she lay on the ground until her mind was blank and her body an empty shell. She wanted to end her suffering right there, but didn't have the energy to even reach for her knife.

A sharp rock jabbed into her hip. She ignored it. A fly landed on her cheek, its jerky steps prickling her skin. She didn't bother brushing it off.

A rock shifted nearby, and Kalish turned dull eyes toward the sound.

The creature picking its way over the scree was like nothing Kalish had ever seen. As long as her arm and lizard-like in form, its plated skin was mottled in perfect imitation of the rocks. Its snout was long and narrow, its front legs muscular and ending in broad feet. Running down its flank was a curious flap of flesh that Kalish supposed must assist its camouflage by blurring the shape of its body. As she watched, the animal picked its way across the rocks, poking its snout into crevices, snuffling gently, as if sniffing for something.

When it stopped and began hurling stones aside, Kalish scrambled to a crouch. The creature would make a good meal, but not if it burrowed out of sight.

Still, she hesitated to kill such a curious animal. What was it doing? What did it smell that she could not? She crept forward while the lizard had its head buried amidst the stones. It kept tossing rocks from the hole it was digging, until half its body had van-ished. If Kalish wanted to eat, she needed to catch this creature now, before it was gone. She eased her knife out of its sheath and sprang forward.

Though it seemed oblivious moments before, as soon as Kalish moved, the lizard sprang from its hole. It darted across the rocks, and then froze, blending seamlessly into the stone. Had Kalish not watched it, she never would have believed there was a lizard there at all. She crept closer, eyes glued to the spot where the animal hid in plain sight. Just when she was within reach, it exploded into motion. It leapt once, twice, onto large boulders until it was above her head height. Then it launched itself into the air, spreading its legs wide. Kalish forgot her pursuit, and her jaw dropped as the odd flap on the lizard's side stretched taut between its legs. The lizard soared down the slope until she lost it among the rocks. In spite of her exhaustion and dehydration, she grinned. A flying lizard! Who would have thought something like that existed? And the skin stretched between its legs? Her thoughts immediately flew to the possibilities—could humans do that? Could you stretch sugarspike fabric between your legs and arms and glide? She imagined scaling a cliff, and then leaping off without the bother and time of hauling a glider with her and assembling it at the top. She began to pace, considering the details. Could you get enough loft that way? How would you steer?

She stumbled into a hole and was brought back to her immediate situation. The lizard's hole was damp and cool. Kalish knelt and scooped more rocks out. The further she went, the more moisture clung to them. At elbow's depth, water welled up, and she laughed out loud. "A flying lizard that can smell water. Oh, wouldn't *that* be a gift for a clan!"

But as she scooped water into her hands and slaked her thirst, Kalish felt less inclined to give anything to any of the Fatecarver clans. She gazed toward the craggy peaks and thought about the lizard. What else was out here? What else didn't she know about? She'd grown up believing that the Fatecarvers, and the Flintcrag Clan in particular, knew everything, were better than any other people in the world. But her brief visit to the Surefoot Clan revealed the lie.

No one travelled into the mountains. No one ventured beyond. But there *was* a beyond, with people in it. Kalish wondered whether there was any truth in the stories of the Treekeepers beyond the mountains. Did they really capture Fatecarver babies and eat them? Did they really make their homes in the tops of trees as tall as cliffs? Did they really worship gods other than the Fates?

Were the Fates even proper gods? After Grandmother Ma's warning about them, she'd begun to question them. The foundations of Kalish's life and beliefs crumbled from under her like a chalky cliff face.

If the Fates weren't gods, if she was banished from her people, what did her own fatecarving mean? Kalish ran her fingers over her cheek where Dayo had traced the outline of wings. "It means whatever I want it to." She scanned the vista of dry buttes behind her. "I don't have to stay here." Her eyes strayed toward the mountains. "I can go somewhere else. I can fly."

She remembered what the elders had said about her storyscar. *You are fated to fly as the kiriki falcons. The wind will be your guide and conveyance. Your understanding will encompass the unknown.* She had wings on her cheeks. She was destined to fly far. Maybe this is what her fate meant. She would soar across the mountains like a falcon, scale rocks with the fluid grace of a lantan. Discover wonders unknown.

SEVENTEEN

Kalish's moment of confidence was short-lived. Water
and food were difficult to come by in the sparsely in-
habited mountains. She learned to catch golo beetles
and ants and some sort of larva that nestled in the
centre of the small, sparse tussocks. On her fourth day
making her way toward the dark peaks in the distance,
the wind picked up and clouds cloaked the mountains'
shoulders. Kalish struggled through a landscape of
slippery scree and sharp rock that cut her hands whenever she fell. In the morning, while the sun shone,
she'd decided to make her way over a saddle that led
toward the heart of the mountain ranges. The saddle
proved more challenging than she anticipated, and she
regretted her decision as the first drops of rain splat-
tered onto her face. She wouldn't make it over before
the storm hit, and there was no shelter on the bare
windswept slope.

She considered going back to the previous
night's camp, but the thought of making the climb
again daunted her. She would push on. She pulled out
her stolen cape—now was the time to test whether it

was really waterproof. She tossed it over her shoulders and pulled up the hood.

As she forged ahead, the wind grew more fierce. It whipped the hood off her head, and rain lashed her face. She pulled the hood back up and bent her head, trusting her feet to guide her up the slope. The rocks grew slick with rain, and rivulets coursed down around her feet. Still she plodded on.

When she finally poked her head above the saddle, the wind nearly knocked her off her feet. She crouched, gripping the ground with her hands, and crawled the remainder of the way to the top.

The view down the other side filled her with dread. As difficult as the climb up had been, the way down the other side was near vertical. This wasn't a pass at all, but a trap. The wind howled, and ice mixed with the rain now. She couldn't stay here. Could she make it down the other side? Far below, she made out a goat gingerly picking its way along a narrow path.

Goat for dinner? Her stomach growled at the thought. She cinched her bundle tighter over her shoulder and lowered herself over the side. Where a goat could go, so could she.

One handhold, one foothold at a time, Kalish made her way down. The wind whipped her cape into a flapping frenzy. Her fingers grew numb, until the only way she knew she was gripping the rock was by watching her hands. Her foot slipped and she struck her knee against the rock. "Spines!"

As she descended, the wind diminished some-what, though the rain kept lashing her. She was soaked from the thighs down, and rivulets of icy water dripped from her hands all the way up her raised arms, but the cape kept most of her upper body and head dry, including the bundle slung over her shoulder, and she was thankful for it.

Daylight was fading by the time the slope finally eased. Kalish stepped onto a narrow goat path and glanced down from her perch. A knot of bushes huddled in a cleft below her, and she struck out toward them. It wouldn't be dry down there, but with luck, there would be enough shelter to keep her alive through the night.

She saw no sign of the goat she'd spotted earlier. Not that she could hunt in this weather or terrain anyway. Nor was there any way to cook in this rain. It would be a cold, hungry night.

Curled in a miserable wet ball on a bed of rock, Kalish slept little. She was up and moving again long before the sun reached the peaks above her. The sky was washed clean, and Kalish could hear the rushing water of multiple streams tumbling down from above. She wouldn't go thirsty today.

Food was more difficult to come by. As she set out toward the next saddle she had to cross, she searched for anything edible, but it seemed the goats had deserted this valley. It was too cold for beetles or lizards to be out and about yet. Kalish pushed on.

By the seventh day, she was scraping lichens off the rocks like a goat herself. They were tough and bitter, but gave her stomach something to work on. She had scaled cliffs, trudged up river valleys, and stumbled across more scree slopes than she thought existed in the world. Her sandals rubbed her feet raw, and the weather grew colder every day. Each time she reached a saddle, she gazed out, expecting the land to drop away into forest. And each time, she was dismayed to find nothing but rank upon rank of peaks rising ahead of her.

Weak with hunger, she slipped again and again, climbing to the ridge she hoped to follow. At the top, she let out a cry of anguish at the sight of yet more peaks to scale.

"I can't make it." She turned to look back where she'd come from. Her homeland was lost behind the many ridges she'd crossed already. Home was at least as far away as the other side of the mountains. There was no going back now. She collapsed on the rough scree and sobbed. Now was the time to leave this body. Maybe for good, as Grandmother Ma had done.

She stepped into the Fatewalker Realm.

Her physical pain eased instantly, but the Fatewalker Realm couldn't erase her anguish. She'd come so far. How could the mountains go on so long? She knew she hadn't lost her way—she was still headed westward. But if she didn't stop to rest in a place with food soon, she wouldn't ever reach Treekeeper lands on the other side. She began to wonder if there even *was* an end to the mountains. Maybe the Treekeepers didn't exist. She understood now why no one crossed the mountains.

She drew up her knees and hung her head. At least she could enjoy warm sun in the Fatewalker Realm. It was tempting to stay here and let her body lie where it was.

"Kalish!"

Her head snapped up.

"Kalish!" It was Dayo's voice. In the blue sky above, a glider spiralled gracefully down toward her. She scrambled to her feet.

Dayo hung beneath a beautifully proportioned glider outfitted with her suspension system. He shifted his weight with ease, bringing the glider out of its spiral into a perfectly controlled landing near her. She scrambled to her feet and eyed him warily.

"I thought I'd never find you." Dayo stepped away from the glider and strode toward her. As he neared, he seemed to register the look on her face, her crossed arms; he pulled up short. "Kalish, I …"

She refused to help ease his awkwardness. She shoved down her own unwilling elation at seeing him and allowed him to shuffle uncomfortably in the tense silence between them.

Dayo focused on his feet. "Kalish. I … I …" He raised his head and peered at her with furrowed brows. "What are you doing here?"

Kalish barked a laugh. "Probably dying. You can take that message back to your clan once you're done gloating."

"Dying? But … but why are you *here*? Why aren't you with another clan?"

Another bitter laugh. "Do you think anyone wants me? You, yourself, said I was a lantan. Do you think strangers from another clan would simply take me in? Surefoot Clan's elders condemned me to death, Dayo. It would have been the same in any other clan. I chose to take my chances beyond the mountains. At least out here, I die on my own terms, not at the hands of my own people. Or is that why you've searched me out? Looking to impress Seeda? Glider not enough to make her marry you? Well, you'd better be quick. I won't last much longer. I hope that glider is as good in real life as it is here, because you'll need it to find me in time to finish me off."

Without waiting for his reply, she slipped out of the Fatewalker Realm and back into her body. The shock of weakness and hunger almost made her flee again. It was tempting to shrug off her body for good, but she didn't want to meet Dayo again. He might be able to find her in the Fatewalker Realm, but the chances of him finding her for real were slim to none. She rose to her feet and staggered. How could she be this weak? She needed rest. Then she'd go on, because there was no choice but to do so. She sank back to the ground and unrolled her blanket. The sun was still high in the sky, and it warmed her face as she wrapped the blanket around herself and allowed sleep to claim her.

She dreamed of warm stew and fire, of bread and meat. She dreamed of flying.

When she woke, the warmth on her face was not that of the sun, but of a small fire. She blinked, disoriented. She was no longer on the ridge, and the sun was long gone. A figure hunched next to the fire turning a pair of sticks propped over the coals. The smell of cooking meat made her mouth water. She shifted, and the figure turned toward her.

"Food's nearly ready." He wrinkled his nose. "Not sure exactly what it is—some sort of rabbit maybe?"

Kalish sat up, wrapping the blanket tightly around her shoulders. A chill had settled into her bones and she shivered. She said nothing, but peered at Dayo. His features looked drawn in the flickering firelight.

"I've been sheltering under the glider wings at night." He nodded toward the ghostly form nearby. "Can't get it too close to the fire, though."

Still, Kalish remained silent. She no longer trusted her friend. And she trusted her own voice less, lest it betray the tumult in her heart.

Dayo turned from the fire, holding out a stick of sizzling meat to her as if she were a wild animal he was attempting to tame. Kalish's stomach growled, and she snatched the stick. Dayo's eyes didn't leave her as she blew on the meat, impatient for it to cool enough to eat.

"I know you don't trust me," he said when her mouth was full. "I don't blame you. I was a fool and an idiot."

"Don't forget *Fate-poxed cactus* too," Kalish growled around her food.

Dayo's shoulders slumped. "That too. I'm sorry."

"Did Seeda finally tell you to get lost?" Kalish let her anger swell and steady her voice.

"Not quite." Dayo poked the fire with a stick. "She's gotten her storyscat. She has the fatecarver mark. She's proofing with Tino."

Kalish might have gloated over Seeda choosing Tino over Dayo, but the knife twist of Seeda as her mother's apprentice and successor silenced her.

"The way Seeda and Tino talked about you …" Dayo's Adam's apple bobbed as he swallowed. "I couldn't listen to it anymore. It was all lies. Cruel lies about my … about someone I …"

Kalish gripped the blanket in her fists, forcing herself to stay where she was. Forcing herself not to go to him. Why should she comfort him, when he was the one who rejected her? He had believed those lies.

He pushed her away, threatened to kill her. "Why are you here?"

Dayo looked her directly in the eye. "Because you're my friend. I couldn't let you die out here alone."

Kalish huffed and stood. "I *was* your friend." She picked up her bundle and moved away from the fire, away from Dayo's glider, settling in the darkness and tossing her waterproof cape over herself. She shut her eyes and pretended to sleep.

EIGHTEEN

It was almost as if Dayo hadn't moved at all overnight. When Kalish opened her eyes in the morning, he was crouched by the fire, this time with a small pot on the coals.

Food. Kalish's stomach growled as she smelled her favourite breakfast—a corn porridge called pola studded with vegetables.

Dayo glanced her way and, seeing her awake, smiled.

Kalish frowned in response. If he thought feeding her was going to make her trust him again … The breeze brought another whiff of stew to her nostrils, and she almost moaned in pleasure. Well, she'd be a fool not to eat, at least. She rose, stretching stiff joints, and stepped to the fire, warming her fingers over its heat.

Dayo stirred the porridge. "I'm afraid I've only got the pot and one spoon. We'll have to share." He gingerly lifted the pot off the coals and set it on the ground between them. Kalish eyed him, and he nodded to her. "Go on. Eat as much as you want. I can make more."

Kalish took a spoonful and shut her eyes as she chewed. Dayo always did make the best pola. And he knew just how she liked it—with extra salt and a bit of the spicy tarantha leaf that bit the tongue and warmed the throat. The agonising comfort it gave threatened to bring tears to her eyes, and when she opened them again, she kept her gaze on the pot. This was bribery. She wouldn't give in to it. She wouldn't forgive Dayo. Not this easily.

She finished the porridge in silence under Dayo's close watch. When she'd scraped the pot clean, he took it and refilled it, setting it back on the fire to cook.

"I refilled your water skin." Dayo nodded to where it lay nearby. "There's a small stream in the gully over there. Goats have been there recently, but I haven't seen any. I reckon we're too close, but it might be worth hunting a bit before we move on."

We? Did he think she'd go with him? Kalish ran her fingers through her limp hair, wishing she had clay to stiffen it. Though she wasn't sure it would stay spiked even if she did—it hadn't been cut in over a moon cycle and was much longer than she liked. Dayo's mother had always cut it for her. A knot twisted in her stomach at the thought of Wathi.

"Mum is talking about moving out of Prime Terrace." Dayo kept his eyes on the porridge. "Her cousin lives in Gully Terrace—I guess she's planning on going there. She was really upset about you being banished. And then when Seeda was marked as a fate-carver ..."

Kalish crouched by the fire, arms wrapped around her knees.

148

"Are you just going to sit there and not say anything?" Dayo raised his eyes to her.

"What do you want me to say? Do you think I enjoy hearing gossip about people I'll never see again? About people who rejected me?"

"My mother never rejected you, Kalish."

And that made it even worse. "But *you* did." Her fists were clenched, nails digging into her palms in a desperate attempt to prevent her from crying. "You pushed me away. You threatened to kill me, even as you asked me to save your life. And after I saved you, your friends nearly *did* kill me. Why are you here, Dayo? Whatever you want from me now, you won't get. I have nothing left to give you." She stood and strode to her scattered possessions and began wrapping them back into a bundle.

"I came to help you, Kalish." Dayo's voice was practically a whisper. "I came to make certain you lived. To make certain you knew you were loved. I don't expect anything from you. Tell me what you need, and I'll do it."

Kalish finished making up her bundle, and slung it over her shoulder. Turning to Dayo she spat, "I need you to go away." She stalked off toward the next ridge, the next hurdle in this journey she expected would kill her. But she wasn't going to accept Dayo's help.

She spent the day scrambling up and down rocky slopes under a leaden sky. The keen wind seemed to slice through her cape and drive heat from her body. By evening, the bravado fuelled by Dayo's porridge had burnt away, and she felt the raw bleeding spots where her shoes rubbed her feet, the ache of thigh muscles on yet another ascent, the shudder in

exhausted knees on a long downhill. She saw nothing
of Dayo.

She curled up that evening in a scrape of a
cave that kept the worst of the wind from her. She
didn't bother with a fire—she had nothing to cook,
and no energy to do anything but spread her cat pelt
on the ground, wrap her blanket around herself and
fall asleep. The pelt was stiff and smelly—she had
never had a chance to properly tan it, and now it was
probably too late to do it. Still, it was warm.

The light of morning revealed a small fire laid
and ready to light and a fat slab of goat haunch prepared and set on a skewer above the fire. Kalish
scrambled to her feet and peered around, certain this
was Dayo's work, but he was nowhere to be seen. She
swallowed a lump in her throat and lit the fire.

The clouds lowered steadily as the morning
progressed, and the temperature plummeted with
them. Kalish wished she'd left home with winter
clothing, but she never expected to be venturing alone
into the mountains. She hiked now with her blanket
wrapped around her underneath her stolen cape. Her
hands and feet grew numb, and when it began to
snow, she knew she had to stop and find shelter. A
rock overhang was the best she could do. She gathered
what fuel she could—some dried tussock, a few twigs
and branches from stunted wind-blasted shrubs—and
built a fire to warm her fingers and toes.

She laid her cat pelt on the ground to shield
her from the cold and shivered herself to sleep listening to the hiss of ice hitting the rocks.

In the night, she dreamed of Dayo, cradling her in the
C of his warm body, wrapping her tight in his em-

brace. Her shivering ceased and she sank into a deep sleep.

She wasn't sure where her dream left off and reality began, but as she slowly regained consciousness, she realised the warmth at her back was another body pressed close. The rock overhang had been walled off and light filtered in through the wings of a glider dusted with snow. Her body tensed, ready to spring up.

"I'm sorry. I'll go if you want me to." Dayo's voice was quiet in her ear. "The snow was covering you by the time I found you. Your whole body was shaking. I was afraid you'd freeze to death." His arm snaked around her waist. "I couldn't bear to lose you again."

It was too much. The comfort of his physical presence cracked something deep inside her chest. For weeks she'd held herself together with nothing but stubborn will, but it wasn't enough. A great pain welled up inside as she let all the grief and anguish of her banishment wash over her. Tears sprang to her eyes, and without warning she was sobbing uncontrollably.

Dayo pulled her tight against himself. "I'm sorry. I'm so sorry, Kalish. My dearest friend, forgive me."

She clutched at his arm, savouring his warmth and pressing herself into him. How long she cried in his arms, she didn't know, but when the storm of her grief passed she lay drained while Dayo slipped out from under the blankets to light a fire and prepare breakfast.

When the smell of corn porridge made her stomach rumble, Kalish threw off the blankets, shivering in the cold air as she stood and stretched as much as the low overhang would allow.

Dayo tossed her a long heavy woollen cape. "Mum sent that for you."

Kalish smiled and blinked back fresh tears as she wrapped the cape around herself. It was warmer than she expected, and she savoured the feeling. "Wathi knew you were coming to me?"

He nodded. "She knew before I did. She started weaving that cape the minute you were gone."

"Did she put you up to this?" The question came out sharp as suspicion chilled her.

Dayo looked up from the porridge he was stirring, and his eyes locked with hers. "No. I came because ... because I wanted to." His eyes fell again and his cheeks flushed. "I guess it took me longer to realise that than it took Mum." He lifted the porridge off the coals and set it in front of her, then sat back on his haunches near the fire, warming his hands.

Kalish took a bite and couldn't suppress her moan of pleasure. Dayo studiously ignored her, but she heard his stomach growl. She held the spoon out to him. "Share with me?"

"You're the woman; you should eat first," he replied without meeting her eyes.

"Oh Dayo, don't be ridiculous. When have we ever paid attention to those rules?"

"I just thought that ... I didn't know if ..." He swallowed and blinked rapidly.

"I never stopped being your friend, Dayo." She checked herself before her voice cracked, and it was a moment before she could go on in a steady voice. "Eat. Let's not waste time arguing. I'm eager to get out of the mountains as quickly as possible."

A ghost of a smile flitted across Dayo's face and he accepted the spoon.

As they ate, Kalish tried to establish the extent of Dayo's help. "What are your plans now you've found me and delivered your mother's cape?"

He shrugged. "That depends on what your plans are."

Kalish sighed. "I'd hoped to get across these Fate-cursed mountains to the other side."

Dayo's eyes widened. "The other side! Why would you go there? What will you do when you get there? You know the stories about the Treekeepers. They're not even our people. They'll kill you!"

"Maybe they will, maybe they won't. Have you ever met anyone who's actually been to Treekeeper territory?"

"No. But that's the point. They're—"

"They're a mystery. I don't know what they're like, how they live, how they'll react to me. What I *do* know is that if I return to Fatecarver lands, I *will* die." She smiled and ran her fingers over her storyscar. "*You are fated to fly as the kiriki falcons. The wind will be your guide and conveyance. Your understanding will encompass the unknown.* That is what the elders said."

"I never heard that part of your Fate. Did they really say that?" A smile crept across Dayo's face.

"They did."

"So that means you're *meant* to go to the Treekeepers!" Dayo leaned forward and ran a finger down Kalish's neck, sending a shiver along her spine. "That's what this plant must be on your neck!" He laughed. "It's a good thing I built this glider for two." His eyes locked with hers.

Kalish didn't dare hope she understood. She searched his eyes for his meaning, and said nothing.

His smile faded. "Do you … do you not want me to come with you?"

Kalish didn't want to make it too easy for him. "If you want to, I can hardly stop you, can I?" Inside, warmth spread through her.

Nineteen

Dayo's glider not only incorporated Kalish's idea for suspending the pilot, but it included two pilot harnesses and a pouch under the wing for storing gear.

"Can it really carry two people?" The wing was longer and broader than any glider she'd ever seen, but she doubted its abilities.

"It can."

Kalish frowned. "Who did you test it with?" She wasn't sure she wanted to know.

Dayo laughed and wrapped an arm around her shoulders. "No one. I wanted you to be the first."

"Then how do you know it works?"

"I loaded it with rocks to test its weight capacity. The deadweight of the rocks makes it hard to manoeuvre. I think with two people, both steering, it'll be amazing."

Testing out a new glider with Dayo. Warmth flooded her chest, and she couldn't disguise her glee. "What are we waiting for? Let's go!"

They packed up their things and prepared the glider, hauling it up to a rise from which they could launch. Kalish fingered the smooth sugarspike fabric of the wing. "How did you get the fabric?"

Dayo blushed. "Um …"

"You stole it, didn't you?" Kalish had always been the one to request the fabric for their gliders—as the fatecarver's daughter, she could get whatever she wanted. Dayo, on the other hand, would have had a difficult time justifying the request.

"Well, I knew I was leaving anyway …" He laughed. "I suspect I'm almost as hated as you are in the terrace now."

"What else did you do?"

Dayo stowed the last of their gear in the glider's storage pouch. "Well, I might have lifted a few other necessary items. And *someone* tossed an incendiary into the fatechamber the night I vanished, but I don't know who that could have been." He turned to Kalish with a sly smile.

"An incendiary!" Kalish laughed. "Oh! Mother must be livid!"

"I wish I could have been there to see her reaction."

"But aren't you worried about what the Fates will do to you for having blown up the fatechamber?"

Dayo snorted. "Your grandmother found me in the Fatewalker Realm." He hung his head and scuffed his foot in the stones. "She told me a lot of things. Had a few harsh words to say about my behaviour towards you, too."

They stood for a few moments in awkward silence before Dayo straightened, still not meeting Kalish's gaze. "Are we ready?" He ran one of the rope harnesses through his hand. "I pretty much used your harness plan, so I guess I don't have to show you how it works."

156

The harnesses suspended them side by side under the wing. Lift-off was awkward as they tried to coordinate their steps for a running launch. Their feet left the ground and their bodies slammed together.

Kalish laughed and almost forgot about steering as they lifted into the air. To fly again, and with Dayo at her side, was almost too much happiness to bear.

"To the left!" Dayo's barked order brought Kalish back to the task at hand, and she shifted her weight left. The glider arced into a broad spiral, rising on an updraft in the morning sun until they had a breathtaking view of the peaks rising rank upon rank around them.

"Woo hoo!" Kalish couldn't suppress her glee. She felt the ripple of the wing through the harness and thought this must be how birds feel, with the wind ruffling their feathers. It wasn't long before she had the feel of the glider, and she and Dayo moved as one, guiding it over invisible hills and valleys of moving air, cresting ridge after ridge heading ever westward toward the Treekeepers.

The ranks of peaks that had seemed so impassable yesterday now glided beneath them one after another. The icy air sliced through even the wool cape she wore, but Kalish didn't feel the cold. Dayo turned to her and grinned, warming her to her toes.

When they finally landed late in the afternoon, Kalish was sore where the harness had rubbed her. Her steps felt slow and heavy compared to the soaring flight of the day. Her fingers were stiff with cold.

"I'll see if I can catch us some dinner," she said, pulling her atlatl from her bundle.

Dayo nodded. "Those funny little rabbit things seem to like flat rocks that catch the sun."

Kalish set off down the east side of the ridge, picking her way among boulders and scree, scanning the landscape for movement. Shadows lengthened, and she shivered as the temperature dropped.

One tall rock was still in sunshine, and Kalish spied a form basking on it—the unmistakable silhouette of a lizard. She crept closer, using the rock to shield her from the lizard's view. As she crept, the sun sank, leaving the rock in shadow. At the base of the rock, Kalish silently set down her atlatl. This was not an animal she wanted to kill. She took a slow breath. *I'm a lantan. I can strike like one.* She leapt from her crouch, snatching at the lizard with both hands.

The cool air slowed the lizard's response, but even so, it was halfway off the rock before Kalish's hand landed on its tail. She seized it firmly, hoping this lizard couldn't shed its tail like the little skinks that lived in the cracks of the terrace walls.

The lizard turned and sank its teeth into her hand. Kalish yelped but didn't let go. With her other hand, she grabbed the lizard around the neck and wrestled it into her arms. She pinned it firmly against her side while it thrashed, its tail lashing her skin with prickly barbs. Its body was smaller than her forearm, and she was able to tuck it under one arm, with a hand controlling its head. She picked up her atlatl and headed back to Dayo.

He was bent over a crackling fire and glanced up at her approach. His brow furrowed. "What is that?"

Kalish smiled. "There's a length of sugarspike cord in my bundle. Can you bring it over?"

When Dayo returned with the cord, he asked again, "What is it? Why did you bring it back alive?"

"This isn't just any lizard. Can you tie that around its neck?" After he'd done so, she continued. "Hang onto the cord while I show you." She carefully spread the lizard's legs, stretching the membrane between its front and rear legs.

Dayo sucked in a breath. "Does it fly?"

"It does. And it can find water underground. I saw one a few days ago. It got me wondering whether I could fashion similar wings for people, so we wouldn't have to carry gliders around. I thought if I saw another, I'd catch it and have a closer look."

The lizard had gone still, and it let them poke and prod it and stretch its limbs this way and that to examine the wing structure. The membrane between its legs was stiffened by what looked like bones, allowing it to spread out further than the legs. Up close, its rock-coloured scales were shot through with flecks of gold. Kalish ran her hand down the animal's smooth, cool side, mesmerised by the feel of it.

Dayo brandished his knife. "Well, let's see how it tastes."

Kalish put her hands protectively over the animal. "Are you kidding? This thing can lead us to water. It can fly." She brushed a hand over its scales again. "And it's gorgeous."

"What are you going to do with it? Keep it?"

Kalish shrugged. "Maybe."

"How will we carry it? Besides, with the glider, finding water shouldn't be a problem. Come on, I'm hungry."

"No way." Kalish stepped further from Dayo's knife. "One of these lizards saved my life."

"And this one will too, by providing a nice dinner for us."

Kalish shook her head. "I can't." Something about the lizard felt sacred. It could fly when all its brethren were earthbound—surely that made it special among lizards.

"Well then, why did you bother to catch it?"

"To show it to you."

"Great. You've shown it to me. Now can we eat it?" He stepped closer, and Kalish backed away again.

"Sorry." She slipped the cord off the lizard's neck and lofted it into the air, trusting it to fly. It snapped open its wings and soared away.

Dayo frowned. "Now what are we supposed to eat?"

"I'll get us something else." Kalish picked up her atlatl and left.

She returned with three of the small rabbits, which Dayo quickly butchered and added to the pot of simmering water he had ready for them.

As evening fell and the rabbit cooked, Kalish pulled out her cat skin to sit on.

"How did you get this?" Dayo asked, stroking the tawny fur.

"Killed it."

"You killed a cat?" Dayo's eyes widened.

Kalish grinned. "With a knife."

"Oh! That's a story I have to hear."

Kalish related the tale of the cat as they ate their stew. Dayo's questions about how she'd ended up travelling with a group of Surefoot men led to some uncomfortable silences. Kalish's anger flared again, and Dayo spent a long time staring into the fire. When her stories ran out and the sky was dark and cold, the

160

silence dragged on. The two children who had slept cocooned together for a dozen years were gone, and Kalish was torn between love and distrust.

"This cat skin must make a nice sleeping mat," Dayo said.

Kalish narrowed her eyes. "If you think you're going to just slot back into your place in my life after betraying me, think again."

"I wasn't saying—"

"Yes, you were. I heard the tone of your voice. You want to go right back to the way things were before—Dayo the protector of little Kalish. Well, I'm not little Kalish anymore. I've been looking after myself for over a moon cycle, no thanks to you. You'll need to do more than fly in and feed me rabbit stew to earn a place at my side again."

Dayo's downcast face and slumped shoulders told her she'd been right about his expectations. His disappointment almost made her relent; her heart ached to have her friend fully restored to her. Flying with him had been an intense joy, but this was *her* journey. His participation in it would be on her terms or not at all.

"There's plenty of room under the glider wings." She stood and bundled the cat skin under her arm. "I'll take this side. Good night." Ducking under the wing, she left him sitting beside the remains of their fire.

Twenty

Dayo was already up when Kalish opened her eyes in the morning. She had no idea where he'd slept, or even if he had slept at all. Even with her cat skin for a rug, she'd been chilly during the night. Dayo must have been freezing. She shucked off her blanket and shivered in the icy air. Frost lay thick over the rocks and glider wings.

"There's no fuel for the fire." Dayo handed her a small, flat loaf of bread that had clearly come from the terrace's ovens. "We'll have to make do with a cold breakfast."

"Thanks." Kalish took a bite of bread. It was stale, but tasted so much of home, it made her chest hurt.

They spoke little as they packed their gear. She regretted her harsh words from the night before.

Tension eased once they were in the air—Kalish couldn't be angry or disappointed when she was flying. They soared into the sunshine and she laughed. Dayo gave her a sideways glance, his mouth turning up at the corners.

They crested the tallest of the mountains that day. By the time they spiralled down to a likely campsite, the ground beneath them was less rock and more tussock. The steep cleft below was dark with shrubs. It was a welcome relief from the stark scree slopes they'd soared over for the past two days.

That night, they ate goat cooked over a fire of aromatic twigs from a bush neither of them recognised. It was warmer than the previous nights, and the air was moist and smelled of damp soil. Still, Kalish shivered in the dark. Dayo kept the fire between them, and Kalish knew the chill was her fault. When they'd finished eating, she drew her cat skin out of her bundle and spread it on the ground. "Will you sit with me?"

Dayo's eyes flicked up to meet hers for the first time since they'd landed. They were warm and brown and filled with an uncertainty that squeezed her heart. She blinked hard and wrapped her arms around her knees. "Please."

Without breaking eye contact, he shifted next to her. She leaned against his shoulder, breathing in the smell of smoke that clung to him. His arm wrapped around her and pulled her close, and she let go of her own knees to encircle his waist with her arms. "I missed you, Dayo. I thought you hated me."

"You were right about Seeda," he murmured into her hair. "I was so stupid. I couldn't see what was right in front of me." He put a finger under her chin and lifted it to press a kiss to her lips. Warmth flooded her body. They'd shared everything, from food to clothes, to a bed for over a decade, but this was entirely different. It was like the winds that swept sometimes across the land in a tight swirling funnel, snatching up dust and shrubs and whipping them round and round in a dizzying, terrifying confusion.

She leaned into that dizzying whirlwind, pressing herself against Dayo and returning his kiss in a way she hoped he couldn't ignore, drawing the kiss out until she thought it would last forever and they were both gasping for breath.

"Kalish." Dayo's voice was rough, and echoed her own longing.

In many ways, the night was like so many before—Kalish slept in a safe nest cocooned beside Dayo—but never before had her skin tingled with every touch. Never before had she paid attention to every detail of his body. Never before had sleep been so far from their minds as they lay down.

She worried they might be shy of one another in the morning, but it felt right and natural to wake beside him and understand how their relationship had changed. From long habit, they eased into the day together. As usual, he was first awake, and she opened her eyes to find him gazing down at her, a smile playing over his lips.

"How long have you been watching me sleep?" she asked playfully.

He shrugged. "A while."

She kissed him and sighed dramatically. "When you could have been up getting a fire going. Just like you to laze around in the morning."

She whipped the blanket off both of them, eliciting a squeal of protest from Dayo. "Come on. If we start early, I bet we can make it to the Treekeepers today." She left Dayo to worry about breakfast, and picked her way to a small stream to fill their water skins. When she returned, the smell of Dayo's porridge was already curling around their campsite.

"Mmm! That smells amazing."

Clouds squatted on the peaks above them as they rolled up their bedding, and the air was oppressive with the threat of rain. Dayo breathed deeply. "Such a strange smell. What do you think it is?"

Kalish tasted the air as it filled her nostrils. "I don't know. It's … a green smell. Do you remember when we were kids? That summer when it rained and rained and rained?"

Dayo's eyes widened. "You're right! The whole valley sprouted that summer. I remember those blue flowers, and the vines that sprawled over everything—all those plants we'd never seen before springing up where there'd only ever been tussock. The smell is the same."

They ate a hurried breakfast, both of them eyeing the clouds. "We're not going to catch any thermals today," Dayo commented.

Kalish shook her head. "But we'll be headed into the wind. That'll give us some good lift."

"As long as it doesn't rain."

Neither one of them had ever flown in the rain. Rain rarely fell in the Fatecarver lands, and when it did it was usually accompanied by fierce winds. There was never any need to take out a glider on a rainy day. Kalish guessed that heavy rain would soak the glider and bring it down. She hoped it would hold off until they'd reached their destination, and didn't stop to wonder how they would know when they'd arrived.

Shrubs in the valleys gave way to trees, with brushy hilltops. The clouds seemed to follow them lower and lower throughout the day. Sometime after midday, it began to rain, spitting in fits and starts, stinging their faces. When they crested a final ridge and saw a huge, tree-covered plain stretching into a hazy blue-green horizon, they both sucked in a breath.

"How can there be this many trees?" Dayo wondered.

"Where will we land?" Kalish worried.

They soared out over the green expanse and, as if on cue, the clouds opened up. A torrent of rain pounded the glider wings and lashed their faces. The wind grew gustier, buffeting the glider. Kalish tightened her grip on the frame and scanned the forest below. "We have to find somewhere to land."

"I'm looking." Dayo's voice was tense.

The glider grew heavy with rain, speeding toward the treetops. Even working together, Kalish and Dayo struggled to keep the craft in the air. Below, the trees stretched in an unbroken mass. There was nowhere to land, and they were dropping swiftly.

"Pretend the treetops are the ground," Kalish suggested.

"What?"

"Land on the treetops. Better than crashing into them."

Dayo nodded, and they hurtled toward the trees. "It'll be faster than we're used to."

Kalish tensed. They sank lower and lower. The trees rushed by beneath them in a blur of green.

"Now!" Their feet practically touched the canopy as they shoved hard on the frame of the glider, forcing the nose up into a stall. Branches whipped their legs. The left wing tip caught on a branch, and the glider lurched and finally smashed into the trees, hurling them face-first into the lashing twigs. Kalish shut her eyes. Leaves slapped like her mother's re-

166

bukes, and twigs stung like switches against arms and legs. Then they jerked to a sudden stop, bobbing in their harnesses, suspended in the midst of the forest canopy.

Kalish opened her eyes. Her skin stung, and her first sight was of her own arms crisscrossed with scratches welling blood. "Spines!" She turned to Dayo. "You okay?"

He groaned and swiped at a trickle of blood dripping over his right eye. He peered up at the shredded glider wing above. "My glider! How will we get home?"

Kalish shook her head. "I don't think we're going home, Dayo. We don't have one to go back to. Come on. Let's get ourselves down from here and find somewhere dry to lick our wounds."

Kalish had never climbed a tree before, and she was worried that the thin branches that held the glider aloft wouldn't support their weight once they were clinging to them. They gathered their things from the storage compartment of the glider and tied them into bundles on their backs.

"We should salvage as much of the glider as we can," Dayo suggested.

"What? While perched up here like birds? No way." Kalish didn't trust the trees at all.

Dayo frowned up at the wings. "How can we leave it there?"

She felt it, too—the pain of leaving the glider behind—but she already had dreams of flying without a glider, like that lizard in the mountains. "What would we do with it in this landscape of trees? Even if we salvaged parts, they'd just be a burden to us moving through the forest. Come on. Let's get down from here."

The most terrifying moment came when Dayo severed her rope harness from the glider frame. "Hang on tight," he warned. Kalish clung to the branches around her. When the rope gave way, the branches bowed beneath her weight. She yelped and scrabbled for footholds among the lower branches as she sank downward. Shifting her grip to the lower branches, she let the others snap back up.

"You okay?" Leaves obscured Dayo from view now.

"I'm good. Be careful when you cut your rope." She frowned up toward the rustle of his movement. A moment later Dayo's form came crashing past her. He settled a few branches below her, gripping a fistful of leaves, and sprawled across a thick limb.

Kalish scrambled down to him. "Dayo?"

He groaned and shifted his grip to a branch above him. Leaves spiralled downward to the forest floor as he pulled himself to a sitting position. "Well, that was graceful." He prodded his ribs and grimaced. "I seem to be all in one piece."

Kalish sighed. "Good thing, because I'm not carrying you down."

The branches were slick with rain, but climbing trees was far easier than climbing cliffs, at least until they reached the trunk. Free of branches for the final span, the smooth bole offered few handholds. Kalish peered toward the forest floor far below. "How can something grow this tall and straight?"

"We could jump," Dayo suggested.

Kalish snorted. "And break our legs. That's way too far to jump."

Dayo shrugged. "Well, let's see who the better climber is." He slid feet first off the lowest branch, scrabbling for toeholds. Kalish frowned down at him.

168

The smooth wet bark offered nothing. She scanned the trees around her. Some were larger, many were smaller, and most had rough bark or vines growing up them that would provide better handholds. They'd managed to land in the worst possible tree. "I think there's a better way down," she called to Dayo.

"No. This is good. There are a few holds." Dayo's voice was strained as he concentrated on his next move. Rain streamed down his face and he blinked the water from his eyes.

"Suit yourself." Kalish shimmied toward the end of the branch until it thinned and bowed under her weight. When she felt one more step might snap the branch in two, she carefully swung herself down until her toes touched the branch of a neighbouring tree below. Only then did she realise the flaw in her plan—she'd have to let go of the branch above before she could grip the branch below. As soon as her weight landed on the branch below, it would dip, and she would lose her footing. She hung for a moment, considering whether she could pull herself back up. Then the branch lurched with a snap, making her decision for her. She let go. The branch beneath her feet wasn't as strong as she'd hoped, and she felt she was in freefall as she scrabbled for a grip at her feet. The branch held, but dipped so far her feet slipped off it, and she found herself bobbing off its end, dangling by her hands, her heart racing.

Hand over hand, she worked her way up the branch to the tree's trunk. This tree had deeply fur-rowed bark, offering plenty of handholds. On the firm surface, her confidence returned, and she quickly spidered down to the ground. Looking up, she smiled. "Having trouble?"

Dayo was only halfway down the smooth trunk of the tree. He craned his neck around. "What? How'd you—" His feet slipped, and in an instant he was plummeting to the ground.

TWENTY-ONE

Every Fatecarver child learns to fall. Stony ground and a life spent in cliff dwellings mean children who are slow to learn don't make it past toddlerhood. Dayo's fall was longer than he would have chosen it to be, but he hit the ground and rolled immediately to his feet, laughing.

"You cheated!"

"I did not. You've said yourself, the most important part of climbing is choosing your route. Obviously, I chose a better route." Kalish stepped over to Dayo and brushed wet leaves from his back. "You're filthy. Come on. Let's find somewhere out of this rain." Dayo glanced up longingly at the tattered glider.

Rain bucketed down, setting every leaf fluttering as fat drops hit them. Dayo hunched in his wool cloak, and Kalish pulled up the hood of her waterproof cape. The roar of the downpour made her nervous—anything, human or animal, could sneak up to them without them hearing. Her eyes darted left and right as they picked their way through dense green undergrowth.

But it was hard to remain wary. Kalish had never seen so much green. She gawked at towering trees, ran her fingers over soft moss-covered logs, and brushed through prickly fern fronds. Filtered through the leaves, it seemed the very air was tinged with life. And the smell—wet soil, rotting leaves, and a thousand other scents she couldn't identify—was an intoxicating perfume.

The rain was relentless. It wasn't long before water was seeping in through the seams in Kalish's cape and trickling down her back. She knew Dayo must be soaked through. They trudged on, water dripping off their noses and fingertips. Kalish's wonder at the sights and smells dulled. She lost all sense of direction as the forest went on forever in a uniform green jumble. She longed for the open tussock lands of home.

The rain slackened and then stopped, and as soon as it did, a hoard of mosquitoes emerged from the green. Kalish slapped at her arms and legs. Itchy welts sprang up wherever her skin was exposed. "How can there be this many mosquitoes?"

Dayo slapped his neck, leaving a red smear of blood. "Do you think there are always this many?"

There were mosquitoes in Fatecarver lands, but not like this. The first time Kalish was bitten, she was so fascinated she didn't swat, but watched the insect feed, its abdomen swelling red before it heaved itself into the air. Now, however, she didn't wait for the whining creatures to draw blood.

The trees continued to drip water as the light dimmed. Somewhere beyond the green and the clouds, the sun was beginning to set. Kalish stopped and ran

172

her fingers through her wet hair, attempting to set it back on edge. It flopped over her eyes and she flicked it away. "We're going to have to find somewhere to spend the night."

Dayo nodded, a curl plastered to his temple from his fraying braid. He looked small and defeated as he crushed another mosquito on his skin, and Kalish wondered if he was regretting his choice to follow her. She might have regretted it, except for her it hadn't been a choice. Not really—die at home in the hands of her clan, or die far away. She'd expected the Treekeepers to do the killing here, but as dark rose around them, she realised the forest itself might be their real enemy. They were soaked, night was falling, and she knew they would never be able to light a fire. Dayo must have seen the worry on her face. He smiled and wrapped a wet arm around her shoulders. "Come on. Some of these big trees have buttresses. They won't keep the rain off, but they'll give us protection from whatever animals prowl this forest at night."

Kalish nodded and smiled back. Her mind leapt to the previous night, and she stood on tiptoes to plant a kiss on his lips. He held onto the kiss, deepening it until she forgot the chill of her wet cape and the whine of mosquitoes. As they moved on, they touched hands, lingering as long as they could before a mossy obstacle parted them.

The tree they found was massive—it would have taken five or six people to encircle it with their arms—and its buttresses were solid walls embracing deep drifts of wet leaves. They ripped branches off the smaller trees, lacing them together over the buttresses to create a sort of lean-to roof. It wouldn't keep rain off if it started pouring again, but it would provide some rain protection and, more importantly, it would foil predators. Together they made a meal of parched corn and leathery dried roots, and then crawled into their makeshift shelter as darkness filled all the space between the trees.

Kalish's cat pelt provided a dry floor, and their wool blankets, while wet, helped keep the chill and the mosquitoes off. The night was warmer than Kalish expected, and the sound of dripping continued through the darkness. As they settled into their damp bed, the black became absolute. Kalish had never seen such a dark night. Her other senses sharpened. Dayo lay warm at her back, his breathing deep and even in his exhaustion. The smell of rotting leaves clung like a cloying blanket over her mouth and nose. The whisper of wind unfelt on the forest floor rustled leaves far overhead.

Some time later, she woke with a start, darkness pressing her chest and pouring in through her eyes as she strained to see anything. A snuffling and shuffling just beyond their shelter made her catch her breath. Dayo was still and silent—awake too, and listening. The animal was big, its steps heavy in the duff. But it wasn't a predator—no hunter would make that much noise. Still, she eased her hand to the knife sheath on her leg, drawing her blade silently. The snuffling grew insistent. With a grunt, the animal shoved at the wall of their shelter.

"Hey!" Kalish jabbed her knife blindly in the direction of the animal. It gave a surprised snort and staggered away. Not far. Within a few moments, it was back, its grunts curious.

"Go away," Kalish growled. A snort like a question answered her, and the snuffling moved closer. Whatever this animal was, it wasn't afraid of her. Not a predator, but probably dangerous, if it was unafraid.

Her heartbeat quickened, and Dayo shifted behind her, reaching for his own knife.

The shelter shivered under the prodding of the animal's snout, less than a hand's breadth from her face. Kalish didn't want to find out what that snout felt like on her cheek. Aiming for the snuffling, she thrust her knife through the branches. The animal squealed, high-pitched and almost human, and thundered away snorting indignation.

As the animal's footsteps faded into the forest, Dayo chuckled. "What *was* that?"

"No idea. It was big though. I'm glad it's gone." Her heart had stopped thudding in her chest, but she was wide awake now. No chance of falling back asleep. If the herbivores in this forest were so unafraid, the predators wouldn't hesitate to attack them. The thought kept her on edge.

Well, if she wasn't going to sleep anyway … she rolled over and wrapped her arms around Dayo, pulling him close. She forgot about predators for a while.

Morning crept slowly into their shelter, as if the trees gathered darkness under their boughs and tried to keep it safe. Above the treetops, the sky was uniform grey, and drizzle ghosted down through the leaves.

They ate another meal of parched corn, Kalish wishing for Dayo's porridge. As they bundled up their gear, Dayo laid a hand on Kalish's arm. "Shh!" He cocked his head into the forest.

Kalish stilled her hands and listened. Threading through the trees was the unmistakable sound of a flute. The tune was strange, rising and falling to a beat that mimicked footsteps. Dayo raised his eyebrows in a question. Kalish took a deep breath, nodded, and they began to wend their way toward the sound.

As they drew closer, a rattling sound and the stomping of feet joined the flute. Ahead lay a clearing filled with people. Without a word, Kalish and Dayo dropped into a hunter's crouch, creeping soundlessly to the edge of the trees.

About thirty people of all ages circled in the clearing. They danced with precision, stepping in time with the flute and shaking leafy branches, the susurration shivering down Kalish's spine. They were dressed in brown capes that draped over one shoulder and some sort of leggings made of a strange, crisp fabric she didn't recognise. More striking than the fabric were the ornaments sewn onto it. Colourful feathers, butterfly and beetle wings, and bright-hued seed pods created a kaleidoscope of colour in the clearing.

In the centre of the group was an elderly man—the source of the flute music. His clothes were heavily adorned with large orange seed pods. How did he walk under the weight, let alone shimmy his body as he did, making the seed pods rattle in perfect time with his song?

The scene was wild and strange, and sent a thrill of fear through Kalish's body. These people were not her own. From their clothing to their dance to their pale skin, they were foreign to her.

She reached out to Dayo, taking his hand and squeezing it. His nerves resonated with her own, vibrating between their palms. He squeezed back and without a word, they stepped out into the clearing.

A child screamed and pointed. The dance collapsed into chaos. Parents scooped up young children, and the whole group backed away from the intruders. Kalish frowned. She'd expected a display of weapons.

176

She'd expected to be killed on sight—all the stories of Treekeepers painted them as fierce warriors, more fearsome than the Fatecarvers. Baby eaters with poisoned spears. But this was a frightened group of gaudily dressed dancers.

The man wearing the suit of seed pods stepped forward, rattling like a lantan with each movement. He barked something at them. Kalish stole a glance at Dayo. "Did you understand?"

Dayo shook his head. "Sorry. We didn't catch that."

"We come in peace. Outcasts from Fatecarver lands. We wish you no harm." Kalish didn't know if they could understand her, but she drew hope from the fact these people were clearly unarmed.

The man took another noisy step forward. "Fatecarvers." He spat on the ground. "You are not welcome here." He spoke slowly this time, and though the words sounded strange on his lilting tongue, she understood. He raised a finger and gave it a flick. Four men melted into the forest.

Kalish swallowed her nerves. "We are no longer Fatecarvers. We seek refuge." Why were the women not stepping forward to negotiate with her? Kalish had adored her father, and she accepted Dayo as an equal, but what kind of people let a man speak for them?

The elderly man frowned. "There is no refuge here for your kind." He looked her up and down and wrinkled his nose, like she was something repulsive.

Kalish scanned the watchful eyes of the women. They offered nothing but hostility and fear. "Perhaps your women would allow us to stay." She gestured to them.

The women muttered to one another, but none spoke. "I speak for the village. You may not stay."

Flummoxed, Kalish glanced again at Dayo. He shrugged. "Well, I suppose we'll leave then." She released his hand and turned to find a pair of spears blocking her way. The four men who had vanished now hemmed them in. One of the spear tips rested just inches from Kalish's chest. It glistened darkly—here were the poison-tipped spears of the stories. She and Dayo turned back to back.

"Let us go." Kalish didn't take her eye off the poisoned spear. "We mean you no harm."

The men holding the spears smiled, and the one closest to her said, "As if you could harm us, little freak." He raised his eyebrows at the elder. "Speaker, what should we do with these creatures?"

The elder considered for a moment. "That one"—he pointed to Dayo—"looks well enough. I will bring the matter of its fate up with the central council at the next meeting. In the meantime, take it to Sintala's family—they need another hand since Albon died."

Dayo was stripped of his possessions and marched out of the clearing. He cast a worried look over his shoulder at Kalish.

"You know where to find me," she called.

One of the men cracked the back of her head with the butt of his spear. "And the freak?"

The Speaker pressed his lips together in disgust. "We'll give it to the trees tonight."

Several in the gathered crowd shuddered. What did it mean to be given to the trees?

"And until then?"

He wrinkled his nose again. "Tie it somewhere outside the village where we won't smell it all day. Maybe on an ant nest."

There was no point in fighting. She had no chance against two men with poisoned spears. Kalish stood still as the men removed her knife and bundle. They tied her hands and feet with some sort of rough rope, and then one of the men bent and grabbed her around the knees. She yelped as he hoisted her up and slung her over his shoulder like an animal he was bringing back for dinner.

"I can walk, you know," she barked when she'd caught her breath. The man holding her simply laughed. The group set off along a narrow path through the forest, a second man following, spear at the ready. Kalish set her arms against the man's back and craned her neck to see. She hoped her elbows dug in painfully as he loped along. She gaped as they passed a structure—presumably a house—made entirely of wood and set in the air on stilts, with leaves for a roof.

They didn't go far before the men stopped beside a small tree. Here, they untied Kalish's wrists, retying them around the bole of the tree, so that her face was pressed against the trunk. They worked quickly and silently.

"What does it mean to be given to the trees?" She asked as they cinched the rope around her wrists.

One of the men grinned. "It means we take you to the nalati trees and leave you there for the night."

That didn't sound too bad. "And?"

The other man leaned down toward her face, eyes wide. "The trees eat you!"

"Nobody survives a night among the nalati. They have teeth like the wild boar and the claws of giant cats." He brandished his fingers to demonstrate the trees' claws.

Kalish snorted. Trees that ate people? Unlikely.

But after the men left, unease began to flutter in her chest. The sounds she and Dayo had heard last night … could they have been nalati trees? Everything about the forest was foreign to her. Maybe there *were* predatory trees. How would she know? Was that why the people raised their houses on stilts? How did a tree hunt? Kalish's mind whirled with visions of gnarled branches grasping and rending flesh.

Before long, more immediate worries pushed away thoughts of carnivorous plants. The rope around her wrists and ankles chafed. She stood awkwardly against the tree, rough bark pressing points of pain along her arms and cheek. When she tried to shift into a more comfortable position, the bark scraped her skin raw. Mosquitoes whined around her head and tickled her immobilised arms and legs.

It began to rain again. Cold rivulets trickled down the trunk and pooled against her body. She wondered where Dayo was and hoped he was being treated better than she was. Her stomach growled and she began to shiver, wishing for her heavy cloak. As the day slowly crept by, her muscles grew sore, her arms bloodied. Mosquito bites tormented her with itching. She sank into misery, closing her eyes and wondering if she could slip away to the Fatewalker Realm without tearing up her physical body when she became unconscious.

She was deep in her own thoughts when something hard pinged against the back of her head. The impact was followed by a giggle, and Kalish

snapped her eyes open. At her movement, a squeal
arose around her. Half a dozen young children who
had been creeping around her leapt back.

Another object impacted her back, and a glee-
ful whoop sounded behind her.

"Stop it!" she growled.

"Stop it! Stop it!" mocked the children. A little
child with a stick darted toward her and swatted her
legs.

"Leave me alone!" Irritation rose hot in her
chest.

"Leave me alone! Leave me alone!" They mimicked her accent, which must have been strange to
them, and laughed.

"Freaky freaky freeeeak!" sang an older child
with long hair. In fact, they all had long hair. Were they
boys or girls? The long hair signalled boys, but the
older one taunting her had obvious breasts, so must be
a girl.

Regardless, they were relentless. Sticks peppered her body as they all joined in. The little child
darted in again, to swat her even harder across the legs
as the others chanted, "Freak! Freak! Freak!"

A tall child with muscular arms took the little
one's stick and dealt her a stinging blow across her exposed cheek. The others cheered. "Again! Again!"

Kalish squeezed her eyes shut, heart hammer-
ing, and the next blow came tearing across her forehead. Then came a flurry of whip-stings—on her
arms, her legs, her neck, her face.

"Stop it!" she roared, impotent against their
torment.

"Stop it! Stop it!" the children roared back at
her. They danced around singing "Freaky freaky

freak!" and swatting her with their switches until Kalish's whole body vibrated with stinging rage.

"Get away from her!" The voice was commanding, and the blows stopped.

"It's just a freak," proclaimed a young voice.

"That's no reason to torment her. Now get! Go play elsewhere."

Kalish opened her eyes to see a middle-aged woman snatch a switch from one of the children and lay about them to chase them off. Kalish took a shaky breath and, to her horror, burst into tears.

The woman followed the children until they'd made good their escape, and then turned back to Kalish. "They will take you to the nalati at dusk. Do not fear. The trees are harmless." She gave a derisive snort. "It's the cats you need to worry about."

Kalish's misery turned to sick fear.

The woman placed a hand on Kalish's shoulder and leaned close. "I will come for you after dark."

Kalish barely had time to whisper a thank you before the woman was gone.

Twenty-two

It wasn't ants or mosquitoes, but flies that drove
Kalish to distraction during the interminable day she
spent tied to a tree. The wounds opened up by the
children's tormenting sticks oozed blood and attracted
swarms of small flies that crawled across her skin and
sipped at the congealing fluid. Their buzzing wings
and pattering feet set her skin crawling, and she could
do nothing to dislodge them without further scraping
her skin and encouraging more flies.

By the time the men returned to take her to
the nalati trees, she welcomed any change, even if it
meant she was to be eaten by some predator. She was
soaked and chilled by the intermittent rain, her skin
itched and stung in equal measure, her limbs ached
from hours standing in an awkward position, and
thirst and hunger gnawed at her strength. Slung over a
man's shoulder again, she hung limply, not caring
where they were taking her.

They entered a grove of enormous trees. Even
in her miserable state, Kalish appreciated their

grandeur. She could never have even imagined trees like this existed in the world. Twenty people linking hands wouldn't have been able to encircle the trunks, and the tops seemed to vanish into the distance when she gazed up at them.

A group of Treekeepers in their strange clothing was already in the grove. They sang an eerie, discordant song that sent fresh shivers down Kalish's spine. The old man was there, shimmying and rattling, leading the singers with his flute. The men set Kalish on her feet in the middle of the singers, and then stepped back. She stood swaying slightly, mesmerised by the singers' movements. They danced and stomped to their strange song, and she noticed they grasped a long vine. Their dance brought them circling in toward her, wrapping the vine round and round her body, pinning her arms to her side and immobilising her legs. Then they bound her to a long pole.

Nalatassa hear our call.
Feed tonight,
Protect us all.
Tree and root,
Limb and bone,
Awake while we are safe at home.

Kalish shuddered again as she caught the words of the song. Then someone shoved her forward to land face down on the ground. The singing abruptly stopped and stillness fell. The light grew dim and the people melted into the forest, leaving Kalish alone on the forest floor.

Nothing stirred as night filled the grove. Kalish managed to roll slightly onto her side, spitting leaves and grit. The great trees loomed above, bending to snatch her up.

A smooth hissing in the dead leaves nearby made her heart beat faster. Had she been worrying about the wrong part of the tree? Was it the roots that entangled a person and dragged them under the earth? She squirmed and the sound stopped. Only her heart pounding in her ears broke the deep silence.

Something skittered across her legs and she started. But it wasn't a creeping root, only a small creature tiptoeing through the leaves.

The rain began again in earnest. Fat drops splatted on her face, and only fear kept Kalish from whimpering aloud her misery.

With the noise of the rain, she didn't hear the creeping footsteps. At the cold touch of a hand she screamed.

"Quiet!" Kalish recognised the voice of the woman who had driven off the children earlier. She fumbled with the vine, unwrapping Kalish and freeing her from the pole so she could sit up.

"My wrists and ankles are tied."

The woman felt her way to Kalish's wrists and severed the rope, then worked on her ankles. Kalish moaned with relief, gingerly feeling the raw and oozing spots.

"Come. We must go before the cats arrive. Give me your hand."

Kalish held out her hand, then hissed in pain when the woman drew a knife across the pad of her thumb. She would have drawn her hand back, but the woman gripped it tightly. "They will expect blood. If they don't find it, they'll look for you in the morning." She pressed Kalish's bleeding hand to the ground before hauling her up and pulling her along. "Drag your feet. Make sure they find your blood. It must look like the trees have taken you."

Snapped back to life by her throbbing thumb and the prospect of escape, Kalish did as the woman commanded, squeezing her wound to increase the flow of blood, and shuffling through the leaf litter. They reached one of the massive trees, and the woman pressed Kalish's hand against the trunk. "There. That will give them what they want. Hurry now." She pulled Kalish through the dark forest more quickly than Kalish liked, but they followed a narrow path, and after a few minutes, when no fallen trunks or large rocks had tripped her, Kalish relaxed a little.

Kalish was just beginning to wonder how far they were going when a house loomed in the darkness. It was on stilts, like the other one she'd seen, and the woman climbed deftly up a notched log propped to the doorway. She beckoned Kalish up behind her.

"Did you get her?" a male voice asked as Kalish mounted to the door.

"She's here," the woman replied.

Kalish stepped through the doorway into the dim light of a lamp. A man sat on the edge of a sleeping platform against the back wall. He nodded at her, but didn't smile. Kalish swallowed her nerves.

"I am Hana," said the woman. "This is my husband Boluso. Sit." Hana waved Kalish to a hide-strewn spot of the floor. Then she drew cloths and a small pot from a basket and sat down beside Kalish, pulling the lamp close. "Let's see to that hand. What is your name?"

Kalish held out her hand to Hana's ministrations. "I am Kalish, daughter of …" Daughter of no one. "I am Kalish."

"And you are a Fatecarver." Hana flicked dirt from Kalish's wound.

"Was. I've been banished."

186

"And what crime did you commit, that you were cast out of your clan?"

Kalish snorted. "They believe I am fated to betray them."

Boluso laughed from the shadows. "They've rather guaranteed that by kicking you out, haven't they?"

Kalish smiled ruefully.

Hana poured water over Kalish's hand, rinsing away the blood. "Boluso and I understand banishment."

"I was expelled from the clan for my foot." Boluso stood and stepped forward into the light. Three toes were missing from his right foot, and a fourth was badly deformed. The skin was a mass of puckered scar tissue. She winced. A good healer would have stitched that wound neatly, straightened the deformed toe. But more perplexing was why an injured foot was cause for expulsion.

"Were you committing a crime when you were injured?"

"Only if failing to keep my axe properly sharpened is a crime. I was felling a tree, helping my brother build his house. My axe slipped."

Kalish frowned. "You were banished because you had an accident?"

"The same thing is wrong with me as is wrong with you, in the eyes of our clan. We are imperfect. You because of your facial tattoo, me because of my missing toes."

Kalish's stomach sank. "You mean you can all read my storyscar?"

Hana shook her head and smeared Kalish's wound with a stinging paste that smelled of pine resin. "No. But Treekeepers believe we are created perfect in form. To alter that form in any way, intentionally or unintentionally, is to anger Nalatassa, our god." Her tone softened. "I don't know what you expected in coming here, but the Treekeepers will never accept you. Your friend, perhaps, but never you." She wrapped Kalish's hand with a length of fabric and gave it a gentle squeeze before releasing it.

"Do you know what's happened to Dayo?"

Hana stood, replacing the pot in the basket. "He is well, but probably tired. He spent the day digging roots."

"Where is he now? I need to find him."

"I don't know where they're housing him. Tomorrow, they'll take him to Council Island to stand before the tribunal."

"Then what?"

"The council will decide what to do with him. It's rare for a Fatecarver to arrive in Treekeeper lands, and even more rare for one to be accepted into the clans, but he is unmarked, and the unmarried women were admiring his dark skin." She shrugged. "If someone claimed him, the council might allow him to stay."

"Claimed him?" Heat rose in Kalish's chest. Dayo was hers.

Boluso must have heard the possessiveness in her voice. "You can do nothing for your friend now. By morning you will be considered dead, and no one must know otherwise or they will not leave you to the kindness of the forest." He limped across the room. "You must be famished." He lifted an overturned bowl off a small table in the corner and broke a chunk of something from a loaf. He handed it to Kalish.

She was starving, and gratefully took the food. She bit into it, expecting bread, but it was some sort of starchy cake, bland and filling. Boluso and Hana watched her inhale the food, and Hana offered her a small bowl of water to wash it down.

"Why did you rescue me, if I'm an abomination to your people?"

Hana took Boluso's hand. "Boluso is an outcast. He, too, was given to the trees. But he survived the night."

"Because she fought off the cats." Boluso smiled at Hana.

"His survival put the council in a bind. The trees didn't claim him, and the clan didn't want him. They turned him out with nothing, to wander the forest alone. We were newly married, and I couldn't bear to be parted from him. I became an outcast with him. The village knows he lives with me, and they insist we remain apart from them."

"Hana is tolerated because she's the best basket weaver the village has. They wouldn't know what to do without her." He kissed her cheek. "But I cannot be seen. I live as a shadow in my own land."

"So you see, we understand." Her manner turned brisk. "Now, it is late and we are all tired. Sleep. You are safe here. In the morning we will discuss the future." She made up a bed for Kalish on the floor and blew out the lamp. Kalish was bone weary, but she had to talk to Dayo. Before she allowed herself to sleep, she entered the Fatewalker Realm.

Leaving her body behind, she slipped out of the hut. The sun shone dappled through the trees, and she sucked in a breath at the dazzling beauty of the forest. But she didn't linger. Two narrow paths threaded through the trees in opposite directions from the hut. Kalish recognised neither, having arrived in the dark, but she knew from which direction she had approached the hut, and she set off on that path.

The ground was soft underfoot, and strange birds called overhead, their songs composed of tones so clear and pure, Kalish couldn't believe they were made by a living creature. The air smelled so strongly of life, Kalish felt drugged by it.

She thought of the clearing where she and Dayo had first seen the Treekeepers, and her feet took her there. She was glad to know the Fatewalker Realm was as unerring here as in her homeland. She would not get lost in this strange land.

Dayo was pacing the clearing when she arrived. He looked up at the sound of her footsteps, and his frown melted into relief. He ran to her and they embraced for a long moment before either one spoke.

"They said you were dead." His voice was husky. "Please tell me you are not."

"I am well. A woman named Hana rescued me. And you?"

"I spent the day digging roots and being ogled by their women." Kalish stiffened at his words, and he chuckled. "Don't worry. They are all pale and weak. I have never seen such women—they are as likely to defer to a man as to another woman." He squeezed her tighter. "They don't compare to you."

"Hana says you will go to the council tomorrow."

"Yes, I'll start the journey tomorrow. It is five days to Council Island."

"Five days!"

"I may not be able to see you during the journey—I don't expect to have a safe place to leave my body and enter the Fatewalker Realm."

"I'll go with you." Kalish pulled away to look into his face.

"You can't. Stay with this Hana. I'll return."

190

"What if you can't? What if they don't let you? What if they give you to the trees?"

Dayo kissed her. "I will meet you here, even if they give me to the trees."

Twenty-Three

When Kalish woke in the morning, her body and heart
both ached. The hut was dimly lit through narrow slits
in the walls. A cacophony of birds outside masked the
silence indoors. Hana and Boluso were gone, but a
bowl of water and more of the root cake had been left
on the table for her.

She needed to pee, and pushed on the wooden
door to go out, but it wouldn't budge. She frowned
and pushed harder. The door held fast. She took a
deep breath and thought. There must be a latch of
some sort. Most Fatecarver dwellings didn't have
doors, except for the grain stores, which had snug-fit-
ting ones to foil rats. She fumbled around the edges of
the door for anything resembling a latch. She found a
set of notches for a bar, but the bar was sitting upright
against the wall.

Of course it wasn't latched from the inside.
She was the only one in here.

Someone had locked her in.

Her stomach lurched. Hana and Boluso had seemed so kind last night. They'd rescued her and fed her. Had their kindness been a ruse? Why not simply let her die in the forest, if they intended to lock her up?

Her mind spun through possibilities. They wanted something from her. But what did she have to give them? They were going to use her in some way—as a slave, or a sacrifice, or a bargaining tool with someone. Fatecarver clans sometimes took hostages in order to pry inventions from other clans. But who would pay to get her back? She laughed, despite her worry. If Hana thought she could bargain with Kalish, she was a fool. What did she know about the Treekeepers? Her mother had told her they ate babies, but did they eat adults too? She shuddered at the thought of being butchered and eaten like a goat.

While her mind played over horrifying scenarios, and then turned to ways she might escape, she mechanically ate the food and drank the water left for her. The light grew. She heard no people outside, only the continued birdsong. Kalish finished her meal and began to search the hut for items to help her escape. A dozen net sacks containing food hung from the rafters—knobbed roots with soil clinging to them, dried meat and fish, odd oblong pink fruits, eggs of varying sizes and colours. She didn't recognise the fruit or roots, and had no idea how to prepare them, but the meat would be good to take with her. On the table were four wooden bowls and an array of spoons—some wooden, others bone—in various sizes, along with a well-worn wooden mortar and pestle.

As her gaze wandered from the useless items on the table, it snagged on a knife jammed in a convenient crack in the wall.

"Aha!" She snatched it up. It was short—a tool for peeling roots, nothing more—but it was sharp and made of a strange shiny material she'd never seen before. It reminded her of the reflective surface of a still pot of water, but was hard as rock. It was beautiful, and the smooth bone handle fit comfortably in her hand. She slipped it into the empty sheath on her leg.

She was peering under the sleeping platform at neat bundles of reeds when she heard someone at the door. She whipped out the tiny knife and whirled as Hana ducked into the hut with a pair of birds dangling from one hand and a basket heaped with leaves in the other. Two children slipped around her and froze when they saw Kalish.

"Good, you're awake. Did you find the—" Hana took in Kalish's tense stance and the knife. "I'm sorry I had to lock you in." Kalish edged toward the door as Hana continued. "We couldn't bear to wake you this morning before we left—you had been through so much yesterday—but we couldn't risk you being seen, and I was worried the Speaker—"

"Hana!" A man called from below, and Hana's eyes widened in fear. The children looked doubtfully into her face.

"Hide!" She hissed to Kalish, pointing. "Under the bed. Keep the knife handy. Children, practise your weaving, there, on the floor."

"But—" The younger one frowned.

"Do it. And say nothing." The children scrambled to comply.

Hana's urgency infected Kalish, pushing aside her anger. Hana turned and stepped out again, shutting the door behind her as Kalish scurried under the bed and pulled bundles of reeds around herself. She listened intently over the sound of the children's frightened whispers and rustling reeds.

"Speaker, you honour me with your visit," Hana said as she descended the ladder.

"My granddaughter says you chased the children away from the freak yesterday."

"And if I did? It hardly matters—the creature is dead, is it not?"

Doubt coloured the Speaker's voice. "Certainly, it is no longer in the nalati grove."

"Well, then—"

"But we seek further confirmation."

"Surely the trees did not reject your offering. If the offering is not there, the trees have taken it."

Kalish could almost hear the Speaker's steely glare, his contempt of Hana. "The signs do not point to the trees. You have shown poor judgement and limited faith in the perfection of Nalatassa in the past. I must search your house."

"My *poor judgement* was love. My *limited faith* had nothing to do with Nalatassa's perfection, only my husband's survival." Hana spat her response. More calmly, she continued, "You are welcome to search the house."

The children fell silent. Kalish's palms sweated as she clutched the knife. She slowed her breathing and pressed herself against the floor. *I am a lantan, still, silent, unseen.* The door opened and footsteps sounded on the floorboards.

"You see? Not even my abomination of a husband is here."

The speaker moved about the room, his costume rattling, so Kalish knew when he bent to peer under the sleeping platform. She held her breath. Her lungs felt like they would burst before she heard him straighten with a snort. "Very well." Then he rattled out the door and down the ladder.

Hana followed him to the door and watched as he disappeared into the forest. When she blew out a gusty breath, Kalish relaxed. "He's gone."

Kalish shimmied out from under the bed and Hana crouched down in front of the children. "I'm sorry I barked at you. You did well."

"Why is the Rattler angry?" asked the younger child, who couldn't have been much older than six years.

"He is called the Speaker—you mustn't call him Rattler. He is angry because he is afraid," Hana replied.

"Of the freak?" The older one pointed at Kalish emerging from her hiding place.

"She is not a freak simply because she is different."

"But Jenjila said—"

"Jenjila was wrong. Just like they're wrong about your papa."

"But why is her face like that?"

"I believe it is what her people do when they come of age." She glanced at Kalish for confirmation. "Just like you will choose your gender and wear the cloak of a man or a woman when you turn eighteen."

Both children frowned at Kalish, clearly unconvinced. "Does her hair not grow? And why is her skin the colour of bark?"

At this, Kalish giggled. She must look as strange to these children as they looked to her.

Hana clapped her hands. "Too many questions. Papa has taken the long path to the river to look for sansan grubs. Go help him, both of you."

The children jumped up eagerly and thundered out of the hut. Hana watched them go with a fond smile, and Kalish's heart ached for Wathi. Hana turned back with a sigh. "I'm sorry about the children. They mean no harm, but I'm constantly fighting against what the others tell them."

Kalish glanced down at the knife she still clutched. "I'm sorry. I—" She'd stolen a knife and threatened her protector with it. She set the knife back on the table.

Hana picked it up and pressed it into Kalish's hand. "No. Keep it. I will try to find you a better one, but until then, you need something."

"Will they come looking for me again?"

"Hopefully not. I expected the Speaker's visit this morning. I'm glad he didn't come earlier, before I returned."

"Am I stuck in here, then?" Her bladder might explode soon. Where was she supposed to relieve herself?

"No. Come. I will show you the safe paths. Then you will help me pluck these birds and prepare the day's meals."

Kalish couldn't help her surprise. "You cook?"

"Of course. How else would we prepare food? Do your people eat your food raw?"

"No. But cooking is men's work."

"Men's work?" Hana looked bemused. "I'd heard the Fatecarvers had strange customs, but I didn't know about that one."

Kalish followed Hana through her morning's work, gathering reeds and hauling water from the river. They met no one, and Kalish knew it was by design.

At the river, Kalish stood with her mouth agape at the deep, clear rushing stream. "So much water!"

Hana cocked her head. "Are there no rivers in Fatecarver lands?"

"There are, but none like this. Ours are dry for much of the year, and if they ever carry this much water, it is the brown of floodwaters after a storm."

"Ah. Our rivers flood too, but they are never dry."

While Hana filled jugs with water, Kalish scrubbed off the filth of days of mountain travel and mishaps, and even found a few handfuls of deep red clay with which to spike her hair after roughly hacking at it with the knife. It had grown so long, she felt shaggy.

Hana glanced suspiciously at her hair as they bent to lift the heavy jugs to their shoulders for the walk back. "Do all the Fatecarvers do that?"

"Only the women. I usually use yellow clay."

"Do your gods require it?"

Kalish smiled. "No. Do your gods require you to wear your hair long?"

Hana nodded. "We are forbidden to modify our bodies in any way, including cutting our hair." She studied Kalish's head for a moment. "It seems a great deal of work. Why do you do it?"

Kalish shrugged. "I guess because we like the way it looks. I've never really thought about it."

"And the men don't wear their hair this way. Why not?"

This elicited a laugh. "Because they're men. Only women cut their hair." She thought for a moment as they walked. "I suppose they couldn't braid the teeth of their kills into their hair if it were short."

Hana's eyes widened. "They braid teeth into their hair? Of the animals they hunt?"

"And the people they kill. It shows off their skills."

Hana was silent for a while, and then spoke hesitantly. "Do your people … kill other people often? Only, we hear stories …"

"What stories have you heard?"

"That you make sport with death, killing one another for slights as small as a strong word or an accidental bump."

Kalish couldn't deny her own people's habit of killing one another, and she had to admit many of her kinsmen and women enjoyed the raids—killing an enemy was a sign of strength and a show of clan solidarity. "Our raids are more for access to resources—water, land, inventions. They're not personal. Not usually, anyway." She considered her own experiences and shuddered. Those attempted killings were personal, at least to her. "I've heard stories about Treekeepers, too."

"Oh?"

"You sneak into Fatecarver lands to steal and eat babies."

Hana laughed. "Who says we do that?"

"Everybody. It's how mums keep their kids from wandering. Every child learns that if they stray too far from home, the Treekeepers will snatch them and eat them."

"Well, we don't eat babies. Just like the trees don't take people at night, no matter how often the Speaker warns us it will happen."

"Do you save everyone they give to the trees? Is that why they still think the trees eat people?"

"No. I can't save everyone. Nor would I want to—some are given to the trees because they have done unspeakable things. But it's not the trees who eat them. It's the cats."

"Why does the Speaker want everyone to think it's the trees?"

"Nalatassa, our god, resides in the nalati trees. If someone offends Nalatassa in some way, it is natural to think the trees would carry out Nalatassa's punishment."

Kalish peered closely at Hana. "But you don't believe in Nalatassa."

Hana shrugged. "I don't think Nalatassa metes out punishment through the trees."

TWENTY-FOUR

The pair arrived back at Hana's house shortly before midday. Hana set Kalish the task of peeling roots and boiling them over a fire in a small mud stove under the house for a midday meal. When Boluso and the children returned, they poured a handful of sansan grubs onto a flat stone set over the fire. The grubs sputtered and popped as they roasted, and the nutty smell made Kalish's mouth water.

The children, Parati and Chen, were full of noisy energy, even after a morning helping their father gather food. When the roots were cooked and the grubs toasted to crispiness, Boluso wrapped a portion of each into a large leaf for each child. The children snatched the parcels and were about to run off into the forest when Hana drew them up sharply with a word. She knelt down in front of the children and grasped a chin in each hand, forcing them to look at her.

"You understand you must not say a word to the other children about Kalish. You may not even hint that you know something of her fate."

The children nodded solemnly. "Yes, Mama."

"You must forget you have seen her, and you must not even bring up the topic. If anyone suspects she is here, they will treat me and your father to the same fate as they treated her. Understand?"

"Yes, Mama." Chen frowned. "Would the trees eat you?"

Parati stood taller. "No, because I would save you both."

Hana pulled the children into a hug. "Keep quiet, and no one will be given to the trees." She released them with a smile and ruffled their hair. "Go now. Have a good afternoon." The children scampered off.

Unease settled into Kalish's stomach. "I should go. I'm putting you at risk."

"Nonsense," Boluso argued. "You would never survive alone in the forest." He handed Kalish a bowl filled with roots and grubs.

"You must at least await your friend's return." Hana's gaze met Boluso's, and something unspoken flashed between them.

"He will come back, won't he?" Kalish's unease grew, and she ignored the food in her bowl as her stomach churned.

Hana nodded. "Yes. He will. Now eat, and this afternoon I will show you how to weave baskets."

The afternoon passed pleasantly. Hana taught Kalish how to make simple baskets and fit them with braided straps so they could be carried on the back. Boluso wove with them, his fingers nimble and sure. While they worked, they peppered each other with questions about their lives and their cultures. The knot in Kalish's stomach eased somewhat.

"How do you protect your village from other clans when your homes have no natural defences?" she asked after describing her terrace and its fortifications.

"Clan loyalty isn't so strong here as it seems to be among the Fatecarvers. If we have a dispute with another clan, the elders consult one another to decide what is to be done. If the clans can't come to an agreement, they take the matter to the central council," Hana explained.

"That's where Dayo's been taken, isn't it? What will happen to him?"

Boluso and Hana shared another glance. There was something they weren't telling her. "The council will decide what to do with him. They will consult tradition and possibly discuss the matter with Nalatassa."

"And what *might* they decide to do with him?"

Hana's hands stilled. "I have heard of Fatecarvers being allowed to join a clan. If he is unmarked, they may decide he can stay."

"But they might not." Kalish knew Hana was trying to keep her spirits up by avoiding the harsh truth. "And then?"

Hana sighed and continued plaiting reeds. "If we are lucky, he will be brought back here and given to the trees."

"If we're not lucky, they'll kill him on Council Island?"

Hanna nodded.

Kalish swallowed and was silent as she fumbled with her basket. They would not kill Dayo if she could help it.

Much later, curled on the floor in the dark, Kalish slipped into the Fatewalker Realm to search for Dayo. Jogging away from the hut through dappled sunlight, she made her way toward the clearing at the centre of the village. As she approached, she heard voices. She ducked behind a tree to listen.

"And what of the woman? She was marked, I assume?" The voice was female.

"Yes. From hairline to neck. And with hair shorn almost to the scalp. We gave her to the trees." The rattle of nalati seed pods gave away the Speaker.

"Good. It is the way."

"Praise Nalatassa."

"You have done well, Gian. The council will take it from here."

"And what of the bladestone you promised?"

"All in good time, Gian. All in good time."

Footsteps exited the clearing, and someone huffed. Then the Speaker rattled toward her, and Kalish shuffled around the tree to keep the trunk between her and the Speaker.

So, the Treekeepers used the Fatewalker Realm too. She would have to be careful not to be seen. She wondered if her mother knew the Treekeepers were here. She hoped not, for the Treekeepers' sake.

The forest grew quiet after the Speaker had rattled away. Kalish manoeuvred into a spot from which she could keep an eye on the clearing in case Dayo appeared. She wished she knew where he'd gone so she could look for him.

Time crawled like the ants Kalish watched creeping in a line past her right foot. There was no sign of Dayo. Her eyes misted and she squeezed them shut to keep the tears from falling. Dayo was fine; she had to believe that. He'd warned her he might not be able to meet her here while he travelled. How could he afford to leave his body when he was sleeping in the open, vulnerable to cats and who knew what other predators that hunted in this forest? She should be glad he wasn't here. He was safer if he didn't try.

Kalish rubbed her eyes and turned to head back to Hana's hut. She tried to convince herself it was for the best Dayo didn't come, but her heart was heavy.

Morning found her bleary-eyed and chafing at her situation. Hana must have sensed her restlessness, because she kept Kalish busy all day, walking several hours to find fiddleheads, and then lifting fish weirs from the river.

Trudging home weighed down with food and her thoughts, Kalish determined to learn more about where they'd taken Dayo. "Tell me more about the central council. Who are they? Where do they meet?"

"They are representatives chosen from each clan. Some are elders, but others are no older than I am. Sintala, from this village, is on the council."

"That's the person Dayo was given to the other day."

Hana nodded. "Her husband died recently. With her duties on the council, she often needs extra help caring for her family."

"Are the council members all women?" The person in the clearing with the Speaker last night had been female, but Kalish had been surprised by how much authority was given to men here.

"No. Of course not. Each clan is represented by one woman and one man—balance is essential, especially on the council."

"And where do they meet?"

"Council Island is in the middle of a great, shallow bay. Five days by boat, more on foot."

"So Dayo has been taken by boat?" Kalish felt a twinge of envy. She'd never even seen a boat, let alone ridden in one. Only a few of the terraces far down on the rivers, where there was reliable water, used boats.

"Yes. Down the Sunsinger River to the sea, then around the headland into Council Bay."

"They take a boat into the sea?" She had never heard of such a thing. The coastline of the Fatecarver lands was composed of steep cliffs pounded by massive waves. Only a fool would take a boat into that punishing water.

"Yes. As long as the sun shines, it is safe enough. Sometimes they must wait for storms to pass, but boats rarely founder between here and Council Bay."

"Is the Sunsinger River the one we were just at?"

"No. I stick to Narrow Creek to avoid the rest of the village. But it joins the Sunsinger River not far downstream from where we fished today."

Kalish didn't know if she could make a five-day journey in one night in the Fatewalker Realm, but she now had the information to try. Late that night, she stepped out of her body and made her way to the Sunsinger River.

If Narrow Creek had impressed her, the Sunsinger River was daunting. It flowed deep and swift between densely forested banks, hissing over rocks at its edges and sucking at Kalish's toes when she dipped them into the water.

A narrow path paralleled the river for a ways, and then curled back into the forest. Kalish pushed on through the undergrowth, frustrated by the slow pace. She'd never make it to Council Island at this rate; no wonder the Treekeepers travelled by boat.

She flopped down on the river bank and put her head in her hands. How could she help Dayo when she couldn't get to him, even in the Fatewalker Realm? Water rushed below her, and it sounded like the whisk of wind at the top of a bluff. She imagined her toes wrapped over the edge of warm rock, the wind ruffling her hair in the moment before she leapt off clinging to a glider. What she would give for a glider right now, and the space to launch it!

You are fated to fly as the kiriki falcons. The wind will be your guide and conveyance. Your understanding will encompass the unknown.

Except the falcons had feathers and wings. They could soar without the need of a glider for lift.

If only she had a falcon's wings.

A rippling shiver over her skin shocked her head out of her hands. She sucked in a breath. Her hands were gone. In place of her fingers were smooth, sculpted grey flight feathers. She lifted an arm, and a rank of interlocking feathers rustled. Her heart raced as she beat the air with her arms … with her wings.

She had wings.

You are fated to fly as the kiriki falcons. Not with a glider. With wings, as the kiriki. She scrambled to her feet, feeling power in the muscles of her chest. A breeze rustled her feathers and, without a moment's hesitation, she leapt into it.

The wind will be your guide and conveyance. She flapped her wings, and it felt as natural as running. Rising above the trees, she caught the stronger winds aloft and soared down the river, following its path to the sea.

Kalish's senses sharpened, and she imagined herself peering down for prey, just as the kiriki did. Other than the Speaker, Gian, and the woman she heard in the clearing, who else walked the Fatewalker Realm within the Treekeepers' territory? She scanned the river for movement.

She was nearly at the mouth of the river, where it emptied into a long, narrow bay, when she spotted a boat moving against the current. She circled down to the trees, perching on a branch overhanging the water. There was a woman in the boat, paddling hard against the water, and making fatewalker-enhanced speed upriver. Kalish followed, gliding effortlessly from branch to branch.

It wasn't long before the woman pulled the boat onto the bank. A man stood waiting for her. Kalish silently swooped closer so she could hear their conversation.

The woman stepped away from the boat and approached the man.

He crossed his arms. "I began to doubt you would show up, Sintala. You're late."

"You know it is difficult when travelling. It wouldn't do to be killed in my sleep, would it?"

"What have you learned?"

"He is from the Flintcrag Clan."

"And?"

"His mother holds no power, but his companion was the fatecarver's daughter."

"Was? Did your miserable village Speaker give her to the trees?"

The woman flinched. "He did."

"And you lifted not a finger to stop it, nor considered spiriting her away in the night?"

"At the time I didn't know who she was. Even if I had known, what could I do? She was tattooed. On what grounds could I possibly have objected without causing suspicion? And how would I have hidden her if I'd taken her? Besides, this companion of hers might serve perfectly well. Surely the fatecarver's daughter's lover has value."

The man snorted. "You know nothing of the Fatecarvers if you believe a man has value. Truly, I question your place on the council. Your predecessor seeded conflict that would tear Fatecarver culture apart, and you undermine it with your incompetence."

"Give me the companion. I know we can use him. You won't be disappointed in me."

"I'd better not be. It would be a shame for you to meet with an accident."

The two parted, and Kalish ghosted after the woman until she reached the sea and drew the boat up at a small village. She entered a large hut and did not emerge, and Kalish knew she'd left the Fatewalker Realm. She also knew Dayo must be there, too. She circled the hut and cried out in frustration. She could do nothing for Dayo, and couldn't even warn him of what she'd overheard.

Twenty-Five

Leaving her wings behind was difficult. When she woke in the morning, Kalish lifted her arms, just to make sure there were no feathers there. She smiled at the memory and itched to return to the Fatewalker Realm to fly again. She heard Hana and Boluso beneath the house, talking quietly.

Footsteps pounded up the path. "Mama! Papa! The Rattler is dead!" The children slept with their grandmother. Kalish understood this wasn't normal Treekeeper practice, but it allowed the children to be part of the community, rather than be outcasts along with their parents. They were breathless from running now, as Kalish descended the ladder.

"He is the Speaker, not the Rattler," Hana admonished. "Show him respect."

"But Mama, Papa! He's dead!" Both children's eyes were wide, and Kalish sensed an equal mix of fear and excitement in the Speaker's death.

Hana frowned. "How can that be?"

"He didn't show up for morning prayers. Mahatu searched for him in his hut, but he wasn't there. Ihan found him face down in the river just now."

Boluso nodded at Hana. "Go. I'll look after the children and draw water."

"I'll help with the water," Kalish added.

Hana quickly took up a stack of small, tightly woven baskets she'd made the day before and hurried to the village.

Kalish swallowed a stab of fear. The Speaker had been murdered. Could it be because someone thought he had killed her? What was going on here, and how did she fit into it?

She tried to hide how edgy she was as she followed Boluso and the children to the stream to collect water. She couldn't help looking over her shoulder at every sound. Her nerves jangled even more when they arrived back home to Hana's account of the morning's discovery.

"It was identical to Albon's death. Remember how Sintala found him in the river with his throat torn out? And in the same spot in the river too."

Sintala. The woman who Dayo was given to, because her husband had died. She was the village's representative on the central council. And she was using Dayo to make up for her loss of Kalish.

"What is this blade?" Kalish was using her small knife to gut a fish for the evening meal. "I've never seen anything like it."

Hana cocked her head. "The Fatecarvers don't have bladestone?"

"Bladestone?"

"It's a strange rock. I believe it comes from somewhere in the mountains. It must be burnt first, and then it becomes malleable."

"Burnt?"

Hana laughed. "I don't really understand the process. They say that on Council Island, there is a huge furnace that burns night and day. Rock goes in one side, and malleable bladestone comes out the other."

Bladestone. It was what the Speaker asked for the other day when Kalish overheard him in the clearing. "Is it used only for knives?"

"No. It makes excellent spear heads, bowls, spoons, and many other things."

Kalish waved a hand around her. "But you use mostly stone, wood and bone."

"Bladestone is rare. Each village's allotment is small, and for people like Boluso and me … well, we have to trade for everything."

Kalish looked at the knife in her hand with new eyes and determined that when she left Hana she would return it.

"Does this go into the pot with the roots?" Kalish held the cleaned fish over the boiling water.

"No, no! Never boil fish!"

Kalish laughed at Hana's consternation. Fish soup was a rare treat for Fatecarvers. "Why not?"

"Fish is always roasted directly over the fire. It is the way."

Kalish had heard that saying—it is the way—several times now. "You've said that before. When we were fishing and when you taught me how to gather reeds. Do all Treekeepers fish, gather reeds and cook in the same way?"

"Yes. It is the way." Hana laughed. "In our tradition, Nalatassa created perfection—the trees, the animals, the people. We are all perfect. Our ways of hunting, fishing, gathering and cooking are all perfect. To change is to question Nalatassa's creation."

Kalish thought of the innovations Fatecarvers were continually developing, the value placed on new ideas, more efficient ways of doing things. Only religious observances remained unchanging. "You question your people's practices around giving people to the trees. Why not boil fish?"

Hana smiled and shrugged. "I suppose it's simply easier to do what I've always done. And there's no reason to question the cooking of fish as long as it tastes good." She reached over to squeeze Boluso's hand. "Questioning the killing of my husband was another matter."

"And questioning my killing?" Kalish still wondered what motivated Hana.

Boluso spoke up. "Once one begins to question the way, it can be hard to stop. Hana and I discussed your situation and decided that, in this case, *the way* was not the *right* way."

"You decided together?"

"How else would we have done it?" Hana asked.

Kalish blushed. "Among the Fatecarvers, men's opinion is unimportant. Only women make decisions."

"Really? What do the men think of that arrangement?" Boluso asked.

Kalish shrugged. "It is the way."

Hana laughed. "Sounding like a Treekeeper already." She peered at Kalish. "You and Dayo have a different sort of relationship, though, don't you? You don't make all the decisions."

"True. Dayo has been my friend since I was very young." She lapsed into silence, thinking about the men she knew—Dayo, her father, Wathi's husband Jenti. How did they feel about being the last to eat, the first to die in battle, the silent observers of the clan's politics? She saw the injustice in Dayo's case—he was special to her—but it never occurred to her that other men deserved the rights of women too. "Are men and women really equal among Treekeepers?"

Hana nodded. "We believe in balance and perfection. Creating children requires both man and woman—balance. Therefore, everything else requires balance too."

"So are boys and girls raised the same way? Taught the same things?"

Hana cocked her head. "Boys? Girls?"

"Boys—children that will grow to be men. Girls—children that will grow to be women. You don't use those words?"

Boluso smiled. "Children are children. They are all the same until they choose to become a man or woman at their coming of age ceremony."

Kalish's eyes widened with astonishment. "But clearly they are different from birth. There's no choice involved."

Hana nodded. "It is true that for most children we can predict what they will choose. But not all. If we forced a woman to call herself a man because she had a penis, it would be denying her perfection, denying Nalatassa's creation."

Kalish couldn't quite wrap her head around the idea. She was quiet as she tended the cooking fish, considering it in relation to herself and the people she
214

loved. It was hard to imagine a boy deciding to become a woman or vice versa in Fatecarver society—boys and girls were treated differently and taught different things from the day they were born. Who would even think to question it? But there were men like Dayo, who broke stereotypes, pushed boundaries. And there were women like her who valued the opinions of men and thought of some of them as equals. Maybe in a society where men and women were already deemed equal, choosing your gender wasn't such a big deal.

The more she pondered it, the more she recognised her own people's failings. Where she had once considered Dayo and her father as exceptions to the rule that men were the lesser sex, she now realised she was wrong. How many more advances would her people have made if men were invited to think? How would it be to live in a society where it didn't matter if you were male or female—a society in which you were valued for being human?

She shook her head. That sort of society would be great, but it didn't exist. The Treekeepers wanted to kill Boluso for having had an accident and being permanently injured. And they tried to kill her because she had a tattoo. They weren't necessarily better than the Fatecarvers; they just had a different set of prejudices.

"You've grown quiet," Hana observed.

"Just thinking." She lifted the finished fish from the fire. "Do you ever consider trying to change Treekeeper culture so Boluso isn't an outcast?"

Hana snorted. "I'd have more luck holding back the spring floodwaters with a fishing net."

After dark, Kalish slipped into the Fatewalker Realm. She was disappointed she didn't immediately transform into a falcon. How had she done it before?

She thought back to her despair on the bank of the river. She'd wished for wings, imagined soaring on them. She closed her eyes and envisioned soaring above the trees on silver wings. It was easy to do, having experienced the sensation yesterday.

She twitched as her skin prickled. Her head felt funny, and feathers rustled as she opened her eyes. She admired her glossy wings, still hardly believing they were hers. Then she launched herself into the air.

Her first stop was the clearing, in the hope of meeting Dayo, but it was deserted. She didn't wait for him, but flew off with supernatural speed, following the directions Hana had given her toward Council Island. As she flew, she scanned below for any sign of others in the Fatewalker Realm.

She quickly passed the mouth of the river into a long narrow bay. Great sea creatures swam below her, spouting water into the air from time to time. Raucous white birds she didn't recognise wheeled around her, as if curious, and then flew off. At the mouth of the bay, Kalish followed the coastline northward, marvelling at the vast stretches of grey sand, the constant motion of the waves. Never had she seen so much water.

She saw no people until she rounded a steep headland into a wide bay. Her falcon eyes picked out an island in the centre of the bay, as perfectly round as a berry. On one side of the island a plume of smoke rose from what looked like an enormous clay oven. That must be the bladestone furnace. Several craft plied the water of the bay, but as she approached the island a group of five women gathered on a dock caught her eye—the Fates. What were the Fates doing here? She spiralled down toward them and settled on the roof of a large wooden structure. The building was different from the hut Hana and Boluso lived in. It sat on the ground and the walls were made with close-fitting boards rather than sticks. Overlapping slabs of wood tiled the roof, and wisps of smoke emerged from a clay pipe sticking up near the peak.

No one gave her more than a cursory glance.

Grandmother Ma had warned her the Fates were not on the Fatecarvers' side, and here they were, at the seat of Treekeeper power.

"Is it really necessary for all of us to go?" War tossed her axe into a waiting boat.

"We're losing control of Point Clan. We need to shore up our pressure there," Love replied, lowering herself into the boat and waving War in.

War followed Love, but argued, "There's hardly any bladestone in Point Clan's territory. Surely we can ignore them."

"Not if we hope to destroy them." Death joined War and Love, making the boat rock dangerously as she stepped in. "You know how those Fatecarvers are—one of them gets an idea and before you know it the whole culture has caught on."

Life smiled as she settled into her seat. "Besides, it's so much fun to watch them slaughter one another. Come on Kara; we haven't got all night." She waved the Unknown into the seat beside her and picked up a paddle.

Kalish's mind whirled. These were the Fates? Plotting to foment trouble between Fatecarver clans? She swooped off the roof and buzzed the boat to get a better look. Life tucked a stray lock of hair up under her spiked wig, the women's fatecarvings were painted on, and Kalish was pretty sure Love's pregnancy was nothing but a sack of leaves tied around her waist. Every one of them a Treekeeper, a fake god.

"Has anyone ever seen a bird do that before?" Death's question startled Kalish out of her musing. She was hovering in front of the boat in the middle of the bay, drawing attention to herself. Quickly she beat her wings and rose high into the air, cursing herself for being so obvious.

She sensed the night was getting on, and the five women pretending to be the Fates were alert to her now, so she headed back toward Hana's hut. In her falcon form she instinctively knew the shortest way to Hana's was across the forest, not back the way she'd come. She struck out, skimming the tops of the trees.

Twenty-six

Grandmother Ma had said the Fates were not helping the Fatecarvers. Were they even real gods, or were they merely Treekeepers dressed up like gods? If the Fatewalker Realm wasn't made by the Fates in order to communicate with Fatecarvers, what was it for? Who created it? It was one thing to think perhaps the gods weren't pleased with her people; it was entirely another matter if her people's gods were actually Treekeepers pretending to be gods.

Once again, Kalish questioned Hana's motivation in saving her from the trees and keeping her at her house. Did she know about the false Fates? Was she part of the plot to destabilise the Fatecarver clans? In the morning, she determined to find out what Hana and Boluso knew.

"What will happen now the Speaker is gone?" she asked as she and Hana walked to the stream to fetch water.

"The council will send us a new Speaker."

"You mean the Speaker isn't someone from the village?" The idea of sending an outsider to a village to provide their spiritual guidance seemed ridiculous to her.

"Speakers are trained on Council Island. They say there is a huge grove of nalati trees there where Nalatassa resides permanently. They train directly with Nalatassa."

"And do they talk with Nalatassa once they leave Council Island?"

"They're called Speakers because they speak with Nalatassa."

"How do they do that?"

Hana shrugged. "It is a secret only Speakers are privy to."

It was a safe answer, but was it true? "In the Fatecarver religion, our fatecarvers speak with the Fates in a place known as the Fatewalker Realm."

"Where is this Fatewalker Realm?"

Should she tell Hana about it? "I'm not sure, but they go there by breathing the smoke from burning piromanga leaves. Do your Speakers use burning leaves at all?"

Hana frowned in thought. "I don't know. The Speaker's hut often smells of smoke, now that I think of it. I guess I never considered how Speakers talk to Nalatassa. They have many rituals that must be done in secret. Most of the time, we see the Speaker only at the morning and evening services."

"And yet you let the Speaker make decisions on behalf of the village? A stranger who you hardly see?" Kalish asked, remembering how she was condemned to death.

"Speakers talk directly to Nalatassa. They know what is right."

"But you questioned the Speaker's decision to kill Boluso and me."

Hana sighed. "You're right. I question the Speaker. I question Nalatassa. Sometimes I wonder if we're all simply being manipulated by the council. Villages specialise in producing one or two products, and those products are sent to the council as taxes. My village is named Weaver's Retreat, because we make baskets. Most people in the village weave all day, with little time for hunting or foraging." Hana gave a little laugh. "In a way, Boluso and I are lucky. As outcasts, we aren't bound by the need to produce the village's taxes, so we can gather and hunt most of our own food."

"If people can't hunt or gather, how do they eat?" Kalish asked.

"In exchange for our taxes, the council distributes products the other villages produce. So Weaver's Retreat gets grain from places like Tanthi Flat, and they get a share of our baskets. We're also supposed to receive finished bladestone goods like spear heads, knives, and wood cutting tools, which are made on Council Island. The council also provides Speakers and the services of healers. But the products we get aren't enough to feed everyone properly, the healers spend a few days here and are gone to the next village, the blades never arrive. I sometimes wonder what the council is doing with everything we send them." They reached the stream and bent to fill their water jugs. Hana laughed ruefully. "Maybe I've been an outcast too long. My vision is blurred by the ill treatment Boluso and I receive."

"Or maybe your vision is sharpened." Kalish watched water flow into the pot she tipped under the water. Unless Hana was an exceptionally good liar, she wasn't working for the council. In fact, she might even be willing to help. "What if I told you your council was pretending to be Fatecarver gods?"

Kalish related what she'd seen to Hana as they returned to the hut.

"But I still don't understand how you saw all this. Did you dream it? You weren't at Council Island last night, I'm certain of that."

Kalish took a deep breath. Did she trust Hana? "Let me show you how to enter the Fatewalker Realm."

Hana's eyebrows rose. "I thought only your fatecarvers could do that, and only by burning piromanga leaves."

"That's what the fatecarvers tell us, and I think most of them believe it too. But there's another way."

They latched the door to avoid being disturbed. "It will look like we are asleep, and no one will be able to rouse us," Kalish explained. Then she talked Hana through the meditation and breathing exercises Grandmother Ma had taught her.

It took Hana a long while to manage it, and Kalish slipped in and out of the Fatewalker Realm several times to help coach her across. It wasn't until Kalish held her hand and led her that she managed it. She stood blinking down at her own body on the floor of the hut.

"That's me? This is so strange."

"Yes, that's your body. Your physical form will stay here in the hut. You always have to come back to your body to exit the Fatewalker Realm," Kalish explained.

Hana peered around the interior of the hut. "It's the same as the real world?"

222

Kalish smiled. "Yes … and no. Come. Let's go for a walk." She unlatched the door and clambered down the ladder.

"How will we keep people out?" Hana asked, waving at the door.

"In the real world, it's still locked." Kalish beckoned Hana toward the centre of the village.

"We can't go this way, Kalish. You can't be seen."

"I won't be. We're in the Fatewalker Realm. The only people we'll meet are others who are also in the Fatewalker Realm."

They strolled the paths of the village, and Hana wondered aloud. "The birds, the insects … are all the animals here? Are these the same animals in the real world or different ones?"

"I think they're the same ones, but I believe the animals exist in both places at once. It's always daytime here, but I've seen nocturnal animals out and about, as well as diurnal ones. We have to essentially leave our bodies to come here, but I think the animals and plants are always here and in the real world."

"You've been here often," Hana observed.

Kalish nodded. "It's where I came to escape pain as a child. It's where Dayo and I go to be free of judging eyes."

"Your families don't approve of your match?"

"We weren't exactly matched before I was cast out. We were friends. And it was mostly my mother who disapproved of our friendship. She believes men are good only for making and caring for children. That her daughter talked with a boy as an equal was disgusting to her. And Dayo's family is quite low, socially speaking, whereas my mother …"

"Hmm?" Hana looked at her expectantly.

"She's our clan's fatecarver."

"Ah, I see. I understand why you might have needed some escape." She cast her eyes around the forest. "And it's … beautiful here. I know it's just like the real world, but there's something different."

"Yes. It's always a sunny day here, for one, but there's something else. Something you can't put a finger on. This place is the *ideal* world."

They met no one as they strolled through the village and down to the river. They spoke little. Hana brushed her hands over tree trunks and plucked flowers, her eyes wide and a smile on her face.

"Can you go anywhere in the Fatewalker Realm?"

"As long as you know how to get there, yes. And travel is faster here. When you run, it's like you're taking ten strides for every one you actually take. And I've never gotten lost, as long as I know where I'm going." She didn't tell Hana about turning into a falcon.

Hana peered at Kalish. "You've been to Council Island. That's why you asked where it was."

Kalish nodded. "I brought you here so you would understand what I've seen, what I know."

As they returned to Hana's hut and their bodies, Kalish told Hana everything.

"So Treekeepers are pretending to be your gods in order to stir up trouble?"

"That's what I gather. And I think it has something to do with getting bladestone. It sounded like the bladestone was on Fatecarver lands."

"But you've never seen it?"

"No. We don't know about it, nor do we use it."

Hana frowned as they re-entered the real world. She sat up and shook her head. "What a strange feeling. My ears are ringing."

"It will pass. I hardly notice it anymore."

Boluso and the children returned shortly after, and for a while their conversation ceased as they all prepared the midday meal. After the children had been sent off to play, Hana asked if they could discuss the matter with Boluso.

Kalish agreed and briefly took him into the Fatewalker Realm. When they returned, he rubbed his face and struggled to sit up. "I feel like I'm going to vomit. You do this regularly?"

Hana laughed. "She claims you get used to it. I'm not sure I believe her."

While Boluso recovered, Kalish related her story to him.

Boluso nodded. "If bladestone is found on Fatecarver land, the council would want it. They're greedy for it. And I can see why they would have counted your capture as an opportunity."

Hana's eyes narrowed as she thought. "You are the fatecarver's daughter, so … she's the one who gave you the tattoo that caused you to be banished?" Kalish nodded. "And you say fatecarvers take direction from the Fates."

Kalish sucked in a breath. "You're thinking Treekeepers posing as the Fates told her to create this fatecarving in order to cause trouble." Then she frowned. "But that makes no sense. How can one person being kicked out of their clan make any difference?"

Hana leaned forward. "Every Fatecarver woman gets a fatecarving. Think how many opportunities that gives for inciting trouble."

"But they can't possibly be messing with *every* fatecarving. And what do they think they'll accomplish with it? If they wanted bladestone from our lands, they could attack us, or trade for it."

Boluso shook his head. "They're distracting the Fatecarvers. Causing just enough strife to keep them at war with each other. They're making you do the work of attacking for them." He laughed. "Look around. We're not a warlike people. If the council tried to attack Fatecarvers, you'd beat us. If you all decided to invade our lands, I doubt we could keep you out. We're simply not equipped for war. By keeping you at each other's throats, the council prevents you thinking about us."

"I suspect they spread the stories about us eating babies too," Hana added.

"And imagine if they tried to trade for bladestone," Boluso continued. "You don't know it exists. What would your people do with it if they knew?"

Kalish laughed. "Make better weapons. You're right. The council has plenty of reason to meddle."

TWENTY-SEVEN

The realisation the Treekeeper council was inciting
conflict among Fatecarver clans only led to more
questions. Now that Hana knew about the Fatewalker
Realm, Kalish could spend more time there, with
Hana keeping watch over her body.

Council Island would hold at least some of the
answers. And Dayo would be there soon. She slipped
into falcon form and sped there as fast as she could.

She was thankful for her bird form—Council
Island buzzed with activity, even in the Fatewalker
Realm. She caught a boat of false Fates returning to
the island, and another leaving. It seemed there were
many Fates, not just one of each. Were *any* of her people's beliefs true?

She scoured the island, taking in the opulence
absent in Hana's village. Solid buildings made of sawn
timber, bladestone stoves for heating the houses and
cooking food, paths paved with cobblestone against
the mud, large and lavishly decorated meeting houses.
Peering through windows, she saw even the most

humble homes were furnished with bladestone utensils and bowls, tables inlaid with brightly coloured
stones and shells, and plump cushions for sleeping on.

The people she saw were dressed in the finest
sugarspike fabric, not the rough barkcloth people wore
in Hana's village. And spaced around the edges of the
island sat catapults identical in design to Fatecarver
machines, but made with larger timber and bladestone
fittings, and polished like deadly works of art.

The Treekeeper council lived well off the taxes
they collected from Treekeeper villages, and they protected that living with technology stolen from Fatecarvers. Anger flared in Kalish's chest.

She spotted the nalati grove in the centre of
the island and circled down into the trees. It was cool
and green, and the towering boles of the trees appeared to hold up the sky. She landed on the ground
and transformed back into her human shape. It was
no wonder the Treekeepers believed their god resided
here—these trees were as magnificent as gods themselves. She rested her hands on a tree trunk and gazed
up, growing dizzy with the sight of white clouds scud-
ding past overhead. Leaning her forehead against the
bark, she almost thought she heard the tree breathing.
Beware, Kalishhhh. The rustle of footsteps blended with
the words, and Kalish whirled to see two men walking
toward her. She transformed into the falcon and rose
to perch on a broken branch well overhead.

The men were deep in conversation and hadn't
noticed her.

"Tofal says their bladestone harvest will be less
this year. They are having to travel further into Fatecarver land to find it."

"Did you tell them the stone is required?"

The first man nodded. "They say the village has lost ten people to the mountains, and unless they start sending children—"

"Well then, they must send children. Tell them the council requires it. Tell them it is the way." He waved a hand. "Promise them more food or something. Just get the stone out of them."

The second man frowned. "Do you think it is wise, this plan for the great furnace, the temple?"

"You have seen yourself how the people begin to dismiss us, tell us they can't send taxes, complain about the services we provide them."

"But what purpose do these large constructions serve?"

"The great furnace will power the saws to cut the trees, and the trees will fuel the furnace to cut more trees. Then we will have wood to build a monument to the council that will impress the people with our greatness. It will show them that Nalatassa blesses us. They will not neglect their taxes when they see how rich we as a people have become."

Wind hissed in the leaves above her like an angry snake.

"And what of the people who depend upon the forest for food? As do we, I might add."

"They can move elsewhere. There is plenty of forest." The man stopped and placed a hand on the other's shoulder. "Do not worry about the people. The more the council can gather here, the more we can send out to the people. Come now, we should return, or we'll be late."

The men turned and vanished among the trees. The branches around Kalish rattled, but no wind ruffled her feathers. She couldn't shake the feeling something was in the nalat grove with her. A presence green and old as the trees themselves. She knew it had warned her in that whisper of a voice. But though she waited for some time after the men left, it did not speak again.

"A machine to cut down trees?" Hana frowned after hearing Kalish's account of her trip.

"That is not the way," Boluso grumbled.

"As we suspected, the council is taking, but not redistributing like it's supposed to do."

"It seems they're waging a war on both Fate-carvers and Treekeepers, without any of us knowing we're even under attack," Kalish said.

The three were silent for a few moments, fingers busy on the baskets they wove. Kalish's were getting better—tighter and less lopsided.

"Did you see your friend Dayo?" Hana asked. "He should be there by now."

Kalish shook her head. She doubted she'd see him before he returned. *If* he returned. It wouldn't be safe for him to enter the Fatewalker Realm on Council Island—there were too many people moving around in that realm there.

Hana threw down her basket. "How could our council do this to our own people? The whole point of the council is to work for the people. How could Sintala and the other council members do this?"

"How much time has Sintala spent here since she joined the council?" Boluso asked. "No more than a few days at a time, and her visits are less and less frequent. You said last time she returned that her own children hardly knew her. How much do you think she worries about what goes on in the villages when she's living in luxury on Council Island?"

230

"But her family is here. Her friends. We chose her to represent us."

Kalish thought of her mother. "Some people don't care about friends and family as long as they have power." Kalish was less worried about what the council was doing to the Treekeepers than what it was doing to the Fatecarvers.

Impersonating the Fates! In order to make her people kill one another. To pit clan against clan. She had to go back and tell them, make them stop fighting and turn their defences toward the Treekeeper realm. She had to save her people.

Her people?

The ones who had rejected her, tried to kill her?

But they had been under the influence of the Treekeeper council. If she could just make them see

…

No. She could never make them see. They would never see anything beyond her lantan eyes, her clanless face that spoke of deceit and betrayal.

And the Treekeepers would never accept her as their own. What was she going to do? Hide in Hana's house the rest of her life?

The only people she had left were Dayo, Hana and Boluso. Outcasts among their own people, belonging nowhere.

Two days later, she was again ghosting around Council Island in her falcon form. By now, she had nearly given up on seeing Dayo. He would be a fool to enter the Fatewalker Realm here.

But there he was, sneaking out of the small house on the corner, pressing himself against the wall.

She keened and circled low to catch his attention, then arrowed toward the nalati grove. He frowned, but after another quick glance around him, sprinted after her.

The grove had been empty a short while ago, and Kalish trusted it would remain so for a while longer. As soon as Dayo was out of sight of the houses, she landed and transformed back into her own form. Dayo, following the falcon, staggered to a halt, his eyes widening in disbelief as she straightened up and shook off the lingering feeling of feathers on her arms.

She smiled and walked toward him.

"But you were ... I saw ..."

"You are fated to fly as the kiriki falcons. The wind will be your guide and conveyance," she explained, quoting the elders.

"But that was the glider!"

Kalish came face to face with Dayo. "No. It wasn't." She read the astonishment in his eyes and wanted to laugh. "Are you going to greet me properly?"

He fell on her, wrapping his arms around her and kissing her. When he pulled back, his eyes were alight with excitement. "Kalish! This place is amazing! And Sintala says she will welcome me into her clan! Have you seen the bladestone? They make the most amazing stuff with it—it's malleable like ... like clay, but harder. And—"

Kalish held up a hand. "Stop right there. You need to know a few things."

"But we can make a life here! And along the coast we could use gliders, though I guess you don't need a glider anymore."

Kalish shoved him away from her. "*We* can't make a life here. As far as they know I'm dead. Remember? They tried to kill me. And they're using you, Dayo. Sintala is—"

"Sintala has been nothing but kind and welcoming. You don't even know her. I've spent five days with her."

"And I've seen her in the Fatewalker Realm, using you as a bargaining chip to make up for the fact she let them kill me. Because they want to use you to help seed conflict among the Fatecarvers so they can continue to steal bladestone from Fatecarver lands, because that's where it comes from. And they're pretending to be the Fates, leading fatecarvers to carve storyscars that cause conflict among clans, *get women expelled from their clans*, and weaken us." Kalish took a deep breath.

Dayo blinked. "But the Fates …"

"Are Treekeeper women with painted faces and fake hair, manipulating us. Grandmother Ma warned me they weren't doing us any favours, but it's worse than that. They aren't even gods." Her voice cracked, and she tried to hold onto her anger, because it was all that was holding her together. In this moment, she knew that no matter what her people did to her, she was a Fatecarver. She would always be a Fatecarver, and her heart ached for her people.

Dayo finally seemed to understand. He nodded toward a downed log, gesturing for her to sit. "Tell me what you've learnt."

She told him everything, both what she'd seen and heard in the Fatewalker realm and what Hana and Boluso had explained to her.

When she finished, he was silent for a long while before speaking softly. "If the Fates aren't real, and your storyscar is meant only to cause trouble, why can you turn into a kiriki? Why is what the elders read in your face true?"

"Everything I've done since they read my fate was based on what they said. And it was no more than what I wanted to do in the first place, aside from being kicked out of the clan. I wanted to fly like a falcon. I wanted to go somewhere and learn new things. *Your understanding will encompass the unknown.* Well, now it does." She sighed. "The question is what do I do with what I know?"

"We can't exactly go charging home telling everyone our entire culture is being manipulated by someone else, can we?"

Kalish shook her head. "But how can we *not* try to tell them? They're being torn apart."

They weren't going to arrive at a solution quickly, and Dayo had been away for too long already. "We'll talk when I return to the village."

"You're sure you're coming back?"

He nodded. "I've made Sintala promise it."

Kalish shook her head. "I think you put too much faith in her word."

"I'll be there."

"Just remember, I'm dead. Don't ask to see me. Visit me in the Fatewalker Realm there—I can show you where Hana lives. That's the only safe way, in the real world."

He nodded, kissed her again, and left.

The five days before Dayo's return dragged interminably. By day, Kalish caught fish, wove baskets, collected roots, and hauled water with Hana and Boluso. At night, she slipped into the Fatewalker Realm. She was drawn back to the nalati grove. There was a pres-
234

ence there—a voice that whispered sometimes, the rustle of the leaves, a rattle of branches. And it knew her name.

There were often people in the grove. Most of them were scheming one thing or another—there was more to Treekeeper politics than Kalish understood. They might not physically fight over land and re-sources, but their verbal battles were intense. On the third night, she found herself alone in the grove. Fly-ing in as a falcon, she landed on the ground and shifted back into her human form. She wandered the grove, still not able to comprehend the enormous size of the trees and how *alive* they seemed. She trailed her fingers along the bark as she circled a particularly mas-sive trunk. It hummed under her touch.

"What *are* you?" she murmured.

Have you not guessed yet, little kiriki? The voice was nothing more than the whisper of leaves, but there was no mistaking its words.

She shook her head and pressed both hands against the bark. It was smooth and warm. "No. You are the trees, or you are in the trees. You are the wind, but more than the wind. You are the hum of life in this forest."

A low rumble of a chuckle vibrated through her hands. *I am all those things and more. I am architect of the Fatewalker Realm and sculptor of the real world.*

"But what *are* you? What is your physical form? Are you these trees?"

I have no form of my own, but inhabit all living things. I am Iskra—the spark. The Treekeepers know me as Nalatassa and believe I am contained in a tree. Fatecarvers have divided me into five Fates so they may count me on their fingers. But I am countless and without borders.

"You are the Fates? The real Fates?"

I am. But a more important question is what are you?

Kalish laughed. "Compared to you, I am nothing. A pebble upon the earth."

And yet you are not. Farseeing falcon, dangerous lantan. If you are a pebble, then you are the *pebble.*

"*The* pebble?"

The pebble dislodged at the top of a scree slope that skips down the mountain, picking up speed and setting other small pebbles into motion until the side of the mountain seethes with moving rock. The pebble in clay that explodes in the kiln and breaks the pot. The pebble that fills the gap between stones.

Kalish sighed. "Actually, I think I'm the pebble everyone sweeps out of their homes with the dirt." She thought of her storyscar. "If you are the Fates and Nalatassa, why do you let the Treekeepers do things like this"—she waved a hand at her own face—"to people?"

Your storyscar is my own special creation. Do not blame the Treekeepers for that.

"*You* told my mother to carve this?" Anger squeezed Kalish's chest.

I did. How else was I to bring you here? As for the others … A sigh whispered through the leaves overhead. *I suppose the fault is my own. I didn't see the danger until it was too late.*

"What danger?"

The danger of being forgotten. You see how few people visit me here, in what you call the Fatewalker Realm. It was not always so. But as your religious leaders grew in power, they wished to hoard it for themselves. They shut you off from me with rules and rituals. And as you retreated from me, so my power waned. Now I am largely confined to this grove, this island. It took great effort to influence your mother into giving you that storyscar. She resisted even my will. She knew it would cause you pain.

236

And then Kalish remembered the conversation she'd overheard on a day that seemed a lifetime ago. Her mother refusing to carve something. They'd been speaking of her? Her mother had fought against the Fates in order to protect her? She swallowed a lump in her throat and tucked the thought away to mull over later. "But why did you do this? Why am I here?"

I think you already know the answer. You will betray your clan. But not because you are of no clan. Rather, you are of all clans, of all peoples. The elders faithfully read your storyscar, but they could not read it all. On your neck are twin plants. Kalish involuntarily ran a finger over the spot where she knew the plants were. *A young nalati tree and a piromanga. Their leaves and branches intertwine as the leaves and branches of the Treekeepers and Fatecarvers are meant to. You will bring these plants, these people together.*

Kalish laughed. "Both of those people want me dead."

Twenty-eight

Dayo rolled his eyes. "I can't do anything without being watched."

A spike of jealousy stabbed Kalish in the gut. "By whom?"

"Kids mostly. They follow me everywhere. But others too."

"Women?" No Fatecarver would look twice at Dayo, but she didn't know about these Treekeeper women.

Dayo laughed. "Are you jealous?" He kissed her cheek, and then said seriously, "Honestly Kalish, I think they look at me like you'd look at a snake with wings. I'm an oddity, and one they don't entirely trust."

They were in the Fatewalker Realm. Dayo had returned to the village two days ago and still hadn't visited Kalish at Hana's house. "Can't you come at night? You know no one is outdoors then—they think the trees will eat them."

Dayo shook his head. "I'm staying at Sintala's house with her mother and father and her children.
238

There's no way to sneak out at night without waking someone up."

"Well you're going to have to do it sometime. We have to get out of here."

She'd related her conversation with Iskra to him, and he'd told her about the huge stores of food, bladestone, and barkcloth he'd seen on Council Island. "The council is hoarding far more than they need, and they waste it on frivolity—it seems like every day is a celebration day, the way they stuff themselves with food and adorn themselves with trinkets." They'd agreed they had to leave. But they hadn't yet agreed where to go or what to do when they arrived there.

"We can't leave until we know more. Sintala is sending her father and me to High Reaches tomorrow to collect bladestone from the village on behalf of the council. Maybe we can find out where it's coming from."

Kalish shook her head. "You still just want to get bladestone for the Fatecarvers?"

"They're stealing it from us. Think what we could do with it!"

"We don't even have the wood to refine it. If we can't melt it down, it's nothing more than rock to us. We've got plenty of that."

"Maybe, maybe not. Anyway, I'm going to High Reaches tomorrow, and I'll let you know what I find out."

Hana was thoughtful after Kalish related her experience with Nalatassa/Iskra in the nalati grove. She wove in silence for some time, and then said, "The question is, how can you possibly unite Treekeepers and Fatecarvers?"

Kalish stopped her clumsy weaving and stared at Hana. "I thought you didn't believe in Nalatassa?"

"I don't believe in the version of Nalatassa I've been taught about—the god who punishes people who are imperfect by making the trees devour them, the god who asks us to put our faith in the council, the god to whom only council members and Speakers can talk. But this Nalatassa—Iskra—you speak of?" Hana shrugged. "They are the real Nalatassa—the god I hear in the singing of the birds, the god I see in the flash of silver fish scales underwater, the god I feel through my fingers as I weave baskets."

Kalish nodded. She understood the feeling. The Fates had always been abstract to her, as they were taught—divine beings who passed judgement and spoke only to and through fatecarvers. But she *knew* the creature in the nalati grove like she knew the spiralling flight of the kiriki, the clatter of goat hooves on rock, the feel of sun-warmed rock beneath her fingers as she climbed.

"So much separates us," Hana continued, "mountains, culture, everything we've been taught." She shook her head. "It seems futile to try to unite us."

Boluso, preparing the evening meal nearby, chimed in. "But consider what we have in common— families, children, the land."

"The land here is nothing like the land of the Fatecarvers," Kalish said. "You take rain and trees for granted here—in Fatecarver lands, both are precious resources, used sparingly."

"Both peoples rely on the land to provide for their needs, correct?" Boluso's knife stilled and he looked at Kalish. She nodded. "We have the same needs—food, water, shelter. That we obtain them in

240

different ways makes little difference." Now he pointed the knife at her. "What is important is that the council is trying to prevent us all from obtaining those needs by stealing from us and hoarding resources for themselves. What we have in common is an enemy."

"Yes, I know that, but what good does that knowledge do if I can't convince others it's true."

"You've convinced me and Boluso," Hana pointed out.

Kalish shook her head. "But you're different from the others. You're outcasts like me."

Hana raised her eyebrows. "Are we really different? I may actually be an outcast because I wouldn't abandon Boluso after his injury, but I'm not sure I felt entirely like I fit in before then. I think we all feel a little like outcasts."

Boluso nodded. "I always wanted to try new things—experiment with new ways of catching fish or snaring birds—but my ideas were squashed because they were not *the way*."

Hana smiled. "And I've been wandering the forest at night since I was a child. But I didn't dare tell anyone because everyone *knew* the trees would eat you if you did. We can't be the only ones who feel we don't fit. We can't be the only ones who would listen to you."

Kalish shook her head. She'd been driven from her own clan, sentenced to die by the Surefoot Clan, and left out for the trees to eat by the Treekeepers. No one was going to listen to her.

Except Wathi had sent her off with provisions and tears. She'd sent Dayo after her. Verlent and her grandmother had stitched Kalish's knee and shown her sympathy on that first horrible day after she was banished. In the Surefoot Clan, Lofi had given her a knife, and Boled had shown her kindness and respect and protected her from Maled and Riven. And after her disastrous meeting with the elders, Zev and Nenu had returned her belongings and wished her well. Maybe she *could* find allies.

But unite Fatecarvers and Treekeepers? The idea was preposterous.

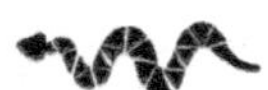

The urge to question her mother had been growing since her conversation with Iskra. What had been going through her head the day she carved Kalish's storyscar? What had she been doing since Kalish was banished? Did she know about the false Fates?

That night, she entered the Fatewalker Realm, changed into her falcon form, and winged her way home. She was surprised at how short the distance seemed to be. Was it because of the falcon form, or because she knew where she was going? Either way it felt like a short flight from Hana's village to her own terrace.

Except it wasn't her own terrace. She had to keep reminding herself as she landed on her favourite ledge and transformed back to her human form, feeling the familiar warm dry rock underfoot. She gazed out over the valley, still achingly familiar, and took a deep breath. The dry air seemed lighter than the humid vapour within the Treekeeper forest. It smelled of dust and sugarspike, and brought tears of longing to her eyes.

Home.

Except not home. She took a steadying breath and made her way toward the terrace. She passed the proofing rooms, wondering who among her friends was occupying them these days. As she entered the terrace, she was shocked to find the unmarried men's room and two rooms beside it reduced to rubble. There must have been an attack since she left. Anger flared against the council, knowing it was likely their work.

She didn't worry about concealment as she padded along the street—the only person she expected to find in the Fatewalker Realm was her mother. She reached the ladder to the main terrace and stopped, taking a deep breath and rubbing her sweaty palms on her thighs. It was possible her mother was sound asleep instead of in the Fatewalker Realm. But the prospect of confronting her still made Kalish nervous.

She descended the ladder and turned toward the fatechamber, straightening her shoulders. She would not show weakness.

"Life, Death, Love, War, Unknown. Guide my steps and let the path be shown. Life, Death, Love …"

Kalish had heard that chant before, but never in Seeda's voice. She skittered to a halt and ducked out of sight to listen.

"Guide my steps—" Seeda let out a squeak of surprise. "Death, you come to me. I am honoured by your presence."

One of the Fates was here? Kalish peeked from her hiding place to look. Seeda was on her knees, bowing her head to a woman whose face was painted to resemble a skull, and whose hair rose stiff and white—goat hair, stiffened with pale clay. How did Seeda not notice she was a fake?

Death spoke. "I grow restless, Seeda. I expected you to complete your task before the five-day was up. I am disappointed."

Seeda's head dipped lower. "I am sorry. I have tried. But she suspects something is amiss. She is always on her guard and will take nothing prepared by my hand."

Kalish frowned. What task had Death given Seeda?

"Surely you still wish for the power I will bestow upon you?"

"Yes, please." Seeda's head dipped so low her forehead touched the ground.

"Then you must perform this task. You must prove yourself worthy. The Flintcrag Clan can be greater than all others, but only with a strong fatecarver. One willing to take the position for herself."

"Yes, my Fate."

"You have one more day." Death turned and strode from the terrace. Kalish was torn between following Death and following Seeda, but Seeda wasn't likely to stick around in the Fatewalker Realm for long. Death, on the other hand, had a long journey to make, and Kalish guessed she wasn't alone.

She transformed into a falcon and glided out of the terrace, circling lazily above Death as she picked her way down the cliff face to her four companions waiting below. She lit in the scrub nearby to listen as Death reached the bottom.

Death shuddered once both feet were firmly planted on the ground. "I hate that climb."

"At least you don't have to do it in the real world," Life answered.

"Has she done it?" the Unknown asked.

Death shook her head.

"You mean Norili is still alive?" Love's eyebrows rose. "I thought you said last time the apprentice was ready and willing to do it." It was all Kalish

244

could do to keep from screeching. She wasn't sure how she felt about her mother anymore, but something primal stirred in her at the thought Seeda was going to try to murder her.

"She was. She is." Death sounded irritated. "I gave her until tomorrow. That gives us time to go to Surefoot and make sure they keep up their raids."

"And if she doesn't follow through with it?" War asked.

"She will. She wants to be fatecarver, and she hates Norili."

The Fates set off, and Kalish circled back up to the terrace. Where was Seeda now? Was she already creeping into her mother's room with a vial of poison or a sharp knife? What if Norili was in the Fatewalker Realm and had left her body unprotected? What if she *wasn't* in the Fatewalker Realm and Kalish couldn't warn her about Seeda?

In falcon form, she swooped around the streets of the terrace. No one stirred. She slipped into the fatechamber, not thinking about how it would look for a falcon—a bird of wide open spaces—to be seen inside a room. It too was empty.

There was nothing for it. She had to warn her mother. She swooped to her room and transformed, standing outside the door. Pressing on it, she was pleased to note it was locked. That meant it was locked in the real world. Of course it was. Her mother understood power. The thought churned in Kalish's stomach. Norili craved power above everything else. Above love, above other people, including, and maybe especially, her.

But her mother hadn't wanted to give her a storyscar that would condemn her. She'd resisted Iskra.

She pounded on her mother's door, calling her name loudly, hoping it would work for her as it had for Dayo when he pulled her into the Fatewalker Realm by calling to her.

"Norili! Norili, I need to speak to you! Norili! Mother! Mother, it's me!"

The door flew open, and there was her mother, wild-eyed and staring. "How did you get here? Tell me you're not here physically. And how did you enter the Fatewalker Realm?"

Ah, yes. Kalish had forgotten her mother didn't know about her and the Fatewalker Realm. Now wasn't the time for explanations. Seeda could be coming at this very moment.

"Seeda's trying to kill you. I just caught her talking to Death, but not the real Death—an imposter."

"What are you talking about? An imposter?"

Kalish waved her hand. "It doesn't matter right now. The important thing is Seeda's going to try to kill you sometime in the next day. She wants to become fatecarver."

Norili snorted. "She doesn't have the skill yet to become fatecarver. I seriously doubt she ever will, in fact. You would have done far better."

It was the first compliment her mother had ever given her, and it stopped Kalish cold. "I what?"

"You would have been a proper fatecarver. An excellent one, no doubt." She smiled without mirth. "I'd like to see Seeda try being fatecarver—she'd be expelled by the elders within a moon cycle."

"Well if you're not careful, that's exactly what is going to happen, except you won't be around to see it."

"I'm always careful." She looked Kalish up and down in that critical way that always shrank her. "You look half starved. Are you okay?"

There was no concern in her voice, but the fact she noticed and asked shocked Kalish so much she struggled to answer. "I'm fine."

"Did Dayo find you?"

Kalish forgot to breathe for a moment. Dayo had set off an incendiary in the Fatechamber before he left and stole a large quantity of sugarspike fabric. But her mother mentioned neither. "Yes. He found me."

Her mother nodded. "I'd best return to my body, and … I don't know where your body is, but I suspect you've got quite a journey back to it."

Kalish's mouth twitched into a smile. This was going to be fun. "It's not so far. Not when I can fly there." She shivered and transformed into a falcon. Norili's jaw dropped open, and Kalish had the satisfaction of seeing pure awe on her mother's face. She beat her wings and lifted off, flapping out of the terrace and into the clear air.

Her mother raised a hand in farewell.

Kalish stooped and sped away.

TWENTY-NINE

Dayo returned grim-faced from High Reaches. He showed up at Hana's hut mid-afternoon, materialising out of the forest so subtly that Kalish blinked a few times before she was certain she was seeing him.

She dropped the knife and root she was peeling and ran to him, throwing her arms around his neck. "You got away."

"I told them I was headed to the river to bathe. One of the women wanted to come with me to make sure I didn't get lost." Kalish stiffened and he chuckled. "I reminded her I knew the way, because I'd hauled water yesterday morning, and told her my gods forbid the washing of anything except our feet and hands, so I wouldn't be long. That put her off—they're very fastidious about cleaning here."

Kalish smiled into his hair, and then pulled back. "Come. You should meet Hana and Boluso, and then tell us all what you've learnt."

Hana and Boluso greeted Dayo warmly, and Dayo thanked them for saving Kalish's life.

248

"You have been to High Reaches," Boluso said. "It has been many years since I was there. The village sits high in the foothills, where the trees are short and twisted by snow and wind."

Dayo nodded. "I wonder that people stay there. It seemed to me that many were underfed, and nearly all the children were coughing."

Hana and Boluso shared a concerned look. "It was not so when I was last there," Boluso said. "High Reaches has the benefit of heat from the earth. Their homes, as I'm sure you noticed, are on the ground, warmed by the very rock they sit on. And the herds of goats that come from the mountains to browse on the trees are legendary in size."

"No longer. Apparently, the council demanded a huge tax of goats several years ago, and it decimated the herd. Few goats frequent the area around the village now, and people grow thin on the tiny fish they can catch in the mountain streams. And even if they had plenty of game, they don't have the time to hunt. The council's demand for bladestone is so high most of the villagers spend all their time chipping rock looking for it, and travelling further every day to find it."

Hana scowled as she lit the fire. "Again, the council taking and not giving back. It is not a true council. It doesn't reflect the people's interests, nor does it distribute resources as it is meant to, so we all have enough. The council seems to exist solely to benefit itself."

"It's nothing we didn't already know," Boluso said. "Though I didn't think it was as bad as you suggest. The question is, what are we going to do about it?"

"What *can* we do about it? We can't exactly attack the council. Kalish, you say Council Island is protected with weapons. None of the villages have weapons—we did away with them generations ago when we established the council to deal with conflicts."

"What if villages simply stopped sending anything to the council?" Kalish asked. "Eventually they'd run out of supplies."

Hana nodded. "It seems like a logical solution, but if a village stops sending their product to the council, the council will stop sending things to the village. If our village didn't send baskets, we wouldn't get grain in return. How would we eat?"

"The same way you and Boluso do—everyone would have time to hunt and forage if they weren't spending all day making baskets."

"Few still know how to live off the forest like Boluso and I do."

Boluso nodded. "Besides, the Speaker holds great power in each village, and from what you've seen Kalish, Speakers are obviously under the control of the council. To convince a village to rebel against the council, they'd have to rebel against the Speaker, against our entire religion and way of life. It's hard to imagine that happening."

They were silent as Kalish finished preparing the roots and put them into a pot with water, placing the pot on the coals as Hana had shown her. Dayo watched with an amused smile. Hana finished the basket she was weaving and tucked in the last loose end. Boluso set a few chunks of squirrel meat on sticks over the fire.

Kalish thought of Seeda and her mother, of the false Fates, of her clanspeople. When would the

250

next raid be? What would the council do to set it off?
How many Fatecarvers would die?

"We need to leave tonight, Dayo."

He nodded. "I have a few supplies hidden
nearby—things Sintala's family won't miss, I hope."

"How will you get away after dark?"

Dayo smiled. "In High Reaches, they brew a
tea from a particular lichen that grows on the rocks
near the bladestone diggings—they use it to help calm
the children's coughs, but it also induces heavy sleep. I
brought some back with me."

Hana smiled sadly. "We thought you might be
going soon. I've made you both baskets you can comfortably carry on your backs and I've filled them with
a few supplies you'll need. And Boluso has wrapped
up food for you that will last a few days at least."

"And there's one other thing." Boluso nodded
at Hana. "Go get it."

Hana clambered up the ladder to the house,
and when she returned she was carrying a familiar
item.

"My atlatl!"

"It was the only thing I could recover. I don't
know who has your knives, and most of your other
things were tossed away or broken for fun."

Kalish accepted the atlatl as Hana held it out
to her. She stroked the worn handle lovingly. "Thank
you. But … how much did you have to trade to get
this?" How would she repay Hana for everything?

Hana waved a hand. "Never mind that. Just
survive."

With her atlatl, she and Dayo could eat and
protect themselves. They might have a chance of sur-
viving in the forest.

Dayo left shortly afterwards, before anyone could notice him missing and seek him out. As Boluso, Hana and Kalish settled down to eat the meal they'd prepared, Boluso's head shot up. "Someone's coming. Kalish—"

She didn't need to be told. She raced up the ladder and hid herself under the sleeping platform among the reeds.

Many feet marched up to the house, and Kalish's muscles tensed. She'd run up here without a knife.

"To what do we owe the honour of such a … delegation?" There was a tightness in Hana's voice that spoke of fear, though the tone was defiant.

The male voice that responded was unfamiliar to Kalish. "Hana, you are charged with the murder of Speaker Gian. You will come with us now, to be given to the trees tonight."

There was a scuffle below, and Boluso growled, "Don't you dare touch her."

More noise of a fight filtered through the floorboards, and Kalish pressed her eye to a tiny crack but saw nothing more than the flash of a leg. Something hit one of the support posts, sending a shiver through the house. The same male voice spoke up as the scuffle died down. "And this … abomination … will be subjected to the same fate as Gian."

"No!" Hana's desperate voice almost pulled Kalish out from her hiding place to throw herself at the villagers below. But she wasn't foolish enough to think she could take on what sounded like a dozen people, without a single weapon. "Give him to the trees along with me."

"We've tried that before. The trees didn't accept him."

More sounds of struggle urged Kalish to act, but she remained motionless. *I am a lantan*, she told herself. *I do not strike until the last moment, when I am sure of my target.* She pressed herself against the floor.

"Where are you taking him? Wait! Boluso!"

The commotion of feet moved out from under the house and split in two directions. When the sounds had faded she began to wriggle from under the bed.

"Who's there?" A voice made her freeze. "Did you hear that, Jumir?"

"Are the kids up there?" asked another voice, presumably Jumir.

"Nah. They're in the village." Then he said louder, "Come down here. We know you're up there."

Kalish crept silently back under the bed. She pulled a bundle of reeds closer to her, and it hissed on the floor. *Spines!*

The floor shook as someone mounted the ladder and pushed open the door. "Anyone here?" The floorboards creaked as he walked around. Kalish shut her eyes and slowed her breathing. *Be a lantan.* She heard him breathing as he peered under the sleeping platform. Reeds hissed across the floor as he pulled aside a bundle.

"Ah!" He lurched back and kicked the reeds back toward Kalish.

The second man ran up the ladder. "What is it?"

The first man laughed. "Snake. Startled me is all."

Kalish's eyes flew open in time to see a mottled green snake longer than her arm glide over the floor and drop through a knot hole.

"Hey, look at what I found," said the second man.

"That's one of those Fatecarver weapons. Where'd you get it?" The man who'd nearly caught her stepped toward the door.

"Down below. Come on. Let's catch up with the others." Both men descended the ladder.

Kalish lay frozen on the floor for some time, ears straining for the sounds of others still hanging around. When she was certain they were gone, she slid out and quickly gathered everything she thought she would need from the hut. She found the baskets Hana had made for her and Dayo. Hana had already loaded them with a goat pelt, some cooking utensils, two barkcloth ponchos Kalish suspected were waterproof, and two of the odd flat hats Treekeepers wore when it rained. Kalish topped them up with dried fruit and fish and a small root cake wrapped in leaves. As she turned to leave, she saw Boluso's spear standing in the corner. She stepped toward it and ran her fingers down its smooth shaft. He would need his spear when she found him. And she might need it to get to him. She picked it up and tested its weight.

The sharp smell of smoke prickled her nose. The smell grew quickly, and Kalish realised the hut was filling with it. She threw open the door and clattered down the ladder to find one of the posts smouldering. In the scuffle below, the cooking fire had been scattered, and a glowing coal had lodged against the post. Kalish rushed for the water pot and was about to quench the fire when she stopped.

254

Hana and Boluso were never going to be able to come back here, even if she did manage to save them both. And a fire might distract the villagers from their plans, at least long enough for Kalish to act. Her eyes darted around to the pair's meagre belongings. She dropped her baskets and the spear, and began loading everything she could into Hana's fish and root baskets. She darted up the ladder and swept bowls and spoons off the table. She scooped up furs from the floor, coughing in the smoke that pooled under the thatch roof.

She gathered knives and fish traps, and hauled them all into the forest. She scrabbled to make a shallow pit in the soil, dropped their belongings into it, and covered it with leaf litter. It wasn't a great disguise, but at least no one would notice it if they casually came by. But how would she tell Hana and Boluso where to find it?

Her mind flew to the sunsinger birds Hana snared. She saved the colourful red feathers to adorn her clothes. Kalish dashed back to the house just as the smouldering post burst into flame. The feathers were in the house. It would only take a moment to run up and snag them. Kalish took a deep breath and scrambled up the ladder.

The heat inside was growing, and the smoke was so thick she could barely see her way. She felt around in the murk for the bag of feathers. It had been in the corner yesterday—she'd put some feathers in it herself. Her lungs were bursting, but she dared not suck in a lungful of the acrid air. *Spines!* The bag wasn't hanging where she'd left it. One of the children must have taken it down. She had to breathe. Now. She couldn't search any longer. She turned and stepped on something soft. She reached down and felt

with her fingers. It was the bag of feathers! She
snatched it up and burst out of the house, practically
tumbling down the ladder, gulping lungfuls of air.

There was a great whoosh as the flames
reached the thatch. With shaking hands, Kalish laid a
discreet trail of bright feathers, tucked in cracks in the
bark of trees, leading to Hana and Boluso's belongings. When she finished, she stashed the remaining
feathers in her basket. She shouldered both baskets,
hefted the spear, and dashed in the direction of the
river, where she thought they'd taken Boluso.

THIRTY

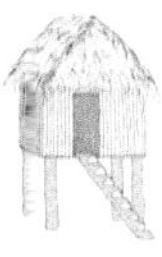

The baskets were cumbersome and hampered Kalish's movement. They were also noisy. When she passed an ancient nalati with a hollow heart, she tucked the baskets inside and marked the spot with a red feather. With nothing but the spear in hand, she moved swiftly and silently now. She searched for clues to where they'd taken Boluso, but the path was thick with footprints that could have been anyone's.

As she approached the river, the rush of water masked other sounds, and she stepped off the path, knowing she wouldn't hear anyone coming until they were too close. She skirted around a pair of houses where, thankfully, no one was home, and soon came to the path paralleling the river's edge. She crouched beside the path, listening intently. The gurgle and plash of water sounded maddeningly like distant voices.

If I were going to murder someone and throw them in the river, I'd do it downstream, away from where people draw water. She turned and followed the water's flow.

It wasn't long before she was certain the voices she was hearing were real. And they were raised in anger. She slipped off the path and crept forward through the undergrowth.

They were crowded together where a small side path provided access to the river down a steep bank—ten, maybe fifteen adults with a few eager children skittering around on the edge of the group, excitement on their faces. As she watched, the children peeled off toward a tree nearby singing, "Freak! Freak! Freak!" That's when Kalish saw Boluso, tied mostly out of her sight, to the tree the children now circled and pelted with handfuls of mud and leaves. Her fists clenched.

She brought her attention back to the adults. Their speech was rapid, and she couldn't catch everything. But it was clear what they were arguing about.

"This is not the way."

"Why not? He should have been dead years ago."

"But Nalatassa chose not to take him. He is the only one who can make these judgements."

"Our Speaker is dead—we must serve justice."

"Are you Nalatassa now?"

She had to act quickly. Once they decided to act, it would be too late. There was no way she could spirit Boluso away without them noticing, and one girl with a spear was nothing against a group of that size. She was thankful she'd let the hut burn. Surely they'd be eager to put out the fire once they knew about it. A fire in this forest must be a fearsome thing. She shuddered and briefly wondered if leaving the fire to burn had been a terrible mistake.

Too late. It was done, and it would help her save Boluso. She took a deep breath, set down the spear, and stepped out of the undergrowth.

"Never mind Boluso. I'm the one who killed Gian," she grinned in what she hoped was a predatory way. "Not Hana, not Boluso. If you want justice, you'll have to kill me … again."

Their shocked eyes and open mouths were almost comical. The momentary stunned silence was broken when one of the children shrieked, "The Fate-carver freak!"

Kalish turned and bolted as the adults burst into action. As one, they surged toward her. She ducked off the path and immediately tripped over a log. *Spines!* She picked herself up and sped on. Undergrowth slashed at her face and slapped her legs. Her own noise drowned out the small sounds of pursuit behind her. What had she been thinking? These people moved through the trees like cats. She would never outrun them crashing clumsily through the forest. She dared a glance behind her. A phalanx of men and women darted gracefully around trees and over logs.

She angled back toward the path. It was the quickest way to lead them to the fire anyway, and she had a better chance of staying ahead of them if she wasn't tripping every ten steps.

Back on the trail, she picked up speed. But even here she wasn't as fast as the lanky Treekeeper men, who steadily gained on her. Soon she could smell the faint odour of smoke. She hoped she'd make it to Hana's house before she was caught. She pushed her legs to move faster, feet slapping wetly on the path.

As she drew closer to Hana's, the smoke grew thick and the crackle of flames was clearly audible. Her pursuers began to shout to one another. Kalish pounded forward, plunging into the smoke, feeling the heat of the flames, hoping to get lost in the confusion of the fire, hoping her pursuers would deem fighting the fire more important than catching her.

Shouts of "Fire!" and "Water!" rang out behind her. She also heard "Fatecarver" and "Freak" among the shouts, but she ignored them all, focusing instead on navigating through the smoke and flames. Hana's hut was fully aflame now, and the heat seared Kalish's face as she ran toward it. Her pursuers were in disarray—running this way and that, some still angling toward her, others breaking off to fight the fire.

One of the posts cracked and broke, burnt through at the base. The entire house began to break apart, showering Kalish with flaming debris. *Spines!* She darted away from the building, skirting around a bush that had burst into flame from the heat. One of her pursuers saw her and veered to intercept her. She dodged him and flew into the forest on the other side of the house. The man followed.

Well, at least it was only one now. The others seemed to have all halted at the fire. But one was enough to catch her, especially since he carried a spear. How could he run so fast through the forest with a spear in hand?

"Lante!" a voice shouted from behind.

Kalish heard the man behind her pause. "I've got the Fatecarver!" he shouted back.

But in the moments he paused and glanced behind him, Kalish put on a burst of speed, ducked behind a tree, and began to climb. She might not be able to outrun this man, but she was confident she could outclimb him. Trees weren't so different from cliffs. The rough bark provided small but useable handholds, and her nimble toes sought out footholds with the

260

desperation of the hunted. She scurried up the tree to the first large branch, and then flattened herself out on it, hoping the man hadn't seen her climb, and hoping he didn't look up.

Be a lantan. She shut her eyes and slowed her breathing, listening intently. The man's pounding footsteps passed the tree and then faltered. *Spines!* Her eyes flew open.

He peered into the forest, then he circled back, scanning the ground. She'd forgotten about her own footprints. Would he be able to track her? Would he guess she'd scaled the tree? Her heart, already working hard after her sprint, drummed against the branch with a wild, percussive rhythm she thought the man was sure to hear.

He retraced his own steps, his gaze on the ground. He passed directly under Kalish and then gave a satisfied grunt. He bent to examine something. Had he found her track? He inched along the ground toward the base of the tree, and Kalish wondered if she was better off staying still, or leaping up and climbing higher.

A whoosh and roar from the direction of Hana's hut saved her from the decision. The man's head jerked up at the sound, and he sprinted back toward the others.

Kalish clung to the branch for a while longer, heart slowly returning to normal. When she was convinced all her pursuers were busy fighting the fire, she slid back down the tree and, giving Hana's house a wide berth, she raced back toward the river.

The smell of smoke permeated the forest now, and Kalish worried she'd started something she'd regret. Fires in Fatecarver lands moved quickly through dry brush and tussock. They sometimes took out swaths of grain, but rarely caused trouble for the terraces, which were carefully kept free of vegetation to prevent sneak attacks. She had no idea what they did in this wet forest. The thought of all the trees around her in flame made her shudder, but surely they were so wet and green they couldn't burn. She hoped not, anyway.

She avoided the paths, but several times had to duck out of sight as people came sprinting past, all headed toward the fire. As distractions went, she'd obviously chosen a good one.

She reached the river and the spot where Boluso had been tied, and her steps faltered.

Boluso was gone. The ropes that had bound him to the tree were gone.

The ground was dark with blood.

Kalish's heart sank. She was too late. Her distraction hadn't been good enough. Someone must have stayed behind to finish the job while the rest pursued her.

"Oh Hana! I'm so sorry," she whispered. She followed a trail of blood to the river bank where it splashed bright onto the rocks and then vanished in the water. She scanned for a body downstream, but saw nothing. Boluso was gone. Her shoulders slumped and she sat on a rock, head in hands, defeated.

Noise on the path behind her brought her back to her senses. Hana still needed rescuing, and she couldn't do that if she were discovered. She scrambled along the bank and hid in the middle of a bush that stung her skin and raised welts on her legs. *Spines! What is this thing?* She rubbed at the welts, but dared not leave the bush as a pair of women passed close by, talking quietly, their footsteps hurried.

Kalish jumped out of the stinging bush as soon as she could, cursing her choice of hiding place. She scooped cool water from the river and rubbed it on her burning skin, and it helped, but only a little. She tried to think around the itching.

Hana was to be given to the trees. So she should be safe until nightfall, wherever they'd taken her. And Kalish knew exactly where she would be taken at dusk. There was no point in her trying to find Hana before then, risking her own capture.

And Dayo? She had no idea where he was—possibly he was helping with the fire. She would have to trust he would find her after dark, too. They'd agreed to meet at Hana's. She hoped the fire would be out, and the area deserted by then.

For now, she needed to lie low. Or rather, high. The safest place might be the trees. She searched nearby until she found one that offered a comfortable perch, and then scrambled up.

Time passed slowly. Kalish's perch wasn't nearly as comfortable as it had appeared from below, and while most of the itchy welts from the stinging plant had subsided, three seemed to only grow worse as the day wore on. She wished she could dive into the Fate-walker Realm, just to escape the incessant itching, but she didn't dare, lest she fall from her perch. Eventually, the smell of smoke lessened, until it vanished entirely, and Kalish hoped it meant they'd managed to extinguish the fire.

Finally the light began to fade. Kalish descended from the tree and stopped first at the river for a drink and to splash water on the itchy welts, and then to retrieve the spear she'd dropped earlier. Then she headed toward the nalati grove.

Watching the ceremony from a distance was almost as bad as being the object of it. Hana was stoic, but Kalish could see the grief in her eyes. They must have told her Boluso was dead. A rock settled into Kalish's stomach. She had failed them both.

The ceremony seemed to go on forever, but as the light began to fail, the villagers nervously skittered away home to shut the forest out for the night. The urge to spring up and release Hana instantly when the last person left the grove was difficult to resist, but Kalish was a lantan. She would wait until the right moment. She crouched until the last scrap of light faded, and then she waited for ten more breaths.

"Hana, it's me," she whispered.

"Kalish! You shouldn't be here."

Kalish snorted as she used the head of the spear to slice Hana's bonds. "Neither should you."

"But if you're caught—" her breath hitched. "They've already killed Boluso, and my house is gone. I may as well let the cats eat me."

Kalish paused to squeeze Hana's hand. "I tried to rescue him, but ..." She finished releasing Hana and helped her to her feet. "Listen. Before the fire spread, I pulled a few things from your house and hid them nearby. Follow the trail of sunsinger feathers from where your house was. They're buried under some leaves—it'll be obvious once you're there."

"But what will I do? Where will I go?"

Kalish gently pulled Hana with her as she made her way toward the remains of her house. "You'll be fine. You've been an outcast for years."

"But I had Boluso and the children. I won't even be able to see the children again. They'll think I'm dead." A sob escaped, and her steps faltered.

Nothing Kalish could say would make it easier for Hana. "The children will be well cared for by their grandparents," was the only positive thing she could come up with. She eased Hana into motion again. "You could come with Dayo and me. I'm not entirely sure where we're going. Probably back to Fatecarver lands to try to help them break from the control of the council." She paused, overwhelmed by the futility of such an effort. "It won't be easy." They padded through the darkness. "Or maybe you can find another village that would take you in." Without Boluso in tow, Kalish reasoned Hana could be accepted fully, but she knew better than to point this out.

Hana didn't respond, and they spent the rest of the journey in silence.

Arriving in the tiny clearing where her house once stood, Hana sucked in a sharp breath. Even in the darkness, the totality of the destruction was obvious. The air was acrid with the smell of burnt wood, and nothing remained of the hut but a pile of ash and charcoal. Hana sank to the ground, shaking with silent tears.

Kalish wondered nervously how long it would be before Dayo arrived. Had his sleeping draught done the trick? When would he be able to slip away? Were she and Hana safe waiting here? She felt an urgent need to leave. She expected the whole village would be out searching for her in the morning, and she wanted to be far away by the time the sun came up.

She realised she'd marked the location of her and Dayo's gear with a feather—invisible in the dark. That had been stupid. There was no way she could find it now. *Spines!* She'd messed everything up. Hadn't been able to save Boluso, had lost what little gear she and Dayo had, and had allowed Hana's house to burn down.

Not that she'd be able to live there now anyway, but …

If only she had thought to retrieve the baskets while it was light out.

Of course! Where was it always daytime? She hurried to Hana's side. "Hana. Can you watch over me while I slip into the Fatewalker Realm for a little bit. Here's the spear."

Hana raised her head and swiped at her face. "Yes. I can do that. Why?"

"I've lost something I need to find."

With Hana on guard, Kalish slipped into the Fatewalker Realm. In the light of a beautiful day, she paced the distance from her body to the tree in which she'd stashed the baskets, counting steps and looking for landmarks she could recognise in the dark. When she returned to her body, she asked Hana to come with her to retrieve the baskets.

Hana kept them on the right path while Kalish counted steps. When she'd reached the right count, she looked toward the sky. "There's a dead tree directly opposite the one I'm looking for. It's got a jagged trunk that sticks up. There!" She pointed, and then turned her back to the dead tree. Stepping off the path, she quickly found the hollow tree and the baskets.

Hana had recovered herself somewhat. "Impressive. Do you think you can do the same with the things you saved for me? I don't think I should be here either when the sun rises."

266

They had recovered all the items Kalish had hidden, and were just stepping back into the clearing when a stifled cry went up. "Mama!" Two small forms hurtled out of the darkness to attach themselves to Hana. Hana bent to hug and kiss them, as all three shed tears. Kalish glanced up to find two men approaching. She breathed a sigh of relief at Dayo's short form. Then her heart seemed to skip a beat as she recognised the second man's limp. "Boluso?"

Hana's head shot up. "Boluso!" He ran to her.

Kalish watched the scene in astonishment until Dayo reached her side. "I thought he was dead. There was blood and—"

Dayo chuckled. "Your little distraction worked, mostly. Well done."

"How did you know?"

"I was there. Hidden, like you. I was trying to figure out how I could take on fifteen villagers at once when you stepped out. It was all I could do to not jump out to protect you." He wrapped an arm around her shoulder. "But I saw what you were doing, so I waited. They only left one man with Boluso. The blood was his. These Treekeepers are poor fighters. How did you get away from them?"

Kalish explained her tree climbing and how she counted on the fire for an additional distraction. "But how did you collect the children, too?"

"Boluso and I have been busy. We've gathered gear for everyone. Only the children and their grandparents know that Boluso and Hana are alive. The grandparents will stay here, but Boluso is hoping Hana agrees to go to another village where they can pass off his injury as a birth defect."

"We should have done that years ago anyway," Boluso said, pulling away from Hana and the children.

Dayo and Boluso produced more baskets of supplies, including fine bladestone knives for both Dayo and Kalish, waterskins, and to Kalish's astonishment, her atlatl. "Where did you find it?"

"The fellow guarding Boluso had it."

They packed their belongings and shouldered their baskets. Even the children carried packs. Their excited whispers made Kalish wonder if they truly understood what was happening.

When the moment for parting arrived, Kalish was strangely reluctant. She'd grown fond of Hana and Boluso. "Thank you." She gave them each a hug. "I'm sorry if we've caused you trouble. You've been so kind and generous. We won't forget that."

Hana nodded. "And thank you both—Boluso and I owe you our lives."

"You will go back to your people?" Boluso asked. "To warn them about the council?"

Kalish sighed. "We have to try."

Boluso nodded. "As will we. Maybe we'll meet again someday."

Kalish laughed. "I know we will. If the council can travel back and forth to harass Fatecarvers, there's nothing stopping any of us from popping in for a visit, right?"

Hana gasped. "That's it, Kalish! That's the way to do it."

"Do what?"

"Topple the council. Unite our people. In the Fatewalker Realm, distance is not such an obstacle— our people can meet, they can see the excesses of Council Island, they can plan. *We* can plan." Determination rang in her voice and brought a smile to Kalish's face.

There was little planning for any of them as Hana and her family limped at Boluso's pace to a distant village where they were unknown, and Kalish and Dayo trekked toward the mountains. Without wings to get them across, they angled northward, to where the mountains were lower. They planned on crossing into Point Clan territory. Kalish remembered the false Fates' comments about losing control of Point Clan, and the stories among Flintcrag Clan painted Point Clan as dangerously rebellious against Fatecarver ways. They hoped to find receptive ears there.

For now, they avoided Treekeeper notice, staying off well-worn trails, travelling at night whenever possible, and hugging the foothills where settlements were more sparse. The land was lush, and they lacked neither water nor food until they began their climb over the mountains. But with Dayo at her side, Kalish didn't despair as she had done when she fled the Fatecarver lands. She was no longer alone. Instead of counting her enemies, she enumerated her allies as she struggled over ridge after ridge.

Dayo, first and foremost.

Hana and Boluso.

Wathi.

Verlent and her grandmother.

Lofi and Boled.

Zev and Nenu.

And maybe even her mother. The thought swelled in her chest.

It wasn't many, but it was a start.

And, of course, there was Iskra. She held the memory of their conversation close to her heart. Iskra had called her the pebble that would set a mountain in motion. The pebble that would shatter the pot. The pebble between stones.

Pebble, kiriki, lantan.

Kalish and Dayo reached the top of a steep saddle of sharp scree, fighting a biting wind that whipped sand into their faces. At the top, she breathed in the scent of sugarspike and dust. Before them lay the stark mesas and canyons of the Fatecarver lands. Something deep inside her sang.

"I never really appreciated how beautiful it is," Dayo said.

Kalish grasped his hand. "Come on. Let's go home."

ACKNOWLEDGEMENTS

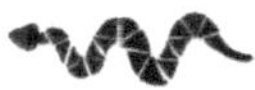

This book started life several years ago as five hundred words inspired by Litopia's monthly flash fiction prompts. I instantly knew that what I'd written was part of a much larger story. Thanks to the many Litopians who have offered support, advice and encouragement to make this book possible.

Thanks to my early readers: Ian, Deryn, Ashlin and Shannon. Thanks also goes to my editor, Belinda, whose falcon-sharp eyes catch so many mistakes.

And thanks to all my young writing students, who challenge *everything*, and keep writing fresh and exciting.

About the Author

Robinne is an entomologist and educator by training, but she has never been able to control her writing habit. She has been publishing poetry and short stories since the 1970s, and has been known to answer exam questions in verse. Her short stories have won multiple awards for science fiction and fantasy writing.

Robinne is blessed to live in New Zealand, where even ordinary life is magical.

Visit her at https://robinneweiss.com.

OTHER BOOKS BY ROBINNE WEISS

Fantasy for ages 8-13
The Dragon Slayer's Son
The Dragon Slayer's Daughter
The Dragon Defence League
Dragon Homecoming
The Ipswich Witch
A Glint of Exoskeleton

Adult fantasy
Squelched

Non-fiction
Insects in the Classroom
Backyard Bugwatcher

Poetry
Pandemic Poetry: Across the Fence